Appointed Vengeance

Wins vs. Losses

The Lawyer Killings Series

Willie Peters

NEWMAN SPRINGS PUBLISHING
320 Broad Street
Red Bank, NJ 07701

First originally published by Newman Springs Publishing 2021

ISBN 978-1-63692-964-4 (Paperback)
ISBN 978-1-63692-965-1 (Digital)

Printed in the United States of America

Acknowledgments

I first and foremost have to thank God for blessing me with talents, gifts, and abilities to achieve the prosperity that you desire for me. Have to thank my parents who loved me and supported me unconditionally my entire life.

My mom, for being that visual and verbal ultimate example and instilling in me confidence, resilience, and determination. Always taught me I can do and be anything I dream of. Thanks to my brothers who always supported me and pushed me. Thanks to my graphic cover artist, my nephew, little Alim. Last but not least, all of my family and friends who loved, supported, and cheered me to the finish line. Would not be possible without.

Readers' Discretion

Appointed Vengeance's aim, goal, and purpose is to raise the awareness in the masses on both sides of the law. This novel's intention is to directly reveal to you, the mass public, that, beyond the shadow of a doubt, people's lives can be dramatically changed.

Appointed Vengeance is an antiprevention novel, and I strongly recommend thoroughly reading this novel. Also take a deep, long, and hard look into the mirror and ask yourself if this is the life that you want for yourself on either side of the law.

Love life to live it long enough to enjoy it.

I was criticized and given up on, but I just worked even harder and prepared even more for my time to be successful. I believed and bet on me. And here I am.

Movie Critic:

> This [a]ction-packed thriller from the visionary writer grips and sucks the reader in with unpredictable and thrilling suspense, [m]aking it impossible to put down.

Book Scene:

> As Richard was climbing out of broken window of [a] gun store with lawyer murder weapons of choice, the police unexpectedly arrive[,] shining spotlights inside the gun store. Richard[,] in a desperate panic[,] falls to the floor[,] hoping he wasn't seen by police.

Readers' Opinions

This crime novel/straight to indy film reading is not only like watching a movie but like actually being in the movie yourself. Unpredictable and highly action packed from beginning to end!

This book takes you inside the mind of the character. It makes the reader feel like he personally knows the character intimately

What I love about this book is that all through it, you can't predict what's going to happen from scene to scene. Just when you think something is going to go this way, the writer takes you on a detour, and the scene twists and turns in a whole 'nother direction. This book definitely grips your attention. I love it!

Appointed Vengeance is definitely one of, if not my favorite book of all times.

One lawyer said,

Appointed Vengeance put the spotlight on an issue that should have had the spotlight placed on it a long time ago. It only takes one crooked attorney to put all our lives in jeopardy! And we would never see the lawyer killer coming!

Several attorneys say,

Appointed Vengeance was beautifully written. It sure got my attention. The point was driven home. And lawyers not living up to the best standards, I think, should really reevaluate their profession and motives.

Several college students studying law were quoted saying,

It's a scary but very realistically possible suspense novel. A narrator that takes you deep inside the mind of each character. And all the characters' emotions and thought process. Every college student across the world is talking about this book right now!

Law professors were among themselves, saying,

A book has never been written this well to captivate the mind of the reader by a rookie, first-time author who surprisingly has the unique writing style of a veteran.

Chapter 1

An upper-class family lived on the outer city limits of Minneapolis, Minnesota, a nice crime-free and close-knit community. The bread-winner of the family was an Afro-American male named Richard Blake Ginn. But all of his friends called him Richy. The name of Richard's wife is Kimberly Ginn. But her friends call her Kim.

Richard and Kim are both in their thirties and have a young daughter together named Jessica Ginn. Richard and Kim have been married since they were in high school together. They were high school sweethearts living the American dream.

Richard was a successful business owner of an automechanic hot rod shop. And an automotive engineer at an automotive plant. Married with a child and living in a big nearly half-million-dollar home. I mean really, what more could a man ask for?

Richard was easily grossing six figures annually. And his wife, Kim, was a stay-at-home mom. Life was good, and they wouldn't change a thing, up until recently. With the economy taking a massive blow. Due to being blindsided by a historic shattering pandemic. A global future full of uncertainty, not knowing what would be the new normal.

Richard's plant, that employed him, had been making cuts and laying off for the last six months. Richard's family had been on their knees at home, praying diligently as a family. Praying that the cuts and layoffs skips over Richard's name. And so far so good; Richard is still making a living.

But the tension level has tremendously increased at home, not knowing if he would receive a pink slip from the company. And money was getting tighter and tighter as each day had passed by. Richard was struggling to maintain his automechanic shop and keep it afloat.

Richard and Kim began arguing about the smallest things now. Many of the arguments were over dinner. Richard hollering at Kim and asking, "Why did you use turkey instead of chicken in the spaghetti, Kim!"

Richard and Kim's marriage had finally crossed roads, confronted with its first real test. And their marriage was on the rocks. It didn't look like they were going to make it. Richy took lesser money, lesser hours, and any other cut that he could think of to keep his job. Richard was the last man standing. And it was really beginning to look like he would be the only one to survive the layoffs and save his family.

Until Richard heard that call over the plant's monitor one day that said, "Rich Ginn, report to the supervisor's office! Rich Ginn, report to the supervisor's office!" Richard knew that it didn't sound good. It didn't feel good either. Richard's whole body went numb. That was the longest walk of Richard's life! Going to the supervisor's office.

It didn't even feel like Richard was in control of his own body! Richard's legs were moving by themselves! It felt like he was taking that walk to the death chamber. And the last two words that Richard remembered hearing was, "We're going to have to let you go...I'm sorry." Richard was completely frozen, paralyzed, heard a repeated hypnotizing echoed whisper, "I'm sorry."

Richard was replaying that whole moment in his mind as he sat in his car, filled with all of his office belongings all around him, from the car seat to the car floor. Richard was sitting inside of his car in the plant's parking lot feeling emotionally drained. His head down, buried onto the steering wheel. Thinking and asking himself, "What do I do now? How am I going to explain this to my wife?"

Richard was thinking about how to pay his car note, his wife, Kim's, car note—roughly $2,000 per month—mortgage, and the private school tuition that his daughter, Jessie, attends, that he's already behind on from taking those cuts to keep his job.

Jessie's school was already complaining that they needed the back payments. Or they would be forced to terminate Jessica's enrollment. Richard was in a deep train of thought, thinking about his life and his future, just as plant security was making a round. Plant security exited his truck, tapped on the driver-side window of Richard's car, and said, "These parking spaces are reserved for employees only, sir. I'm going to have to ask you to leave."

Richard thought, *I haven't been let go from my job but for twenty minutes tops! And this is the same guy that talks college football with me every morning!*

But Richard just started his car up and shoved all of his office property that he had accumulated over the years, out of the back seat onto the floor so that he could see out of his rearview mirror. Then Richard drove off.

Richard had arrived to pick his daughter up from school. Jessie excitedly opened the car door, happy to see her dad. Jessie screamed, "Hiii, Daddy!" And she hugged her father, Richard, as tight as her little arms could squeeze him. Totally unaware that her daddy had just gotten permanently laid off from work. But Richard just acted as he always did when he picked his daughter up from school. Richard kissed Jessie on top of her head and fixed her pretty hair back into place.

Richard asked Jessie, "So…How was Daddy's little girl day today?"

Jessie, with a big loving smile, with dimples, excitedly answered, "Fiiiiine!" She dragged the word like the spoiled little girl that Richard had raised her up to be.

Richard's family was his only real true pride, joy, and happiness. And although he and Kim were going through their differences due to the stress, it was unmistakenly evident that they still truly loved each other.

And they believed that the storm that they were faced with, they would weather it too. Just like all the other storms that they were ever faced with. Richard and Kim told each other, "We'll just keep praying, and we'll make it through this one too. Together as a family."

Richard and Jessica pulled up into the driveway, finally home, and they went inside. Jessica hugged her mother and quickly ran into her room to play with her dolls. Richard walked into the living room, kissed Kim on her cheek, and said, "Hey, honey." Then Richard sat down onto the couch. But Kim could tell something was wrong with Richard.

She looked at Richard with concern and asked, "What's wrong, baby? Is everything all right?"

Richard answered, "I…really don't feel like talking about it right now, hun. We'll talk later on. I really need a nap."

Richard dozed off and fell asleep until about 9:30 p.m. Kim was in their bedroom at that time, getting ready for bed, when Richard walked in with a glass of vodka in his hand that he had almost just downed in two big gulps before he entered into the bedroom that Kim was in.

Kim looked at Richard and could instantly tell that he was drunk. But Kim still decided to ask Richard again, "What was wrong with you earlier, Richy? You didn't look right!"

Richard took one more big swallow, finishing the rest of the glass off. Richard answered, "It was nothing, baby. Just nothing…I need you right now. And I'll feel so much better. You know it's nothing that you can't fix." Richard was hinting around to sex. And Kim knew exactly what Richard was hinting to as she seductively grinned and growled at Richard.

Kim lifted the cover-up showing her completely nude body, waiting on Richard to climb into bed with her. Richard eagerly took all of his clothes off first, and then he climbed on top of Kim. Kissing all over her naked body starting with her earlobe, then her neck, Richard gently made his way down to her breast as he caressed them both at the same time, with his lips pecking at them.

Richard was taking his time, anticipating the moment of passionate lovemaking. Then finally Richard kissed down Kim's stomach as Kim began moaning, anticipating Richard getting closer and closer to her vagina. Her magical spot. Kim was gripping the back of Richard's head as he was giving her intense oral sex.

Richard and Kim were making hours and hours of hard passionate love, as they have been doing since they were in high school together, skipping class to go back to Kim's parents' house. Richard and Kim weren't feeling more in love until now. Their emotions were running high and wild at an all-time high.

Hours later, they finished making love and just lay there, sweating, exhausted, and out of breath. Kim was cradled and tightly cuddled up in Richard's arms. They both were staring up at the ceiling in complete silence and thinking about their future together.

Kim rolled toward Richard and looked him into his eyes, visibly full of fear of the unknown, and said, "I'm scared, baby. If you lose your job, I'm afraid we'll be homeless. I'm scared for Jessie. I want her to have a better life than I had."

Richard was just lying there, letting Kim talk, scared to cut her off by telling her that her biggest fear was now their reality. Richard was trying to find the right time to cut Kim off and tell her that he, in fact, officially lost his job earlier in the day.

But it seemed like no time was a good-enough time to break the news to Kim. So Richard just kept stroking Kim's hair and listening to her talk. Richard was looking into Kim's eyes and letting her vent. Until she finally paused and said to Richard, "I love you, Richy."

And that's when Richard took that as the best time to build up the courage to tell Kim. *It's now or never*, Richard thought to himself. Richard began talking. "See, that's what I wanted to talk to you about, Kim. They called me into the office at the plant today…and let me go."

Kim, with a confused expression on her face, asked, "Huh? What? What do you mean! What are you talking about, Richy!" Kim pushed Richard away from her. She jumped up off his chest and sat up, putting her robe on.

Richard explained to Kim a little bit slower, making sure that she heard every word that came out of his mouth. Richard sat up onto the edge of the bed and said, "Kim, my supervisor called me into his office today. He told me that the plant no longer needs me. I mean…What could I say, Kim?" Richard paused for a brief moment, head down, and continued, "What could I do! I tried, I tried!"

Richard and Kim both were hollering back and forth at the top of their lungs. But Richard tried to keep things at a calm level as he said, "Don't worry, Kim…I'm going to take care of you and Jessie. Like my life depends on it. We still have the hot rod mechanic shop so…Whatever I have to do."

But Kim was too busy hysterically crying and screaming—"God! Why!"—to even hear Richard's plea to her. Richard tried to speak again to comfort Kim.

He said, "I'm going to look for some jobs on line." But Kim just broke out into a tirade, violently attacking Richard.

Kim was wildly windmill-slapping Richard while swinging her arms. Kim was scratching and hitting Richard. Richard was fighting to restrain Kim, pinning her down onto the bed, tightly gripping her wrist. Then Kim broke out into a verbal assault, attacking Richard's manhood.

Kim screamed, "I always knew you were a piece of shit! I should have never married your good-for-nothing ass! Broke motherfucker! Can't even take care of your family like a real man! Here's a newsletter, Jessie ain't your daughter, dumbass! I just didn't want to break your li'l soft ass heart!

Kim smirked sarcastically. "You're a real fucking loser! Jessie is Jeff's daughter!

Jeff was Richard's best friend and his best man at Richard's and Kim's wedding. But rumors circled that Kim was cheating on Richard with Jeff early in the relationship but were later proven to be just rumors. But the possibility of Kim cheating on Richard has always been in the back of Richard's mind.

Jessie was the sole reason that Richard had married Kim. Richard thought, *And now she wants to throw it in my face that Jessie isn't mine?* That was a low blow that ripped Richard's heart clean out of his chest. Not to mention during Richard's and Kim's argument, they didn't realize that during the loud commotion, Jessie awakened from out of her sleep.

Jessie was standing there, by their bedroom door, listening to every word that Kim had said about her not being Richard's daughter. Jessie was also watching her father straddle over her mother, pinning her wrist down to the bed.

Jessie was watching her mother struggling to free herself from Richard's hold. Kim was fighting Richard as she and Richard noticed Jessie standing in the doorway. Richard and Kim both said, "It's okay, go back to sleep, Jessie." Not wanting Jessie to see her mother and father fighting.

Richard had finally let go of Kim so she could get up. Kim snatched her blankets and pillows from off of the bed, headed to go sleep on the living room couch, but not before looking at Richard with a deep hatred and said, "I hate you! Fucking loser!" And she spit into Richard's face, then slammed the bedroom door behind herself. *Wham!*

Richard used his T-shirt to wipe Kim's loogie from out of his eye and off of his cheek. Then he threw his T-shirt at the bedroom door behind her.

Richard stood there for a few seconds, staring at the door and thinking about his wife, his daughter, his future, possibly losing his house, losing his job, maintaining his hot rod business, and his life.

Richard's thoughts and his mind were clouded, flooded, and racing, filled with confusion as tears streamed down his cheeks.

Richard kneeled down onto the bedroom floor and reached up under the bed for his fifth of vodka that he had stashed. Then he sat down on the edge of the bed. He continued drinking out of the bottle until he fell back and blacked out on the bed.

Chapter 2

Richard woke up the next morning groggy with a massive hangover. It was around 8:00 a.m. when the sounds of a loud police radio standing over him were going off.

A voice over the police radio said, "I'm in the suspect's bedroom now. I have visual contact. Over." Richard looked up, rubbing his eyes, trying to get his vision into focus, still groggy from the vodka hangover.

Richard was rubbing his eyes, thinking it was a dream or a nightmare, until he saw the two all-blue police-officer uniforms standing on each side of him. Both police officers had their Tasers in hand and ready to pull the trigger on Richard.

Richard said, "Wait, wait, wait! What's this all about! Wait, first of all, how did you guys get into my house!" Richard was crawling backward, away from the police's grasp and toward the headboard.

One of the police officers named Trau was Vietnamese. Officer Trau said, "It's okay, Mr. Ginn. Just remain calm. We just want to question you about a disturbance complaint that we received last night. And we'll be on our way, sir."

Richard was visibly furious and hurt that Kim would even allow the police officers into their home while he was sleeping. But Richard went along with the police officers anyway. Hoping that would encourage the police officers to leave out of his home that much quicker.

Then Officer Trau said, "This is strictly for your safety and ours, Mr. Ginn." But the other police officer was still uptight and nervous, observing Richard's every movement. His hand was still on the trigger of his Taser, aiming at Richard's torso. Officer Trau repeated, "Again this is just strictly for your safety and ours, sir. Just a formality." The officer went on, saying, "I'm going to have to ask you to put your hands behind your back for me, please."

Richard was becoming upset as he asked, "All of this for a fake disturbance call? Come on, man! Is this really necessary, Officer? Really! This is some bullshit!"

Officer Trau replied, saying, "It's just a formality, Mr. Ginn. We just need to question you. And we'll be on our way, sir."

While Officer Trau was pleading with Richard, Officer Trau's partner widened his stance, trying to get a more focused aim to tase Richard if Richard wasn't compliant to their orders.

You could see the forearm muscles tighten in Officer Trau's partner's arms. He was ready to tase as he barked commands at Richard. "Just do as you're fucking told! Do it now! Give me a fucking reason to trade my Taser for my Glock! Please!

Officer Trau, frustrated at his partner for instigating and antagonizing a hostile situation, looked over at his partner and said to him, "Knock it off, Rick!" Then Officer Trau looked back at Richard and said, "Come on, Mr. Ginn, we'll be in and out of here. Just cuff up for me."

Richard stood up and began putting on his underwear, sweats, and his T-shirt that he had wiped Kim's spit off of his face with. Then Richard began to put on his shoes. Richard reluctantly turned around for Officer Trau to put the handcuffs on him.

As Richard walked past the bedroom mirror in handcuffs, he glanced into it to see himself in handcuffs. A day and time where he had thought he would be the last person on the planet to see himself in handcuffs!

When Richard glanced into the mirror, he noticed the scratches that Kim had put on him last night, when she was scratching, punching, kicking, and slapping him while Richard tried to hold her down and stop her from fighting him.

Richard had scratches all over his upper arms, chest, shoulders and a couple scratches visible on his face. Richard looked bad! As he thought to himself, *Damn...this shit doesn't look good! Especially after that O. J. shit. They always believe the woman nowadays. But I just hope the police don't believe that I beat Kim up. And even if they do, I know Kim would stick up for me and tell them the truth.*

Those were all of the thoughts going through Richard's head. As he walked from the bedroom, down the stairs, and through the kitchen, where Kim and Richard's daughter, Jessie, was standing by the dining room table.

Jessie was holding on tight to Kim's leg, almost hiding behind her mother. Richard glanced over at both of them and walked on outside to the police car where all of Richard's neighbors were outside, standing on their front lawns, watching the commotion that their neighborhood wasn't accustomed to seeing.

Richard's neighbors have never seen police cars unless their children or grandchildren were police themselves, just visiting.

Richard was embarrassed; he walked out of his home with his head down, desperately trying to avoid eye contact with all the rest of his neighbors staring at him.

Officer Trau opened the back police car door. Richard climbed into the back seat of the police car and sat down. He was furious and just ready for the circus to be all over with. And the sooner the better. All of Richard's and Kim's friends in the neighborhood knew about their current money struggles of late. But all of their friends have extended their hands out to the Ginn family.

Officer Trau placed Richard into the back of the police car as he stood just outside the police car door while the door was still ajar. By this time, Kim, Jessie, and Officer Trau's partner that begged Richard to do something stupid so he could use his Glock instead of his Taser, they all were standing in front of the house. Officer Trau's partner was standing in front of Kim with his notepad and pen in hand moving feverishly. He was trying to keep up with every word that came out of Kim's mouth. The only time it seemed the officer could catch up was when Kim briefly stopped talking to take a long drag on her Newport cigarette.

Kim inhaled, pulling on her cigarette until it lit up bright red. Just before the long ash on the end had fallen off. Richard looked up at Kim, confused and angry. Angry that Kim wasn't moving quick enough to explain to the police that this was just one big misunderstanding.

Richard was thinking, *What could she possibly be telling them for this long?* But an even better question that Richard asked himself was, *Why is she even talking to the cops! And all over a li'l argument last night! If Kim wanted to press charges, it's nothing for her to press charges on me. But I didn't do anything.*

Richard even began to wonder and ask himself, *I wonder which neighbor called the cops on me?* All of his neighbors were staring, and Richard couldn't pick one out of the crowd. Richard thought that they were his friends. He felt beyond betrayed.

The officer that was standing next to Kim walked over to the police car that Richard was handcuffed in the back seat of. Officer Trau got out of his patrol car that Richard was seated in and met his partner in front of the police car. Officer Trau's partner was flipping through his notepad of notes that he had written down while listening to Kim.

Officer Trau's partner was explaining to Officer Trau as Officer Trau was nodding his head up and down, affirming that he understood every detail given to him by his partner. Officer Trau patted his partner on the back, as if to say job well done. Then Officer Trau's partner drove off in a separate squad car.

Richard was watching the whole thing unfold from the back seat of the police car. Richard thought to himself, *The cops are going through all of this? To the highest extreme over loud noise?*

Officer Trau got back into his own squad car, flipped through some more papers, inhaled a deep breath, and after dramatically exhaling, he looked back at Richard through his rearview mirror.

Officer Trau said to Richard, "Okay, this is what we have here, Mr. Ginn." Officer Trau paused for a brief moment, thinking of what words to choose next for Richard.

That's when Richard thought, *Man, just hurry up with the loud disturbance ticket. So I can go back into my house and get ready to go up to my hot rod shop. Check on things around the business and go job hunting. I need to pay these bills!*

Officer Trau said, "Okay, Mr. Ginn...you are being charged with rape, assault and battery, and kidnapping. Your wife, Kim Ginn, is the victim that wishes to pursue charges against you."

Richard was dumbfounded and speechless! He couldn't believe what he had just heard. Richard asked, "Rape! On my wife! Come on, please tell me that she isn't doing this to me!"

Richard continued under his breath faintly, "Please tell me that the cops don't believe this make believe made-up rape story? It's got to be a mistake! Kim loves me...right? Kim wouldn't do me like this. Would she? She wouldn't do this to me."

Richard continued, "Damn, how could this cop lie to me? He didn't have any intentions on cuffing me just for questioning. This motherfucker knew all along that he was arresting me for rape!"

Richard was sitting in the back of the police car, trying to make sense of what just happened and what his ears had just heard. Richard thought, *This motherfucker lied. And Kim lied too! That piece of shit knew damn well that he wasn't questioning me for my side of the disturbance call. They are the police! It says right on the outside of this car to protect and to serve.* Richard was becoming more and more angry with those thoughts racing through his mind.

Richard said to Officer Trau, "Wait a minute, Mr. Officer Trau, it has to be some sort of mistake or something here. Kim is my wife. We're married. I can't really rape my wife, can I? Yes...We did have sex last night, consensual sex. I did not and never would rape my wife. Officer! You have to believe me!"

Richard was adamantly trying to convince Officer Trau of his innocence. But Officer Trau responded by saying, "Well...I don't know what to tell you, Mr. Ginn—" Before Officer Trau could finish, Richard desperately cut him off again, trying to plead his case.

Richard said, "The only thing that I am guilty of, sir, is loving my family! And trying my damnest to provide the best for my family! Not to mention being the best husband that I can possibly be for the same woman that's sending me to jail right now!"

Richard continued, "You have to believe me! You just have to!"

Officer Trau just replied, "I'm not the one to do your convincing to. Mr. Ginn…you need to convince the judge. You need to convince the jury. I'm just doing my job, sir."

Richard dropped his head down heavily in disbelief. Speechless. Officer Trau went on, saying, "Now I have to read you your rights, Mr. Ginn." Officer Trau began reading Richard his rights. And the last thing that Richard remembered hearing was the last part of his rights. "If you can't afford an attorney, one will be *appointed* to you." Eerie words that echoed in Richard's mind and would ultimately haunt him and severely cripple society for a lifetime.

Chapter 3

Officer Trau asked Richard, "Do you understand your rights?"

Richard answered, "Yes, I understand my rights," sarcastically angry.

Officer Trau put his squad car into drive and radioed in to the police station. "Over."

The dispatcher answered, "Copy that."

Officer Trau began pulling his patrol car away from Richard's house. Richard took his last plea attempt to Kim, who was still standing in front of their house.

Richard put his lips up to the crack in the back window of the patrol car and hollered one last desperate plea to Kim, "Kim, please straighten this out! Please! It's just a big MISUNDERSTANDIIIINNNGGG!"

Richard's voice was faintly fading away the further the car drove off down the street, with fall leaves in the middle of the street, blowing up into the air, as the patrol car sped through the beautiful brown and burnt-orange fall-color leaves that blanketed the street.

On the ride to the police precinct, Richard envisioned his entire life and everything that he had worked for flash right before his eyes.

Richard loved Kim and didn't understand why she would lie like this. Richard figured that Kim was just mad and that she would eventually calm down and call the police station and tell them that she was just upset. And that's why she lied. Richard felt a relief, drawing the conclusion that, *This will all be over as soon as I get to the police station*. He let out a sigh of relief.

By the time that Richard and Officer Trau arrived at the precinct for booking, Richard had already forgiven his wife, Kim, in his mind. And as Richard was getting booked and fingerprinted, he was intrigued by the new state-of-the-art fingerprinting computer.

The fingerprinting process wasn't like the ones of those old cop shows that Richard used to watch, where the police used the old black fingerprinting ink. Richard thought to himself, *Wow! Technology is becoming more and more advanced today.*

A female deputy appeared and asked Richard, "Please stand up against the *x* on the wall. And face the camera for this mug shot. Richard was extremely embarrassed. He couldn't get over the fact that he was getting booked and fingerprinted for rape—for raping his wife at that. Richard slowly followed the lady deputy's order. Feeling mentally exhausted and drained, Richard backed up to the wall. The lady deputy snapped Richard's mug shot.

After taking Richard's mug shot, the lady deputy ordered Richard to, "Turn and face left for me, Mr. Ginn." She snapped the left mug shot of Richard's face. Then she ordered Richard to, "Turn and face right for me, sir."

Richard was sarcastically taking as long as he possibly could in following the deputy's orders. Richard's stomach was turning, and he was beginning to feel extremely sick at the thought of being in jail for something that he didn't do.

Richard attempted to hold his composure until he couldn't anymore and—"Blahhhhh uuhhhh." It all came up when he looked up and saw his mug shot on the computer screen! He held his vomit in his mouth until he got to the holding cell.

The holding cell was jam-packed with what seemed to be twenty other guys, lying wherever they could squeeze in at for room. The rock-solid hard concrete floor was top-of-the-line luxurious, compared to the iron bench for sitting or standing up for seven or more hours straight.

There were even men lying underneath the toilet where Richard swiftly made his way toward to spit out the vomit that he had been holding in his mouth since seeing his mug shot on the computer screen.

The man that was asleep underneath the toilet, where a big dark golden-yellow puddle of piss rested underneath, angrily hopped up to his feet. The man was still very visibly drunk from last night.

After losing and fighting for his balance and stumbling, he finally was able to stand. And when he did, he said to Richard, "*Que onda? Hey! What's up with that, homes!*"

The man spoke with a deep Southern Mexican raspy accent. The drunk man was pointing his finger in Richard's face, touching the tip of Richard's nose. The man was a heavyset Hispanic male, towering over Richard's five-foot-ten inches and 190-pound frame— almost double Richard's size.

Richard came from a totally different background than most of the men in the holding cell with him. Richard wasn't used to the verbal or physical aggressiveness from the Hispanic male.

Richard had never been in a fight his entire life. Richard was shaking to the point that his knees almost buckled and gave out on him as Richard just stood there with the Hispanic male's finger still touching his nose.

Richard quickly apologized to the clearly frustrated stranger. Richard said, "I am terribly sorry for that. I apologize to you, sir." Richard spoke in the softest most humble tone possible. Richard went on, "And I promise that it will not ever happen again. *Ever*! *I promise, sir*!"

Richard was praying that the man accepted his humble apology while everyone else in the holding cell stared at Richard, like they were more than anxiously ready to hurt him as well.

All of the other men in the holding cell were angry at Richard too for waking them up from out of their sleep. And there were other men angry at Richard for interrupting their collect calls to family and friends that they were feverishly trying to collect money from to bond out of jail. But Richard quickly defused the situation by apologizing to all the other men in the small shoulder-to-shoulder holding cell as well.

The Hispanic male lay right back down into his comfortable spot underneath the toilet, where the stench of dark-gold piss mixed with alcohol reeked! But it didn't seem to bother him at all because it had become a normal routine for the man. The Hispanic man quickly fell back to sleep after he snuggled down into the concrete floor.

Everyone else followed the giant Hispanic man's lead. They either went back to sleep or continued pleading on the phone for bond money. Some men were even begging their girlfriends for some type of forgiveness.

Richard spotted a little opening on the bench for himself. He was going to sit down and wait for a phone to get free so he could call his wife, Kim, and get back home. After an hour had almost passed, and Richard nodding in and out of his sleep, Richard heard someone hang the phone up.

The loud *bang* from the telephone had woken Richard up. Richard wondered why the man was so visibly angry as he stared at Richard with fire burning deep in his eyes while walking past Richard.

Richard quickly looked down at the floor, not trying to make eye contact with the man. As Richard slithered his way through and around all the other men crammed shoulder to shoulder, Richard was tight-rope walking to the phone. Richard was desperately trying hard not to step on or bump anybody lying on the floor.

Richard picked the phone up and called his house. *Ring. Ring. Ring.* After three tries of calling home and Kim not answering, Richard hung the phone up and thought, *I'll just try again around four o'clock. Hopefully Kim answers by then. Or I will be heading to the county jail, along with everyone else that can't seem to make bond.*

The more Richard thought about it, he couldn't take that chance. He started asking himself, *Who can I call? Who can I call?* His mind was racing as he was tapping the phone against his chin and going through names that he could call for bond money.

Richard called one of his buddies that was lucky enough to keep his job at the same plant that just had let Richard go. Richard said to himself, "Oh, I can call my buddy John to get me out! And I'll just pay him back as soon as I can!"

Richard spotted a clock on the wall just outside of the cell in the hallway. It was twelve noon. Richard said to himself, "Good! We're on lunch break right now!"

Richard called John up at the plant, and John eagerly agreed to come help his friend Richy out. But John couldn't resist asking

Richard why he was in jail. Richard told John that he would explain later. He just needed him to come get him out of jail first. They both hung their telephones up.

Twenty minutes had passed, then a lady deputy came to the holding cell's jail bars and called out Richard's name. She hollered out, "Mr. Ginn? Is there a Mr. Ginn?"

Richard sprung to his feet quickly and answered, "That's me! Right here! I'm Mr. Ginn!" He was waving his hand, trying to catch the deputy's attention. Richard was thinking that it must be his buddy John, there to bond him out.

The lady deputy replied, "Mr. Ginn, it's time for you to see the judge, sir." With calculated flawless precision, Richard slithered and tiptoed his way over, around, and through all of the bodies crammed into the jam-packed holding cell.

Richard was whispering, trying not to wake up the guys that were sleep or disturb the guys that were still on the telephone. Richard whispered, "Excuse me, excuse me, pardon me, sir, pardon me—" While the men just lay there, looking up at Richard and hoping that he would make the mistake of accidentally allowing his shoe to touch their clothes.

Richard was successful, he made it through the men who were obstacles of land mines like his life depended on it. And he was glad that he had made it through.

*****

Richard went to see the judge. He waited his turn behind all the other people being arraigned. One man for identity theft, another man for computer hacking, a younger black lady that couldn't have been no more than twenty years old. She was being arraigned for trafficking 250 pounds of marijuana from Arizona.

Richard was also behind a parole violator, but the one crime that seemed to catch Richard's attention the most, a little child-faced eighteen-year-old kid. He was charged with carjacking, sexual assault, and attempted murder.

Richard thought that the kid looked too young and too innocent to be charged with those type of heinous crimes. But the judge
set the kid's bond at $1 million cash surety.

Then it was Richard's turn to stand in front of and face the judge.
Richard got arraigned on rape, assault, and kidnapping charges. And
the judge ordered Richard to stay away from his wife and daughter.
"Until court proceedings are resolved."

The only thing that Richard was allowed to do was get his car
but only in the company of a police officer. And that's if he's fortu-
nate enough to make bond.

Richard's bond was set at $5,000, 10 percent. But if at any time
Richard violates the stipulations of his bond, then his bond would
automatically be revoked. And Richard would be ordered to sit in jail
until his trial date.

The judge asked Richard, "Mr. Ginn, do you fully understand
the stipulations of your bond, sir?"

Richard confidently answered, "Yes, ma'am, I do."

The judge responded, "Then you are free to go, Mr. Ginn."

Richard walked out of the courtroom feeling extremely relieved
that the judge didn't set his bond at an unreachable amount. Especially
since losing his job in the thick of the pandemic.

Richard thought that $500 wasn't too bad and that his buddy
John should be able to handle that. Richard was escorted directly
back to the holding cell where he stood right at the door, waiting to
hear his name because that meant his buddy John had bonded him
out. Richard wasn't taking any chances of going back through all of
those people lying on the floor.

The clock on the wall was now reading 3:45 p.m. Richard was
beginning to wonder what was taking his buddy John so long to get
there and bond him out. Richard began to panic. He was nervous
that if John didn't get him out by 5:00 p.m., that he would surely
end up in the county jail. And Richard was definitely not trying to
go to the county jail.

Chapter 4

Richard had seen and heard too many stories of what went on the inside. And it was fights, stabbings, and rapes. Richard kept staring back at the clock which seemed as if it was moving fast-paced at double the normal speed. The time was now 4:48 p.m., and Richard heard the county jail deputy's belly chains. The chains were rattling and jingling at a distance down the hall and getting closer. He thought for sure it was over.

The lady deputy arrived at the holding cell bars and told everybody, "Step out and line up to be cuffed up. Off to the county jail." Richard stepped out of the holding cell and into the line with everyone else waiting to be cuffed up. A male deputy from the county jail put handcuffs on Richard. As Richard held his arms up high in the air, the county jail transportation deputy locked Richard's handcuffs with his key.

Right then the lady deputy standing next to the male deputy hollered out, "Ginn! I need Ginn! Where you at!"

Richard tried to raise his hand up, but the handcuffs connected to the belly chains wouldn't allow him to fully raise his hand. So Richard loudly said, "That's me, missus! Right here, right here!"

The lady deputy responded, "Looks like today is your lucky day. Somebody must looooove youuuuuuu!" With a big joking smile on her face, the lady deputy looked over at the male deputy doing all the handcuffing.

She said to him, "Mr. Ginn has been bonded out. You can take those off of this one."

Richard let out a huge sigh of relief—*whew!*—exhaling almost all of the air in his body. And just like that, Richard was a free man again. But for how long? Richard didn't know.

Richard exited the elevator where his good friend John was sitting and waiting for his buddy Richard. John wanted to make sure Richard was all right. John stood up as Richard was quickly approaching him. Richard shook John's hand and said, "Thanks, John. I promise to pay you back!"

Richard hurriedly told John, "I will fill you in on what happened in the car! Come on!" Richard was anxious to fill John in. They both got into John's car as a police car pulled up next to the driver's side of John's car. The police officer rolled his police car window down.

The police officer said, "There's already a police officer at your residence so that you can secure your vehicle with supervision. But your bond restrictions states that you can't stay. That you must leave."

Richard exhaled with frustration and replied, "The judge had already explained it to me, sir. Thank you." Richard tapped John on the arm and said, "Let's go." And John was off in his new Dodge Challenger Hellcat, driving through the downtown green traffic lights, headed to Richard's house.

Richard explained the whole situation with Kim to John. John was listening to Richard in total disbelief about how Kim lied to the police about Richard raping her because he had lost his job. John didn't even question if Richard was being truthful. John knew that his buddy Richard wasn't capable of such a terrible accusation on his wife. John believed that his friend was an innocent man.

John couldn't believe what Kim had done because everything that Richard had done was for his wife, Kim, and his daughter, Jessie. Richard loved his family and Kim way too much to even think of doing something like that.

John arrived at Richard's house where a police car was parked in front, waiting. The police officer kept occasionally looking up into his rearview mirror, back at John and Richard parked behind him. But the police officer never exited his police squad car. The police officer was just making sure that Richard followed his bond restrictions and that Richard left the property like he was ordered to do.

Richard exited John's car and looked at the police officer. The police officer looked back at Richard through his rearview mirror but still did not exit his police vehicle. He just nodded his head, as if to give Richard the go-ahead.

Richard hurriedly exited his friend John's car and made his way to his brand-new Impala SS that was parked beside Kim's car in the driveway. Richard pressed the car alarm button to disarm the car alarm—*chirp, chirp*—while John was still parked behind the police car. John was making sure his buddy Richard left the house with no altercations.

Richard pulled the door handle to his car. He wanted to get into his car as quickly as possible before his wife, Kim, came out of the house and started a confrontation, risking his bond being revoked. But that's when Richard realized that he had no money at all when he reached into his pocket to pull his keys out.

John was slowly beginning to drive off once he had seen Richard getting into his car. Richard hollered, "John! John! John!" John heard Richard hollering. John looked back and stomped on his car brakes—*urt*! Richard ran up to John's passenger side window of his car. Richard asked John, "I need some money! Do you have any money on you?"

John reached into his pants pocket and pulled out about $600 that was left over from posting Richard's bond. John answered, "This is all that I have, Rich." As if John wasn't sure if it was enough to help Richard out. John extended his hand toward Richard; his palm was up, filled with mostly one-hundred-dollar bills, with fifties, twenties, and ten-dollar bills mixed all in as well.

Richard quickly reached inside of John's passenger side window one hand at a time. Richard was grabbing and stuffing as much money as he could at one time, stuffing the money into his pants pockets until he grabbed it all. Even quickly picking up the money that had fallen onto the passenger seat.

Richard squatted down to eye-level with the car's passenger side window. He looked his buddy John directly into his eyes, with the deepest of sincerity, and said, "Thank you, J, don't worry, I will pay you back as soon as I can…I promise."

John looked Richard directly back into his eyes, being the real, true, and concerned friend that John was. He said to Richard,

"Richy, don't worry about it. Just be careful. You hear me? Just please be careful! If you need anything—I mean anything—don't hesitate to give me a call, okay?"

Richard, without saying one word, just nodded his head up and down, as if to say, *I will.* Richard turned and began to walk away. That's when John called Richard's name again and said, "Richy… anything."

Richard turned around and quickly began walking back toward his car. And that's when Richard had noticed his daughter, Jessie, staring at him. Jessie was standing in the living room behind the big bay window.

Richard stopped dead in his tracks, noticing his beautiful daughter staring at him getting into his car. Richard stared back at Jessie in a deep daze. Jessie was waving bye to her daddy and smiling like she missed him.

Richard was waving back at Jessie and hoped that she could read his lips when he said, "Daddy loves you." Then Richard kissed the palm of his hands and blew her a kiss.

Just as Richard had blown Jessie a kiss, his wife, Kim, had appeared in the window to see who Jessie was waving at. As soon as Kim saw it was Richard, Kim quickly grabbed Jessie and snatched her away back from the window.

The police officer that was sitting in his car saw Richard waving at his daughter. The police officer exited his car like he was angry with Richard. In a loud aggressive tone, he hollered at Richard, "All right! Let's go, Mr. Ginn!" Richard looked back at the police officer and quickly snapped out of his deep daze.

Richard hopped inside of his Impala SS, started the car up, and backed out of the driveway. Richard sped off down the street, blowing the fall leaves up into the air behind him. *Vroom!* He was gone.

Chapter 5

After Richard's friend John had posted bond for him, while being processed out of the precinct, the lady deputy handed Richard an attorney business card so that Richard could seek legal representation for free if he couldn't afford an attorney.

The lady deputy told Richard, "Call no later than a week from today if you want an attorney to represent you for your preliminary examination."

The date that Richard was released on bond was November 15. Richard didn't have a clue what a preliminary examination was. He had never been in trouble before in his entire life. So just the sound of *preliminary examination* terrified Richard in the worst way. Richard still had his cell phone. It was sitting in the passenger seat in his car.

Richard had been out of jail and out on bond for about four days now. Richard was using some of the money that his friend John had given him to sleep at a low-budget, crime-riddled, prostitution, high-drug traffic, and rodent-infested motel.

Richard wasn't comfortable there at all! Totally opposite of the struggle and blemish-free lifestyle that he dedicated his life to build. But for $30 a night and on a $600 budget, he couldn't complain!

Richard thought to call the attorney that was on the card that the lady deputy at the jail had given him, just to let him know that he *would not* be needing his services and that he had his own family lawyer that had been representing his family for years.

Richard sat up from lying down in the motel room bed, walked over and closed the door to his room first. It kept blowing open all through the night from the broken latch that didn't lock.

The strong night wind kept blowing and pushing his shoe out of the door. And the fat healthy mice weren't any better! They were running rampant in fierce competition with the army of roaches scrambling on top of each other!

Richard sat back down on the bed. He leaned up against the headboard. Then he reached for his pants and pulled the attorney's card out of his pocket. The attorney card read "Geofrey Davis Attorney at Law" across the top of the card.

The middle of the card read "Criminal defense lawyer for..." The card listed all of the more serious crimes: murder, armed robbery, great bodily harm, concealed weapons, etc., including what Richard was charged with—sexual assault.

To Richard, it wasn't even an option to have this Geofrey Davis guy for his lawyer to represent him. Richard was a firm believer in "you get exactly what you pay for!" And since this lawyer wouldn't be getting paid by Richard, Richard thought, *That lawyer could care less if I get found guilty and sent to prison. He's not making or losing a dime representing me.*

Richard felt more confident, assured, and at ease paying good money for what he wanted. The only thing that Richard forgot about was he lost his job! And he had no real source of income coming in.

Richard couldn't rely on his automechanic shop. Business was slow to none due to the pandemic. And the shop was on the verge of being lost. Richard was in debt.

But one thing in Richard's favor was that the family lawyer knew that Richard was good for the retaining fee that he would ask for his legal representation.

Well, at least that was what Richard was hoping for, that the lawyer would know that he was good for the money because Richard always has been throughout all their years of business dealings.

Richard thought, *I'll just explain my situation to the family lawyer...and* I know *that he would be patient enough to go to bat for me.* So the money was the least of Richard's worries.

Richard called this Geofrey Davis guy to fire him before he even hired him. And Richard did just that. And Geofrey Davis was beyond more than okay with Richard not needing his services too. Richard heard the subtle excitement, but Geofrey Davis quickly switched back to a calm professional emotion, preserving his game face.

Richard thought that Geofrey Davis sounded as if the less work that he had to do for *free*, the better off he would be. So Richard was beyond more than okay with Geofrey Davis not representing him too.

Richard immediately began dialing his family lawyer next. And Richard was right! The family lawyer eagerly agreed. He was going to represent Richard at his preliminary examination, free of charge. But the day of the preliminary examination, the family lawyer told Richard to "Have ten thousand for me to represent you at trial…if it goes that far."

Richard agreed to have the $10,000 the day of the preliminary examination if after the examination, findings went that far. But if it didn't go to trial, the family lawyer told Richard, "Consider this a favor for the family."

Richard told the family lawyer his case identification number which was written on the back of the court-appointed lawyer's attorney card. The same card that the lady deputy had given him when he posted bond. Richard wanted the family lawyer to properly be prepared.

Then Richard told him the date of his preliminary examination. It was scheduled for November 23. Richard and his family lawyer both said, "All right. See you on the twenty-third." Then they both hung their phones up.

Richard left his motel room, headed to his bank to withdraw the $10,000 out of his savings account. But the lady bank teller working at the window was confused because Richard's bank account balance read all zeros, indicating that Richard didn't have any money in his bank account. Richard didn't even understand.

Richard told the bank teller at the window, "Wait a minute, ma'am, this must be some type of mistake or something." Richard, with disbelief and concern on his face, was confused.

Richard quickly dumped all of his bank account cards out onto the counter, even the savings account card that he had started for his daughter, Jessie. Richard was beginning to panic, as all of his bank account cards were falling out everywhere as he pulled them out. Richard even began to get loud and rude with the lady bank teller. He was causing an embarrassing scene by now.

All of the women in the bank were staring at Richard. They all were grasping their purses intensely tight to their bodies. Richard was looking like a crazy and dirty homeless man. His normal clean-shaven face was now a big scruffy beard that was now hiding his face.

Richard's clothes, that once stayed nice, clean, and pressed, were now a yellowish brown, underarm-stained dress shirt and filthy dress slacks. Richard's clothes looked ragged, like he wore them for years.

After Richard's rude comments, the bank teller woman said to him, "Please calm down, sir. We'll figure this all out. I'm going to get my supervisor. Just one second, please."

Richard was so angry that he had made the bank teller lady nervous. She was visibly shaken, not knowing if she would hit the panic button on him or not, meaning a robbery was in progress. The bank teller woman's hand remained on her panic button, nearly from the first time that Richard had stepped into her line.

The bank teller woman didn't get a chance to get her supervisor from the back. He was already watching the commotion from the back. The supervisor was watching Richard from every angle on the bank's security monitors from the very first time that Richard had stepped inside of the bank.

The lady bank teller's supervisor immediately appeared from out of the back of the bank to see exactly what the commotion was all about. Richard explained to the supervisor that he wanted to make a withdrawal from his bank account, but for some odd and strange reason, his bank account was reading all zeros.

Richard had been saving money in his bank account from out of his paychecks for years. And he felt that there was not any reason for his account balance to be reading all zeros. The supervisor said to Richard, "Follow me, sir."

Richard eagerly followed the supervisor to the back office of the bank where the supervisor pulled out a chair and asked Richard to sit down. The supervisor then got onto his laptop and punched Richard's name into the bank's system.

Richard was leaning forward, attempting to look over the supervisor's shoulder. Richard wanted to see what exactly he was looking at for himself. Richard was curious as to why the supervisor was shaking his head in disbelief.

The supervisor just kept using the computer's mouse, scrolling down and looking at Richard's transactions and mumbling to himself quietly, "Mmm, mmmm, mm! Mmmmm. That's not good... that's not good at all."

Richard leaned up a little closer, still not able to fully see the entire computer screen until he just finally stood up, towering over the supervisor's back and said, "What! What is it! Where's my money!"

The supervisor answered, "I see exactly where your money went, Mr. Ginn...and you're not going to be happy about it either."

Richard, visibly frustrated, replied, "I just want to know where my money is, sir."

The supervisor answered, "It shows here that your wife, Kim, came in the bank on the fifteenth and withdrew everything that you had, Mr. Ginn. And that's why your account is showing all zeros for account balance."

Richard was paralyzed, numb, and speechless. He fell completely silent and began to think to himself, *The fifteenth? The fifteenth? That was just literally a few days ago! As a matter of fact... that is the same day that I went to jail! Nooooo, she didn't? That dirty little*—Richard said to the supervisor, "No, no, no. Wait a minute. She can't do that, can she?"

The supervisor stood up, turned and faced Richard, then said, "Unfortunately yes...yes, she can. Because you and your wife have a joint account together. Remember?" He looked Richard directly eye to eye.

Richard stood there, feeling helpless, thinking about what his next move would be. Finally Richard just shook his head in disbelief, let out a deep exhale—*whew*—and said, "Okay, thank you, sir. I apologize for the misunderstanding and inconvenience."

Richard then turned around, looked at the lady bank teller that he first tried to get his withdrawal from, and said to her, "I'm sorry, missus. I really am. Thank you." And Richard walked past her standing in the doorway. And just like that, Richard was back in his car.

Richard was just sitting there, dumbfounded, still thinking about what he should do next, asking himself, "What can I do next? What can I do next?" Richard was hurt, lost, and confused. To think that Kim would do him like that. Finally he started his car up and drove off. Richard put his left blinker on and jumped right into the flow of traffic.

Richard went back to his motel room and thought long and hard, trying to figure out why his wife, Kim, would do him like that, as if she was trying to do her best to send him to prison, knowing that he didn't do what she was accusing him of. Richard was deeply hurt as tears streamed down his cheeks.

Richard worked tirelessly hard to provide for his wife, Kim, and his daughter, Jessie. Richard did whatever Kim wanted. No matter how daunting the task was, Richard always delivered. All Richard ever wanted to do was make his wife happy.

Richard was back at his motel room, asking himself, "And she really done me like this? After I told her I just lost my job?"

It was extremely difficult for Richard to make sense of it all. He sat down on the edge of his bed, still stumped on what to do next. His preliminary examination was in the next couple of weeks. And he didn't even know how he would come up with the $10,000 for trial. If it were to be a trial, Richard wanted the money to be handy just in case.

*****

Those couple of weeks Richard had talked about had passed quick! It was now November 23, and Richard still couldn't come up with that ten grand! Richard thought again, *My only other option is to explain to the family lawyer that I need just a little more time to get the money together. And hopefully he'll understand again and work with me.* At least that was what Richard was hoping for.

Richard pulled up to the courtroom building and saw his family lawyer's Mercedes Benz parked in front. He was drinking expensive coffee and reading a local Minneapolis E-News. He had been waiting in his car for Richard to pull up.

Richard parked his Impala SS, hopped out, and greeted the family lawyer with a firm familiar big handshake. The family lawyer barely recognized Richard in his worn and tattered clothes. His big scruffy beard and long hair were not the norm for Richard.

It took the family lawyer a couple seconds to recognize Richard. The family lawyer was trying desperately to make Richard's face out. Richard still was shaking the lawyer's hand when the lawyer, with a confused look on his face, asked, "Richard?"

Richard smiled and answered, "Yes…It's me. I know, I know."

The family lawyer shook Richard's hand and asked, "Richy… what happened?"

Richard answered, "I'm kinda going through a little situation right now. That's why I need your help! But I will explain later!" Richard said to the family lawyer, "I couldn't come up with the $10,000 yet. But if you give me a little more time, I'm positive that I can get it."

The family lawyer told Richard, "I'll just get your preliminary postponed for the day. Just to give you more time to get things situated." The family lawyer told Richard that he would just tell the judge that he needed more time to properly prepare. And that's just what the family lawyer did, just that.

The family lawyer said to the judge, "I just recently received Mr. Ginn's caseload, Your Honor. And if it's not too much to ask of the court, I would like to request an extension to be properly prepared."

The judge granted the family lawyer's request. And Richard felt relieved, walking out of the courtroom while telling his lawyer, "Thank you. I really do appreciate you being so patient with me. And I promise to have that ten thousand for you our next court date." Then Richard and the family lawyer went their separate ways until the next prelim.

The judge set the preliminary examination date back one month from the day. The next preliminary examination date was set for December 23, exactly one month away. Richard went out looking for a job, trying to come up with the ten grand. Or at least some of it.

But with no luck. Still in the thick of the pandemic, nobody was hiring. People were losing not only their jobs but their businesses as well. So nobody was hiring.

Not a day went by that Richard wasn't thinking about his wife, Kim, and their daughter, Jessie. He worried about how they were doing and if they were all right. Richard was sitting in his motel room for endless hours. He was staring out of his motel room window and observing all of the criminal activity just on the other side of his motel room door.

The motel parking lot was full of hand-to-hand drug transactions. A lot of strange men and women pulling up in their cars with the lights off and handpicking prostitutes. Richard was staring at the interactions in between daydreaming, thinking about his wife and daughter.

Richard picked his phone up off the bed and held it for a second. He was contemplating on calling his wife, Kim. And after only a few seconds of thinking about it, Richard finally mustered up the courage to call his own house.

Richard dialed the first three digits of their house telephone number. Then he paused for a brief second, Richard thought that it wouldn't be a good idea to call. Richard said to himself, "Nahhhh, I would be in violation of my bond." Richard quickly hung his phone up.

Richard was still sitting there in complete silence, staring out of his window at all of the drug dealers running up to every car that they thought wanted to buy drugs.

Richard was also staring at all of the prostitutes trying to get into any and every car that they wanted to spend some money on sexual favors. Richard was still thinking about his wife and young daughter.

Richard sat back in his chair, tilted the chair back onto its rear hind legs, and was tapping his cell phone up against his knee. And it was killing Richard. He couldn't resist the temptation any longer of hearing his wife, Kim's, voice. Richard said to himself, "If I could just hear your voice so that I would know that you are doing okay. Then I could sleep at night with a clear conscience."

Richard had been tossing and turning, getting very little—if any—sleep for the last few nights. Richard couldn't fight the temptation any longer. He picked his telephone up again. Richard dialed the entire telephone number to his house.

The telephone rang. *Ring. Ring.* Richard's wife, Kim, picked the telephone up and answered, "Hello?"

But when she answered hello, Richard could hear Kim and another man giggling in the background. Richard heard the man saying to Kim, "Come on, baby…hang the phone up. I'm ready—" Richard immediately hung the phone up. *Click!* He was instantly infuriated, holding his phone as it hummed with a dial tone.

Richard asked himself, "Why is Kim doing me like this? What did I do to deserve to be treated like this? All I ever tried to do was love you, Kim. Kim, why!"

Richard was feeling extremely sad and helpless until he snapped out of it. Richard picked his big fifth of 100-percent-proof vodka up from off of the dresser and turned the bottle up, guzzling mouthfuls until the vodka was leaking out of the corners of his mouth and choking him.

That was Richard's way of running from the pain of things that he didn't want to face—picking the liquor bottle up and drinking to numb the pain. And after Richard's first initial big gulp, he was right back to infuriated! Only now, from the vodka, his anger was intensified!

Richard was fuming, thinking, *What man did Kim have the nerve to have in my house! In my bed!* But what had angered Richard even more was when he wondered, *What man does Kim have around my daughter!*

Richard didn't waste another second. He hopped into his impala SS and tore through the city streets of Minneapolis, all the way across town to his once-home to check on his daughter. Richard turned onto the street that his house was on. He slowly rode past, trying to look into the gigantic bay window in front of his home. Richard wanted to see what was going on. He also wanted to see who was that strange man's voice that he heard giggling with Kim in the background of his home.

As Richard rode past, he didn't see any other car parked in his driveway. All Richard noticed was that his wife's car was parked in the driveway where it's always parked at. So Richard continued passing by slowly and looking into the den. Richard was hoping to see his daughter. But the lights were off, so she was probably asleep.

Richard came to an almost complete stop in front of his house. And that's when he noticed that his porch light had come on, and the front door had opened up. But before he could see who it was that was coming out of the house, Richard stomped on and accelerated the gas pedal, speeding off down the street while looking back at his house through his rearview mirror.

That's when Richard saw Kim come out of the house onto the front porch in her nightgown, and some strange guy had come out of the house behind her.

The strange man had wrapped his arms around Kim and looked down the street in Richard's direction. Kim and the strange man was trying to make out whose car that was in front of their home. The strange man said to Kim, "It must have been the pizza man, honey. Now bring your sexy ass back in here!"

The strange man firmly gripped and cupped both of Kim's buttocks with both of his hands. The strange man was standing in front of her. As she jumped up into the man's arms and wrapped both of her legs tightly around his waist. He gleefully carried Kim back inside of the house. Richard watched it all unfold through his rearview mirror as he continued driving down the street. Richard was hurt with how Kim could move on that quick.

Richard drove back to his motel room and finished off the rest of that bottle of vodka. He drank and guzzled until the vodka was all gone, and he had passed out.

*****

A few weeks had passed, then a whole month had quickly flown by.

It was now Richard's preliminary examination date, December 23, and Richard still couldn't come up with the $10,000 for the lawyer. Times were too hard. And he couldn't get that type of loan from anybody.

Everybody that Richard had known from his small circle of family, friends, and coworkers, they all were saving their money and everything they own in the pandemic because they didn't know when or if their turn would come for poverty to strike. Some of Richard's family and friends were losing their jobs and homes.

The friends that Richard thought could help him out, he called them. But they all said the same thing. "I'm saving everything that I have right now. So I really don't have it to loan."

Chapter 6

Richard was stumped. So he went into his bathroom, grabbed his razor blade out of the medicine cabinet. Richard pulled out his shaving cream, and he began shaving. He wanted to shave off the big scruffy beard that he wasn't used to seeing on himself. Richard didn't even recognize himself anymore. He wanted to appear presentable for his preliminary examination.

Richard didn't want to look like some crazed killer. Richard showered and put a clean change of clothes on. His buddy John had given him some clean clothes out of his own closet.

Richard was ready for his preliminary examination. But he didn't have that $10,000 that the family lawyer had requested. Richard hoped that he would understand and help him out as long as he could to help keep him out of jail.

Richard dreaded the thought of going to jail. Not only didn't Richard have that ten thousand for the lawyer, but that $600 that his buddy John had loaned him was running low by now also. With Richard buying food, paying for his motel room, and buying gas, Richard was close to being broke!

All Richard had to his name was about $175. Richard didn't know what he was going to do once that money was gone.

Richard grabbed that $175 from off of his motel room dresser. He glanced into the dresser mirror, making sure that he was looking respectable and presentable. Richard straightened and tightened his tie up. He got into his car and headed toward the courtroom.

Richard was scheduled for his preliminary examination for the kidnapping and sexual assault that his wife, Kim, had lied and accused him of.

Richard thought to arrive early so that he could fill the family lawyer in on his money situation. Richard prayed that the family lawyer would understand and be patient with him for just a little while longer to help him stay out of prison. Richard's fingers were crossed.

Richard was extremely grateful as he thought, *Well, even if he doesn't want to help me out at trial, at least he did help me out at my preliminary examination. And free of charge at that.*

Richard went on, saying, "And the family lawyer is just that good to get the entire case dismissed. So I am really liking my chances!"

So that was exactly what Richard had banked on because of the simple fact that he couldn't come up with the money that the lawyer had requested Richard to get to represent him.

Richard knew that the prosecutor's case was weak because it was built solely on lies. The lies of Richard's wife at that. Richard truly believed that the judge would definitely see right through it and dismiss his case today.

Richard thought, *I can't see them taking me to trial for this BS, so I really don't see the need to come up with the $10,000 anyway.*

Richard pulled his car up to the courthouse and parked. Richard didn't see his lawyer waiting for him anywhere as he did the last time they were supposed to meet. Richard was beginning to wonder if maybe he had misheard the date that he was supposed to show up.

Richard got out of his car and looked around with a puzzled look on his face. And that's when the family lawyer appeared out of a shiny brand-new metallic-gray Range Rover, parked directly in front of Richard's car.

The family lawyer's car was a different car from the last car that Richard had last seen him in. Richard said to himself, "The last car that he was in was a Mercedes Benz...ooooh, that's why I didn't recognize him."

They shook hands and greeted each other. The family lawyer jokingly said to Richard, "Hey, Rich, maaaan, you really clean up well. It's almost scary how many faces you have."

They both laughed as Richard replied, "I know, right? But look, I really need to talk to you."

Richard placed his arm around the family lawyer's shoulder and began to whisper into his ear as they began to walk off.

Richard was explaining to the family lawyer that he hadn't come up with the $10,000 yet. The family lawyer was just nodding his head to every word that Richard was saying to him. They were both walking through the court building toward the courtroom.

When the family lawyer and Richard both entered into the courtroom, they heard the bailiff call out, "*State of Minnesota v. Richard Blake Ginn.*" Richard and the family lawyer stood up at the defense table. They were acknowledging that they both were present in the courtroom.

Richard was feeling very, very confident. And why shouldn't he? Richard had one of the state of Minnesota's most feared, most known, respected, biggest, and most powerful attorney standing beside him. And he was ready for war!

But what Richard's family lawyer said next totally blew Richard's mind! Richard was blindsided.

The family lawyer cleared his throat before he began to speak. "Mmm…mmmm…yes, Your Honor, I am here in behalf of my client, Mr. Richard Blake Ginn, for the record."

The young female judge, which looked to be in her late thirties, responded, "Please continue, Counsel."

The family lawyer proceeded, and what he said next, Richard couldn't believe what he was hearing. The family lawyer said, "Yes, Your Honor, thank you, and I really do apologize for not addressing the court in an timely manner. But I would like to withdraw my name from representation of Mr. Ginn due to a conflict of interest, a breakdown in the attorney-client relationship.

Richard couldn't believe what he had just heard from whom he thought was a family friend and whom he thought was his lawyer. Richard thought that the family lawyer understood his circumstances because he was explaining the situation to the family lawyer earlier. And he was nodding his head as if he understood every word that Richard was saying.

Richard thought that the family lawyer was willing to work with him and be patient. Richard, with a puzzled look on his face, was thinking, *Conflict of interest? Yeah, the conflict of interest was that*

I didn't have his damn money! And that was the damn breakdown in the attorney-client relationship!

Richard was listening in total disbelief, his jaw dropped as he fell desperately silent. He looked back and forth, and back again, between his lawyer and the judge. Richard was listening intensely to every word that his lawyer was saying to the judge.

Richard was furious and thinking, *Breakdown in attorney-client relationship? How? We were just laughing and joking on the way inside of the court building. Yeah…the breakdown in our relationship wasn't until I said I couldn't come up with the ten grand.*

The judge was listening to every word that Richard's attorney was saying to her. She had a dormant look on her face as she glanced back and forth from Richard to his lawyer, and from Richard's lawyer back at him. Her face was as stiff, still, and emotionless as concrete.

The judge asked, "Are you sure that this is what you both think is best?"

The family lawyer answered, "Yes, Your Honor, Mr. Ginn and I talked just prior to this examination. And that was when we both agreed that this decision is in his and my best interest."

Richard was looking over at his lawyer with his eyes wide open, not even flinching to even blink, knowing that his lawyer had just lied. Richard's lawyer had just lied to the judge. And right in front of him! Under oath at that! Richard was thinking to himself, *We both agreed? When! Where was I at! I didn't agree to anything! And you are supposed to be a lawyer? Some lawyer you are!*

The judge began talking again. She said, "We are still going to proceed with the aaaahhhh…" The judge quickly thumbed through a stack of papers that were sitting in front of her at her bench. The judge continued speaking, "We will proceed with the preliminary examination today. Since everyone is already present today."

The judge went on, "Does Mr. Ginn have legal representation present with him here today?"

The family lawyer answered, "Yes, he does, Your Honor."

The court-appointed lawyer that Richard was given when he had posted bond stood up. The judge had said to the lawyer that stood up, "Approach the bench and state your name for the record, sir."

The lawyer that stood up grabbed his briefcase, approached the bench, and stood directly next to Richard as Richard's family lawyer took a step backward. He was given the new lawyer space to stand. Richard looked up and down at this strange guy that was now calling himself Richard's lawyer.

The new lawyer began speaking to the judge. "Your Honor, I am Mr. Ginn's court-appointed attorney, Geofrey Davis. I was given Mr. Ginn's case the day that he was charged with sexual assault. Your Honor, Mr. Ginn's attorney had notified me a couple of days ago... on the twenty-first to be exact. He indicated that he would no longer be representing Mr. Ginn any further. And he asked me to be present and make an appearance today."

The judge was listening and occasionally taking notes. The new lawyer, Geofrey Davis, went on speaking, "So I will be representing Mr. Ginn here today for his preliminary examination. And for his sexual assault trial also. If necessary, if it goes that far, Your Honor."

Richard was listening to his new lawyer, Geofrey Davis, and was surprisingly feeling impressed. Geofrey Davis's whole demeanor, standing confidently, articulate as he spoke to the judge, really impressed Richard.

Richard had let his guard down a little, feeling as if he could trust this Geofrey Davis guy. And that he might have gotten lucky, not needing the ten grand after all. Richard thought to himself, *Looks like I saved myself ten grand aaaaand got the case dismissed at the same time.* Richard liked his chances with his court-appointed lawyer.

Richard went from a tired and worn-out posture, as he stood next to Geofrey Davis, to now an overly confident stance. Richard's entire demeanor was extremely clear and spoke volumes. Richard's body language was indicating that he was now ready for war!

The judge looked over at Richard's family lawyer and said, "You are now dismissed, sir."

And the family lawyer replied, "Thank you, Your Honor." Then he bent over to pick up his briefcase. And as he was exiting the courtroom, the family lawyer had patted Richard on his back and said, "Good luck, Richy...I'm sorry. I really am."

Richard, still visibly angry at the family lawyer, pretended as if he didn't hear a single word that the family lawyer had just said to him. Richard just kept staring straight ahead, never blinking one time. Richard was waiting on the next phase of the court proceedings.

The judge said, "I think that we wasted enough time here this morning. And if it's not too much of a problem, and if both parties don't mind, I would really like to move forward with this preliminary examination." The judge was being sarcastic, growing visibly impatient with all of the antics.

Richard's lawyer, Mr. Davis, replied, "Yes, Your Honor. I apologize. I am ready to proceed."

The judge looked over at the prosecutor's table and asked, "If it's not a problem with you either, I would like to continue."

The prosecutor's table stood up and answered, "Yes, Your Honor, we are ready to proceed!"

Mr. Davis looked over at Richard and whispered, "Come on, Richard, let's take a seat."

Richard leaned over to Mr. Davis's ear with a puzzle and concerned look on his face and asked, "Is this preliminary examination part of my trial?" Richard wasn't familiar at all with the law or how the judicial system worked.

Richard's lawyer, Mr. Davis, didn't know that Richard was unfamiliar to the judicial system until Richard asked that question, which his lawyer, Mr. Davis, thought was a very stupid question. And that's when Mr. Davis's red flag went up about Richard's ignorance.

Richard's lawyer, Mr. Davis, smelled blood. And Mr. Davis knew, without a doubt, from that point on that he could basically say and do whatever to Richard. And Richard would willingly go right with it and go without any problems.

After Mr. Davis had heard Richard's question, one could easily see the frustration and impatience all in Mr. Davis's face. And it was also clearly evident to Richard as well. Richard thought to himself, *Come on, that is the first question that I had asked, and you're tired of me already? I didn't ask one hundred questions, that was my very first question. And this moron is already exhaling deep breaths? As if he is tired of me within these first five minutes!*

Geofrey Davis just remained silent, ignoring Richard. He didn't even think twice about answering Richard's question. Richard thought to himself, *If I had the money to pay you, I bet you wouldn't be tired of me then!* Mr. Davis was acting as if he didn't have time for the questions.

After a few seconds had passed, Mr. Davis had finally answered Richard's question. Mr. Davis sarcastically answered, "No…It's not a trial, Mr. Ginn. It's just a preliminary exam to determine if the judge thinks that it is enough evidence to send the case to trial and if it is a possibility that you committed these offenses. Guess what? Yep! You guessed it, buddy…you will be going to trial for raping your wife!"

After making light and joking about Richard's situation, Mr. Davis went on speaking to Richard. He said, "The prosecutor isn't going to present all of their evidence against you today. They are going to present juuust enough evidence to question if it is a strong possibility that you could have committed this crime. This offense."

The preliminary examination proceeding went so quickly that Richard didn't even notice that it was all over until the judge said, "The trial date is set for March 5, right after New Year's."

During the preliminary examination, the prosecutor went straight for the home run hit, no questions or doubts about if it was a possibility. The prosecutor went for something that could not be disputed—Richard's semen, swabbed and taken with a forensic rape kit from the inside canal of his wife's vagina.

It was withheld as evidence in the rape kit exam that the doctor performed on Richard's wife the morning of the alleged sexual assault. And that was all that it took, and a trial date was set. But if Richard would have had better legal representation, it would have taken much more concrete evidence than that to bound him over.

But his court-appointed lawyer, Mr. Geofrey Davis, didn't even attempt to put up a fight in the least way. But Richard never knew a difference. Remember, this was a whole new world and language barrier for Richard.

Richard didn't know it, but that wasn't the prosecutor's best evidence against him. Richard still couldn't believe what his wife was doing to him. Richard thought that the prosecutor had to know that his wife was setting him up.

That his wife, Kim, was lying! Because that was his wife. And she convinced herself that she could get away with it. But the female prosecutor didn't care. She was desperately trying to make an example out of Richard. She wanted Richard locked up and sent away to prison for a long time.

The prosecutor told the judge, "Your Honor, just because Mr. Ginn is married to his wife, he feels as if he is entitled to have sex with her whenever he wants to. And if she dares tell him no, then ol' Richard here…" The prosecutor pauses and glances at Richard sarcastically as she continued, "just takes it from her."

The prosecutor looked over at Richard and said, "That right there, Mr. Ginn, if you didn't know, is called rape! *R-a-p-e*—rape! but I am almost certain that he wouldn't know that with his little business and all of his big money from his pretty engineer salary." Then the prosecutor stopped right there and sat back down.

Richard leaned over toward his lawyer and whispered, "This is my wife we're talking about here, for Christ's sakes! It was consensual between the both of us. I can't rape my wife! She is lying! You can't get this dismissed?"

Mr. Davis let out another exaggerated dramatic exhale, still seeming overly frustrated with Richard's questions. Mr. Davis was growing even more impatient. Mr. Davis answered, "No! We can't get it dismissed, Mr. Ginn! The judge has already set the trial date. And you are now in circuit court!"

Mr. Davis was aggressively whispering in Richard's ear. Splashes and sprays of his saliva were coming out of Mr. Davis's mouth as he was barking into Richard's ear.

Richard couldn't believe what was happening to his life. Richard was thinking, *I am actually looking at going to prison for a crime that I didn't even commit?* The judge had bound Richard over to circuit court and adjourned the preliminary examination. It was all over just that quick.

Richard and Mr. Davis had walked out of the courtroom together. They walked through the halls toward their vehicles. They both stopped in front of the court building. They observed the flow of the lunch hour traffic going back and forth and all of the state workers smoking cigarettes on their lunch break.

Richard looked Mr. Davis directly into his eyes and said, "Mr. Davis, please help me, sir…believe me when I tell you that I am an innocent man, sir! Please! I did not—I repeat—did not rape my wife! I don't have any money right now to pay you, but God as my witness, I promise to pay you. But you have to help me!"

Mr. Davis placed one hand onto Richard's shoulder and said, "It's really not for me to believe you, Richard, you don't have to convince me. You have to convince those twelve people that are deciding your fate. I don't know, we'll see."

Mr. Davis patted Richard on his back, then he got into his car. And he was off into the busy, bumper-to-bumper lunch rush hour traffic.

Chapter 7

March 5, was the trial date. And it will be the beginning of a new year in a couple of days. That meant that Richard had roughly two months before trial.

Richard stared at the calendar on his wall as each day had passed by. To Richard every day felt as if he was on death row. Just counting the days down until his execution, which was his trial date.

Richard finally landed a job at a construction site. He knew a few people, made a couple of connections, and they looked out for him. Richard thought, *It doesn't pay much, but it's enough to pay for my gas, buy a little food to eat, and a place to sleep.* So Richard still didn't complain.

It definitely wasn't the life that Richard had grown accustomed to living or the life that he had worked till exhaustion to enjoy. But Richard was making it. His construction site boss was paying him $100 per day—under the table. Richard didn't think that was adequate enough pay for the hard labor that he did.

Especially since the weather was in the early stages of waist-high snow and extremely strong and below-zero cold wind of Minneapolis, one of the top states to be hit the hardest in the country by the winter season. Richard hated it!

Richard had thought plenty of times about calling his wife, Kim, or stopping by the house and asking her, "What would it take for me to do for you to consider getting me out of this mess?" But Richard didn't want to risk going to jail for violating his bond stipulations. Richard couldn't trust what his wife would do now.

Richard still couldn't believe that his wife was treating him like that. Richard had apologized several times for his infidelity on her. Richard had cheated on his wife. He tried to explain to Kim that it was something that just had mistakenly happened and that he had no feelings whatsoever for the woman that shared the same name as his wife.

Richard tried to explain to Kim, "She was just a girl that I hired up at the shop to do desk work." But Richard paused and relived that very same moment, replaying it in his mind. He went on, "Or maybe it's the waaaay that Kim had found out about me cheating on her that got her hell-bent on getting me to prison?"

It was much, much more than Richard just losing his job. *Ooooooh…now it all comes out.*

Richard had cheated on Kim too? That explains everything! The exact reason why Kim was hell-bent on bringing Richard to his knees. She was a woman scorned. And that's why Kim was trying to take Richard's mechanic shop from him that he owns.

The mechanic shop is where Richard's mistress worked and where Kim had caught her husband, Richard, cheating at.

It was after business hours, closing time, when Kim had showed up to bring Richard some food to eat. Kim was thinking about Richard and that he probably hadn't eaten all day. So Kim took her husband some food up to the hot rod mechanic shop. And that's when Kim caught her husband with the other woman.

Kim had her own set of keys to the shop too. Kim left their daughter, Jessie, waiting in the car while she ran into the shop for a brief second. The only two cars parked in front of the shop were her husband's Impala and the newly hired in phone receptionist's car, which was parked a space over from Richard's car.

Kim knew the phone receptionist; she was a nice cute little young lady. She was determined and ambitious about having a successful future. She was in her first year of college, enrolled at the University of Minnesota. And all this young vibrant girl wore were the university shirts, hats, etc. She was proud of her school.

Richard's wife, Kim, had really hit it off with the new receptionist from the first day that they had met each other. Maybe because ironically, the young girl's name was Kim as well.

But Richard's wife, Kim, was the only reason that the college Kim had even gotten hired for the job. And if it wasn't for Richard's wife speaking up for her, Richard was adamantly against hiring the college Kim at his shop. But Richard's wife, Kim, had really admired the fact that Kim was going to college and trying to do something positive with her life.

Richard was totally against hiring Kim at first because she was a young girl, and he felt his shop wasn't a place for a woman. And another reason was that she had no prior experience in automechanics. This was Kim's very first job ever. And if it wasn't for Richard's wife, Kim, speaking up for her, she definitely would not have gotten the job.

Kim felt betrayed and backstabbed by a young lady that she had considered to be a close friend and that she had also believed in. She felt like the good deed that she had done had ultimately blown up in her face. And came back to haunt her.

When Richard's wife, Kim, had entered into her and her husband's automechanic shop, she called out Richard's name because she didn't see him at first. Kim hollered, "Richy! Richy!" And still no answer. Kim thought, *Maybe Richy is in the back somewhere.*

Kim didn't see the college Kim at the desk going through receipts like she almost always did. So Kim continued walking through the shop toward the back. But this time, Kim called out Kim's name. "Kim! Kim! Are you in here?" But again no answer from Kim either.

Kim had thought for a second, *Now that's strange.* Now Kim was beginning to wonder if Kim and her husband were okay. Kim was hoping and praying that no one had come into the shop and hurt them in a robbery. Kim thought, *Please don't be shot or dead somewhere! Please, God! Please!* Kim mumbled, almost a whisper, to herself.

Kim was thinking about all of those episodes on crime shows where people's businesses got robbed, and the workers at the place of business got shot and killed.

Kim was very slowly and very cautiously walking through the big shop. Kim was peeking her head around corners and calling out both of their names, "Richy! Kim! Kim! Richy!" with each step that she took through the shop. And Kim was occasionally looking down onto the floor for any signs of blood.

Kim was walking with her cell phone clenched tightly into her hand, just in case she had to quickly dial 911 for an emergency, just in case her husband, Richy, might be lying somewhere, bleeding to death. The food that Kim had brought up to the shop was getting cold.

But the food was the least of her worries at this very moment. It was still sitting on top of the receptionist's desk. And the food was becoming more cold with each second that had passed.

The closer that Kim had approached the back of the shop, she was hearing little sounds of pants and moans from a female. Then Kim was faintly hearing the moans and groans of a man as she was zeroing her ears in and tracking the sounds.

Kim was thinking, *Ooooh no! Please be alive! Please, Richy, I need you!* Kim thought for sure that her husband was lying in a huge puddle of blood. The mere thought of envisioning her husband shot and helplessly dying had tears forming and streaming down her cheeks.

Kim heard her husband's moan like he was in some sort of pain and dying slow. Kim panicked and began to dial 911 into her cell phone. All Kim had to press was "send" to the emergency dispatch. Kim picked up her pace and began to walk a little faster toward the commotion in the back bathroom.

Kim was headed in the direction of the faint moans that she was hearing from her friend Kim and from her husband, Richard.

Kim turned the corner in the shop where the pants and moans grew much stronger, louder, and more intense. Kim saw that the bathroom door was slightly ajar. Kim gently pushed the bathroom door an inch open. Then she called out her husband's name, "Richy?" Kim was frantic and terrified of potentially finding her husband shot and covered in his own blood.

Kim built up her nerves and pushed the bathroom door open as she held her breath, and tears poured down both of her cheeks. Kim called her husband's name, "Richy?" But when the bathroom door flew open, Kim wasn't expecting to see what she saw.

Instead of finding her husband lying there, shot and dying, in a big puddle of his own blood, Kim was witnessing the entire backside of her husband's buttocks. Richard was completely naked from the waist down. His pants and his briefs were dropped down to his ankles.

Kim saw sweat beads streaming down her husband's legs. And he was deep in between some woman's legs that were spread as far apart as they could possibly spread. And Kim saw the woman's nails were as deep as they could dig, clawing into her husband's back.

Richard had the woman sitting up on the sink, she was bent into the corner, as deep as she could go. And Richard was thrusting deep inside of the woman. He was giving the woman all that he could give her with each thrust and her exhaling intense moans and groans she let out, thrust for thrust.

Kim was listening to the woman, being sexually pleasured, scream, "Oh! Yeahhhhh! Fuck me, baby! Fuck me harder, Richy! Please! Fuck me! This pussy is good, ain't it? Whose pussy is it?"

And Richard, being sexually pleasured as well, was answering back, "This pussy is mine! This is all my pussy!"

Kim could see Richard's buttocks contracting tightly, as if he was orgasming at the same time that Kim was calling out his name.

Richard's wife, Kim, was trying to look over his shoulder to see who this girl was. She was hoping that it wasn't her friend Kim whom she had gotten the job for.

Richard's wife, Kim, had stood up on her tiptoes, and that was when she instantly saw who the girl was. The girl was her friend Kim, the girl she had indeed gotten the job for. And her friend Kim was looking as if she was enjoying every inch of her husband's penis and his long stroke to match as her eyes rolled up into the back of her head. And she was breathing hard, as if she couldn't catch her breath. And her face had tightened up each time that Richard went in and thrusted deep inside of her.

Richard's wife, Kim, had seen that both her husband and her friend were soaking wet, sweating profusely, when they both were startled by the unexpected sound of Kim's voice.

The college Kim had quickly pushed Richard up from off the top of her and quickly pulled down her University of Minnesota hooded sweatshirt. She was trying to cover up the lower half of her naked body that Richard had previously pulled up to kiss her on her pretty, firm, and perky breast.

After Kim had pulled her sweatshirt down, she grabbed her panties and her University of Minnesota sweatpants from off of the bathroom floor. She was nervously putting her panties on so fast that she didn't even notice that she was putting them on backward.

While Kim was putting on her sweatpants, she just kept repeating, "Kim, I'm sorry. I'm so sorry, Kim! It just happened!" She was begging and pleading to Kim as she tried to squeeze past Richard's wife, Kim. The college Kim was trying to get through the bathroom door to leave the shop.

She was praying that she didn't accidentally brush up against Richard's wife, Kim, but definitely praying that Kim didn't beat her ass on her way out of the small bathroom doorway.

Richard's wife, Kim, was hurt and crying, staring at Kim with an evil eye. She was extremely furious and feeling like the world's biggest fool for even being concerned that her husband might be hurt! Richard's wife, Kim, was thinking, *All I wanted to do was bring my husband something to eat.* But all along, Richard was cheating on his wife, Kim.

Richard had pulled up and buttoned his slacks by now. And he was nervously trying to fasten his belt. All Richard kept saying to his wife, Kim, was, "Baby, I'm sorry! It's not what you think! I love *you*, Kim! You have to believe me! She came onto me! That's your friend...and she knew better!"

Richard was walking behind his wife, Kim, toward the front of the shop. Richard was begging and pleading to Kim for her to believe him and forgive him.

But Richard's wife, Kim, wasn't trying to hear anything that Richard was saying. She just wanted out of there and away from Richard before she ended up hurting him or who once was her friend Kim. But the other Kim was long gone by now.

Richard's wife, Kim, had walked past the front desk where the food that she had brought to the shop for Richard had sat. The food was cold by now. Kim walked past the food, spit on it, and with all the strength and anger that she could dig deep to find, she slapped the food and the huge supersized cup of Coca-Cola.

The supersized cup of soda flew all over the desk, all over the shop's receipts for the day, the smartphone, and onto the wall, where it all eventually ended up all over, staining everything in its path. *Slap! Bam! Splash!*

Richard and Kim's daughter, Jessie, was staring at the both of them as they were exiting the shop and staring at her mother crying. She didn't know what had just happened, but she knew that something was terribly wrong. Kim got into her car, slammed the car door, and took off. She was driving erratically, speeding out of the parking lot. *Urrrrrtttt!*

Richard just stood there, staring at his wife and daughter driving away.

While Richard slept on the couch at home, Kim didn't speak to him for a couple of weeks. Though Richard persistently kept trying and pleading with Kim. He was desperately trying to apologize, but she still wasn't giving Richard a chance. Richard was talking to her and doing nice things around the house for her.

Richard was also cooking for his wife, Kim, and running hot bubble baths for her that went cold. His attempts went unnoticed and fell on deaf ears at first. But eventually Kim began to slowly give in, and Richard took her out for dinner one night to a nice romantic and elegant restaurant.

Richard had gone above and beyond his way to make sure it was special. Kim had finally forgiven him. They had worked through their differences for the sake of their marriage and to keep their family together. They did it for their daughter, Jessie.

Things at home went back to normal besides the few times that Kim couldn't eat every time she thought about her husband cheating on her with one of her closest friends. Kim constantly looked in the bathroom mirror and asked herself, "What am I not doing for him? I must be ugly to him now? I know what it is, I'm not pretty anymore. It's my fault. I could've done more."

Kim truly believed that she went the extra distance for her husband to make him happy. And she actually did. But she just couldn't answer or understand why her husband would cheat on her. Kim constantly stared in the bathroom mirror, constantly thinking that she was ugly.

Kim obsessively kept asking herself, "What does Kim have that I don't have? She's not even cute. Ugly bitch! And my dumbass husband couldn't even cheat on me with somebody that looks better than me! Or at least as good as me! Stupid ass didn't even cheat up another notch, he cheated down!" Kim was furious at Richard every time that she thought about Richard cheating on her.

Kim thought that she could stay strong. And she thought that she could forgive Richard for the sake of their family. But every time she had thought about what Richard had done, her stomach would turn instantly, making her nauseous. Kim would automatically vomit.

Kim had forgiven Richard, but how to get even was always in the back of her mind. She was constantly thinking of ways how to make Richard feel the pain that he had caused her to feel. Kim had lain in the bed, sleepless many nights, beside Richard, thinking long and hard, *How can I get even? How can I make him feel the pain that this bastard made me feel?*

The best and only way that Kim could think of, she didn't really know if she should do it or not. Until that very day to get even had come. And Richard's wife had gotten revenge. She had gotten even.

Richard sat in his car in the darkness of the night, waiting at the traffic light. Richard was thinking about his life and how it had ended up being what it was now. At that very moment, Richard was totally embarrassed, to say the least.

Richard didn't mean for things to happen the way that it did. And Richard regretted the poor decision to cheat on his wife that he had made. Richard, being a man that firmly believed in and stood on his values and morals, had always thought if you cheat on your wife, you cheat on your kid too.

Richard stayed true to his word and his family for all of those years, up until that one mistake that he had made. He had gotten weak and slipped up.

After a few seconds of cars blowing their horns behind him, Richard had noticed that the traffic light was green, and he was holding up a long line of cars in traffic. He took his foot off of the brake pedal and mashed on the gas as the light was turning yellow and stopping all of the other cars that were behind him waiting.

Richard drove back to his motel room and went to sleep. He had plans of waking up in the morning and going to his daughter, Jessie's, school. Richard wanted to see his baby girl, he hadn't seen her in a while due to his wife, Kim, and his bond restrictions.

Richard wanted Jessie to know that he loved her and that he missed her tremendously. Richard thought, *I never want my daughter to think, not even for one second, that her daddy doesn't love her.* Richard thought about Jessie all night and how happy he was going to be in the morning when he saw her pretty little face.

Richard pulled Jessie's picture from out of his shirt pocket where he had always left her picture since he had left home. Richard kissed the picture of his daughter and stared at her until he eventually fell asleep.

Richard woke up the next morning and headed up to Jessie's school. Jessie was ten years old and in the fourth grade. Richard knew that he had to be careful going anywhere near the school or anywhere near his daughter. That would surely get him locked up. But Richard was thinking, *But I haven't seen my daughter in so long. I have to see my baby.*

Richard felt like seeing his daughter was definitely well worth the risk. Richard further thought, *How can they tell me that I can't see my daughter?* as he sat in his car parked about a half of a block down the street from the school.

Richard said to himself, "I didn't do anything wrong. So how can those bastards keep me from seeing my daughter?" Richard got out of his car, hoping he wouldn't be seen by school security or by any of the school teachers that knew him because they all knew that he was charged with raping his wife and headed to trial soon.

The snow was covering the sidewalks and the streets from the heavy snowfall of last night. And it continued to have heavy snowfall off and on all morning. Richard stepped out of his car, looked around, he didn't notice anyone looking in his direction.

Richard quickly cut through an area of big pine trees. He stopped in the middle of the big pine trees for a second, trying not to be noticed. Then Richard looked toward the direction of his daughter's classroom. Richard could easily see his daughter's teacher teaching the class. And Richard also observed a few students inside of the classroom, they were also visible from where he was standing.

Richard looked around once more, making sure that no one was around. Then he would cut across the children's playground to his daughter's classroom window. At least that was Richard's plan.

Richard was just about to step out of the pine trees when he heard a walkie-talkie radio. He quickly stepped back into the thick brush of pine trees. Richard was trying hard not to be seen and hoping that the school security guard didn't see him. Richard was out of the security guard's view in just enough time. Richard thought, *Whew! That was a close one!* as the school's security guard was walking around the school's perimeter, checking all of the doors.

The security guard stopped at one of the classroom windows; he was smiling and waving at a little girl that was inside one of the classrooms. She was waving at the security guard as he walked past.

Richard was kneeling down onto one knee, waiting on the security guard to finish making his rounds. And when the security guard continued making his way around the school, Richard took that as an opportunity to take his chance to see his daughter, Jessie.

Richard was extremely excited and couldn't wait to see his daughter, Jessie. Richard's heartbeat was racing superfast. He was anxiously anticipating finally seeing his baby girl. Richard thought, *It's been a long time...too long!*

Richard successfully made it to his daughter's classroom. Richard got up to her window, poked his head from around the side of the building to the front of the classroom window. And the only thing that was visible was half of Richard's face if anyone from inside of the classroom would have seen him. Richard was discreetly looking into his daughter's classroom.

Richard looked up and down, frantically searching each aisle of students. He was looking for Jessie until he spotted her. Jessie was seated in the fourth row, second aisle from the window, and sitting at the last desk. Jessie was doing her schoolwork as she was writing on lined paper. Richard softly tapped onto the window. *Tap, tap, tap.*

He was desperately trying to get Jessie's attention without her teacher noticing, who was sitting at her desk grading papers.

Jessie didn't hear the soft taps at the window. So Richard tapped onto the window again. Only this time, he tapped a little harder. *Tap! Tap! Tap!* Jessie jumped as the louder taps startled her.

At first Jessie didn't know where the taps on the window had come from. She looked much further down toward the other end of the window. She was listening to the taps on the glass, trying to follow them. It was hard for Jessie to see Richard, with only a small half of his face visible. Jessie finally noticed something poking out. What she saw was half of Richard's face that had caught her attention.

By the time Jessie had figured out where the taps were coming from, she saw something written into the frost on the outside of the classroom window. Richard had used his finger to write, *I love you, Jessie* into the glass of the classroom window. Richard wrote the letter *I* with a heart symbol up under it. And up under the heart, he wrote the letter *U*. Up under the letter *U*, Richard wrote *Jessie*.

Jessie was staring at it all written into the glass. But she had a confused look on her face, though, as if she didn't seem to recognize the stranger standing on the outside of her classroom window.

Richard finally stood up so Jessie could see his whole face and recognize that he was her dad. But Jessie still didn't recognize the strange man standing on the outside of her classroom window.

Jessie just stared at Richard, as if he was a stranger. To Jessie, Richard had looked as if he was homeless man. A stranger trying to kidnap some kids. Richard scared Jessie to the point where she didn't know what else to do but scream. And that was exactly what she did to get her teacher's attention. Jessie screamed, "Mrs. Paaaaaarks! Mrs. Paaaaarks! Mrs. Paaaarks! Look! Look! It's a stranger on the outside of the window!"

Richard heard his daughter screaming at the top of her lungs, trying to get her teacher's attention. Jessie was raising her hand and pointing toward the direction where Richard was standing in the window. But by the time Mrs. Parks had looked up, Richard had scraped the window clean of what he had written and ran off as quickly as he could before Mrs. Parks could see him or call for the school's security.

While Richard was running to his car, Mrs. Parks was on the telephone. She was calling school security to check the school's grounds.

As Richard was running and getting closer to his car, he pushed his car alarm button, disarming his car alarm so that he could enter into his car without the siren sounding off. Richard jumped into his car and quickly drove off before he could be seen.

Richard drove a few blocks away and pulled his car onto a little side street. Richard threw the gear shift into park and then adjusted his rearview mirror so that he could look at his reflection into it.

Richard was puzzled, trying to figure out what was so different about the way that he looked. Richard asked himself while looking into the mirror, "Why didn't my own daughter recognize me? Why didn't Jessie recognize her own father?" Richard was absolutely stumped.

Richard reached up, held the mirror with one hand, looking at himself up close, up and down, and from one cheek to the other cheek, from side to side. Richard was sitting upright to see his entire face in the mirror. And Richard's other hand was rubbing and feeling all over his facial features.

Richard rubbed back and forth, from one side of his face to the other. He stared into the mirror and carefully rubbed both of his cheeks and his chin. Richard kept asking himself, "Why didn't my own daughter recognize me?"

It took Richard a moment, but he had come to the conclusion, saying, "That's what it was! I have a full-grown beard! And this beat-up red-and-black flannel!" while he was staring down at the tattered red-and-black flannel. Richard had grown accustomed to his new look since being out on his own and barely surviving from day to day in a cheap motel.

But ever since his daughter could remember, she was used to seeing her dad clean-shaven first thing in the morning. No facial hair except for his mustache that stayed neatly and perfectly trimmed.

Jessie was also used to seeing her daddy neatly dressed. Dress shirt and freshly pressed slacks, not some dirty, rickety, and tattered beat-up flannel. And since it was cold outside and snowing, Richard had a winter skull cap pulled extremely low and tight to his head.

When Richard was living at home, he never wore winter skull caps. Richard thought to himself, *This is why...ooooh!* Once Richard had figured it out, he quickly overcame the pain and confusion of his daughter not remembering her daddy.

Once Richard had thought about it, even he had to admit that he looked like some crazy and strange homeless man. Richard figured that his daughter would tell Kim about what happened at school this morning. And Richard was right. Jessie couldn't wait to tell her mother about everything that she saw at school.

Richard didn't even recognize his own self when he looked into the mirror sometimes. Richard put his car into drive and made his way to work. He was already running late by now. Richard arrived at the construction site and put in about ten hours, two hours was in overtime. Richard thought, *I needed the few little extra dollars anyways.*

Now that Kim had cleaned out their joint bank accounts, and Richard had the hot rod mechanic shop in her name, he wasn't seeing any money from the business either. That was pretty much Richard's entire routine as he approached closer and closer to his trial date.

Richard was working long hours at the construction site and, every now and then, going back up to Jessie's classroom window, looking inside. Only this time, he was clean-shaven, no beard.

Richard had also gotten his hair cut. And he had stolen a dress shirt from out of the grocery store that sold clothes as well. Richard said to himself, "I am making sure Jessie recognizes me this time." Richard risked going to jail a couple of times just to get that dress shirt.

Richard walked into the grocery store with no plans whatsoever of stealing a dress shirt. But the first couple of times, he came really close but couldn't quite muster up the nerve.

The store's security was onto him. Richard dug deep down into his pockets and pulled out a small amount of cash. Richard counted up the loose dollar bills, the crumpled-up five-dollar-bills, one ten-dollar-bill, and some loose change. It all added up to a little more than twenty dollars, maybe eighteen dollars and some change.

Richard depleted that $600 that his friend John had loaned him when he had bonded Richard out of jail.

Richard was in a serious dilemma, and he had a choice to make as he sat out in the front of the grocery store, stumped, trying to decide what to do.

And the decision that Richard had come to grips with was spend all of his money on that dress shirt to look presentable for court so that his daughter, Jessie, could recognize him and because paying for the shirt was just the right thing to do. Richard thought, *I never ever stole anything my entire life. I've always worked extremely hard and earned everything that I have gotten this far.*

Or on the other hand, Richard thought, *I can steal the shirt and still keep my money to get gas and buy some food to eat.*

Richard stared at the loose dollars crumpled up tightly in the palm of his hand before he finally built up the nerves to enter the grocery store.

Richard quickly stuffed all of the cash back into his pants pocket. With his adrenaline pumping on high and his heartbeat racing, as it was pounding, he got out of his car and walked into the grocery store.

Richard was so terrified at the very thought of stealing that he had begun getting dizzy and lightheaded as he was entering the store's entrance. Richard was desperately trying hard not to pass out or faint just before he even got into the store.

Richard stepped inside of the store and looked around at all the customers and departments inside of the store. To Richard, it seemed as if he was living out a bad dream. To Richard's eyes, everybody inside of the store was moving at a superfast pace. But actually that was still just the fear from the thought of himself about to steal for the first time in his life!

Richard was so nervous and scared that he didn't realize that he was looking suspicious. And him looking suspicious was causing a scene and drawing the shoppers' attention.

Richard was so nervous that he didn't hear the little girl sitting in the shopping cart being pushed by her mother say to Richard,

"Hi, mister!" Richard didn't hear what seemed to be a little four-year-old girl as he walked past, focused on the task at hand.

Richard's eyes were wandering back and forth, looking for the clothing aisle. Richard just kept walking without speaking to the little girl. The little girl kept smiling as her mother kept pushing her in the shopping cart. And the little girl's older brother was playing with his toy airplane and following closely behind their mother.

Richard finally spotted the clothing aisle that had the dress shirts, dress slacks, ties, and socks, etc. Richard was still extremely nervous, though, as he looked around, making sure the coast was clear, and nobody was watching him and that he wasn't being followed by store's security. The coast was clear.

Richard walked down the clothing aisle and stood in front of the shirt section. He thumbed through a few shirts. He was trying to make it look like he was a legitimate shopper looking to purchase a shirt.

Richard stood up onto his tiptoes, thumbing and looking through the shelf just above him while he was peeking out of each corner of his peripheral view, making sure that the coast was clear to stuff the shirt into the inside of his coat.

Richard quickly grabbed the shirt from off of the shelf, but then he paused for a brief second. Richard envisioned himself in handcuffs and being escorted by a police officer, holding in his hand that very same dress shirt that Richard had tried to steal.

Richard envisioned himself in the back of a car and off to jail again. Richard thought, *No...I can't do it!* He got cold feet and placed the shirt back onto the shelf and turned away to walk off.

But then Richard had instantly thought about his daughter, how much he loves her and hadn't seen her in such a long time. Richard thought, *And when I finally did get a chance to see my baby girl, she didn't even recognize her own father.*

Richard instantly became saddened. It hurt Richard that his very own daughter didn't recognize her father when she had seen him. Then instantly fury came over Richard as he thought, *Damn that! My daughter is worth the risk!*

Richard immediately stopped in his tracks, he turned around and started walking back, with conviction, toward that shirt that he had grabbed and abandoned just a few seconds earlier.

Richard made sure that no one was in front of him looking. Then he looked behind himself and over both of his shoulders, making sure no one was behind him looking, either.

Then Richard struck quick! He snatched the shirt from off of the shelf, lifted the front of his winter coat up, and then he stuffed the dress shirt into the front of his underwear, making sure that the elastic band of his underwear held the dress shirt securely in place, reassuring that it wouldn't fall. It was secure.

While Richard was stuffing the shirt into the front of his drawers, he was looking back and forth over both of his shoulders. Richard had the jitters, but you could see the look of anger all in his face, at the fact that his daughter didn't recognize him. And that gave him unstoppable courage and justified stealing the shirt in his mind.

But Richard didn't look at it as stealing now. Richard looked at stealing the shirt as getting even. And once the shirt was tightly in place and secured, Richard frantically pulled the front of his winter coat back down. And he made sure that he didn't look suspicious if the shirt that he had just stolen was bulging out. Richard exhaled a deep breath, gathered himself, and began trying to walk as normal as possible toward the parking lot.

As Richard was nervously walking toward the parking lot, he noticed a shortcut through the kids' toy section of the store. Richard thought, *This way is much faster than the way that I came into the store. And I wouldn't look suspicious coming from the kids' toy section.*

Richard swiftly began walking through the kids' toy section without trying to cause attention. And so far so good, his plan was working smoothly. Richard had finally gained his poise by now. The shoppers weren't moving as fast to Richards eyes as they were when he had first entered into the grocery store.

Being angry that his daughter didn't recognize him and justifying himself stealing really helped make Richard calm, determined, and focused. He saw the store's entrance doors from afar. He was still making his way quickly but calmly through the toy section.

Richard was almost to the doors and out of the store. *Just a little bit further,* he thought. And Richard would be home safe in the parking lot. *I'm parked just on the other side of those doors,* thought Richard.

As Richard was just emerging out of the kids' section, it was totally quiet with no movement at all. All you could hear were the pet birds and guinea pigs at a distance in the animal section. Richard said to himself, "If I could just make it to the other side of those doors…"

Right then, two ten-year-old kids playing in a camping tent jumped out from out of nowhere and, at the very top of their lungs, screamed as loud as their screechy high-pitched little voices could reach, "RAAAAAAWWWW!" They saw Richard as a goofy man coming from a mile away.

The kids startled Richard so much that he stumbled, tripped, and fell into a bunch of toys that were spread all over the floor on display. Richard and the kids had caused somewhat of a scene as customers looked back into that very direction and also came from other aisles to see what the noise and all of the commotion was about.

The kids popped out from out of the tent and were rolling all over the floor. They were pointing and laughing at Richard hysterically as Richard lay there on the floor, in pain, rolling from side to side, grabbing his lower back, wincing and moaning. Richard was lying there, trying to figure out how he let two little kids get him like that. And that really made the two little boys laugh even harder.

Richard slowly began to get up onto his feet. He was mad and thinking, *Damn…How did I let two little kids scare me like that?* Richard was staring at the kids and shaking his head in disbelief. That's when the two little kids' mother, who was in the next aisle over, knew it was a good chance that the loud commotion was probably her two mischievous sons.

The kids' mother quickly ran over to the toy section where she saw Richard trying to stand to his feet. The mother immediately grabbed Richard's arm and tried to help him to his feet. The boys' mother was straightening Richard's coat and his hat out for him while she was concerned and asking him, "Are you okay, sir? I am terribly sorry about my sons. I really am. Please forgive them."

The little boys' mother kept brushing down the front of Richard's winter coat with both of her hands. Richard, fearing that the woman may accidentally knock the stolen shirt from out of his underwear, quickly grabbed both of the woman's hands before she accidentally knocked the shirt out.

Richard nervously said to the woman, "It's okay, ma'am. It's all right, honestly." Richard kept repeating himself to the woman as he was nervously walking away before the store's security showed up, and he potentially got caught.

While Richard was walking away, he kept talking to the woman, smiling at the kids, and trying to make as little of a scene as he possibly could. Richard politely but nervously smiled and convincingly said once more to assure the kids' mother, "It's okay. Trust me. They're just kids having fun." And Richard quickly walked away.

But he could see more people than usual standing in front of the store's entrance doors. Richard thought, *That just doesn't look right. Something is not right with those people.* To Richard those very same people looked like plainclothes police officers that were stalling for time and waiting for Richard to walk through so that they could catch him red-handed.

Richard thought against it and leaned toward his gut feeling. *Nah, my chance is blown now. It's over*, thought Richard. Richard quickly rerouted to another aisle, out of the eye sight of the strange people that were standing in front of the store's entrance.

Then Richard detoured to another aisle with intentions of abandoning the shirt that he had stolen that was still safely tucked into his drawers. Richard pulled the shirt from his underwear, threw it, and kept walking, all in the same motion, without breaking his stride. Then Richard headed back toward the same entrance to leave the store where all of those same suspicious people stood around waiting.

It was a real good thing Richard followed his gut feeling and threw the shirt when he did because his intuition was right. Those suspicious-looking people standing at the front of the store's entrance were doing just that—waiting on Richard to exit the store with the stolen merchandise. Those strange-looking people were the store's security team.

They noticed Richard immediately as soon as he got out of his car in the store's parking lot. Something didn't look right to them about Richard. He was acting too nervous and suspicious. And that's what caught the store's attention. The security camera zoomed in on Richard before he even entered through the store's entrance doors.

Richard said, "Whew! I really just dodged a close one! Man!" He continued walking through the store's security team. They were staring at Richard as he walked past them.

The store's security had received the call on their earpieces that Richard had ditched the merchandise and to "let him go." Richard felt relieved but disappointed. He was very relieved that he didn't end up in jail but disappointed that he didn't get the shirt.

Richard thought, *I don't know if the kids helped me escape from going to jail or if they blew my chances to get the shirt.* Richard got into his car feeling like he lived to fight another day.

After a few more failed attempts at trying to get a nice shirt, Richard finally found the right store that was a little bit easier to shoplift from. And he got a shirt. Richard was going back up to his daughter, Jessie's, school off and on. He was still writing into the winter's frost on the school window what he had always written into it. The letter *I*, and up under the letter *I*, a big heart shape, and up under the heart shape, the letter *U*. And lastly up under the letter *U* was his daughter's name, *Jessie*.

Richard would occasionally show up at his old house unannounced without being noticed. He would tap onto his daughter's bedroom window, leaving the same writing into the winter's frost of her bedroom window. Richard would stand there in Jessie's window, blowing Jessie kisses and forming his lips to say the words to his daughter, "I love you, Jessie."

And Jessie would always say the same words back to Richard, saying, "I love you too." She moved her mouth as Richard read her lips. Jessie would kiss the palm of her hand and blow a kiss back at Richard every time. Richard and Jessie's bond and love were unmistakenly strong and evident.

It felt good to Richard. He had all of the material things that a man could ever want. But nothing could compare to the love that Richard had for his family. Richard would die one thousand times if he had to, without question or doubt, just so his family could live. Nothing or nobody could ever replace his wife, Kim, or his daughter, Jessie.

Even though his wife, Kim, was lying and trying to destroy Richard and possibly send him to prison. But Richard was still madly in love with his high school sweetheart/wife, Kimberly Ginn. Richard thought, *I would forgive her at the drop of a hat. If only she would just talk to me.*

Chapter 8

Kim was still harboring ill feelings of revenge. And she was still acting as if she didn't want to have anything to do with her husband, Richard.

Richard would even go up to Kim's bedroom window at night. And he would sneak a peak at Kim watching television, eating, and talking on the telephone while painting her toenails.

Richard even stared at Kim while hiding under her window outside for hours at a time. Richard sometimes watched his wife come from out of the shower dripping wet and with nothing on covering her body but a bath towel tightly wrapped around her naked body, revealing her shape and every curve from her breast down.

Richard had vomited once right outside of Kim's bedroom window just from the thought of losing her and the queasy thought of another man sleeping in his bed while he would be away, serving hard time in prison.

One night Kim had heard a strange noise outside her window. It sounded like someone was throwing up. Kim quickly walked away from looking into her dresser mirror to check it out. But whatever it was long gone by the time Kim made it to her window. Kim turned her light off and went to bed.

Richard went back to his motel room, and he tossed and turned all night. His mind was racing, thinking about his wife, Kim. As soon as the sun had risen, and it felt like people were out and about, Richard had finally made up his mind to call his wife, Kim, and try to talk to her. Richard picked his phone up off of the bed and dialed Kim's number. The phone rang and Kim answered, "Hello?"

Richard began talking to Kim in a very humble but confused tone. Richard said, "How you doing, Kim?"

But Kim angrily responded, "Who is this! I know good and damn well that the other person on the other end of my phone isn't trying to violate his bond and go back to jail!"

Richard panicked and nervously answered, "No, no, no, Kim! Please don't. I'm not trying to violate my bond or go back to jail."

Kim replied, "Then what in the hell are you doing on the other end of my line, Richy!"

Richard quickly answered in a soft-spoken and humble tone, "Kim...I just really wanted to talk to you, babe...I love you—"

But Kim quickly and sarcastically answered back, saying, "Yeah, sure you love me...honey, you love me so much that I caught your dick up in another bitch! Huh? Yeah, Richard, you must really loooove me! If that's love, then I would really hate to see what you would do to me if you hated me!"

Richard answered Kim, saying, "No, Kim, that was just a very, very, very stupid mistake that I made. And that I truly, truly regret. I'm sorry. I told you that I was sorry, Kim...what else could I do?"

Richard could hear Kim take in a deep breath and let out an even deeper exhale on the other end of the phone before she answered, saying, "Look, Richard...I really have to go...and if you just so happen to call again, I am going to call the cops on you myself, sweetie. Take care, hun." Then Kim hung her phone up on Richard just as she heard a word about to come out of his mouth.

Richard hung his phone up and just sat there in darkness in his motel room. The only light that illuminated his motel room was the light that shined through his curtains from the motel parking lot.

Richard was sitting in the dark and thinking to himself, *How in the world could I have been so stupid? That was so, so stupid! Stupid of me to have sex with that girl! And cheat on my wife.*

And now Kim was burying Richard at all costs, accusing him of raping her, a rape that he didn't even do.

Chapter 9

It was literally one week before Richard was scheduled to go on trial for allegedly raping his wife that she falsely accused him of because she caught Richard cheating on her and wanted to get even. And this was her way of revenge.

And Richard's court-appointed lawyer, Geofrey Davis, still hadn't contacted him or let Richard know anything about his court proceedings yet.

It had been a little more than six months since Richard and Geofrey Davis had spoken. And with one week to go before trial, Richard was beginning to become a little more nervous and uncertain about his future.

Richard's phone began ringing while he was in the bathroom showering. *Ring. Ring. Ring.* Richard faintly heard his phone ringing from afar. Richard could tell by the sound of the ring that it wasn't the motel's telephone that was ringing. It was his cell phone lying on top of his pillow, ringing on the bed.

Richard quickly turned the water to the shower off. He was moving extremely fast, trying to get out of the bathtub. He was trying to walk and wrap the bath towel around his waist at the same time. Richard was desperately trying to make it to the telephone before it stopped ringing.

Richard tripped and almost stumbled getting out of the bathtub. He was slipping on the water that was on the floor. Richard finally grabbed the phone on its last ring, but his wet and slippery hands were fumbling the phone, trying to get a handle and trying to turn the phone on all at the same time.

Richard finally caught the phone on its last ring. He answered, "Hello?" But it was too late. All Richard heard on the other end of the telephone was a loud dial tone. Whoever it was had hung their phone up, thinking Richard must have been busy or that he must have left his phone somewhere.

Richard had a feeling that the person that was trying to call him was his court-appointed lawyer, Geofrey Davis, because not too many people knew his phone number. And all of his friends and business associates that used to call him had all stopped calling since they all have heard about the rumor of their friend Richard being charged with raping his wife, Kim.

Everybody that Richard thought were his friends had all turned their backs on him and had all cut ties with him as well. Richard's friends didn't want anything to do with a rapist. All of Richard's friends had abandoned him except for his best friend, John. John had Richard's back and believed in his friend Richard's innocence 100 percent.

Richard would never forget his friend John's words in the most trying time of Richard's life. His friend John had told Richard, "I'll always be here for you, Richy! You're my friend. And I am going to help you out any way that I possibly can!" Richard felt relieved that someone believed in him and his innocence.

Richard thought, *Dammit! That was my attorney calling, I bet! And since I don't have any money to pay him, he probably won't waste his time calling me back.* So Richard just continued to dry off and put his clothes on. And as soon as Richard buttoned up his slacks, before putting his shirt on, the telephone began ringing again. But this time Richard caught the phone before the first full ring was finished.

Richard was overly excited and somewhat louder than usual at the fact that the telephone rang again. Richard answered, "Hello!" Richard was listening intensely, anticipating whose voice would be on the other end of the telephone. And the voice that was on the other end of the telephone was exactly who Richard hoped it would be—his court-appointed lawyer, Geofrey Davis.

Geofrey Davis answered, saying, "Hello, can I speak with Richard Ginn, please?"

Richard anxiously replied, "This is he. Who is this? Mr. Davis?"

Geofrey Davis answered, "Hey, Richy, how you been holding up, pal?"

Richard, still excited by the sound of his lawyer's voice, replied, "I'm doing all right, I guess…just been wanting to know, where do we stand on this trial situation? We only have…what, three…four days left?"

Richard took a quick glance at his calendar with all of the days marked off with an *x* up to date.

Richard's lawyer answered, "Yes…about three…four days. I apologize for lack of communication, not keeping you posted on where you stand as far as trial is concerned."

Richard's lawyer, Geofrey Davis went on, saying, "I have been really busy as of late for some reason or another. But the reason that I called you today is, you are right, we have about three days before we are set to go to trial. I conversed with the prosecutor, and I have some good news and some bad news for you, Richard."

Richard replied, "Some good news and some bad news?" Richard didn't understand what Geofrey Davis was implying.

Geofrey Davis answered, "Yes, Richy, which do you want first?"

Richard answered, "It doesn't really matter, does it?"

Geofrey Davis answered, "Well…Richard, here's the bad news, in a sense. I guess it all depends on how you look at it. I spoke with the prosecutor, and I really fought my ass off for you, Richard…I really did!"

Geofrey Davis really wanted Richard to believe that he was going to bat for him. But in all actuality, Geofrey Davis could care less about if Richard went to prison or not. He just wanted Richard out of his way and off his caseload as soon as possible so maybe he could make some money off of a *real* client worth working for. And to Geofrey Davis, a real client was a client that could pay him money.

Richard cut Geofrey Davis off in the middle of their conversation. Richard interrupted by saying, "I really appreciate you fighting your ass off for me too. I really do, Mr. Davis. All of your help. And when I get things back in order, after we beat this case…" Richard, smiling with confidence, continued, "I'm going to pay you, I promise!"

Geofrey Davis cut Richard off and said, "Don't worry about it. If you do, then you do. But if you can't then…" Geofrey Davis paused briefly before he continued talking with Richard, "Don't worry about it, Richard." Geofrey Davis knew that one of his attorney's bar conduct clearly states that "no lawyer shall accept funds for pro bono defense cases."

Geofrey Davis began talking to Richard again. He was repeating himself, making sure that it was clear and that Richard understood when he said, "Yeah, I worked my ass off. But I got a deal for you. And I really think that it's in your best interest." And by Richard not knowing the law, he was listening to his court-appointed lawyer's reasoning.

Richard's heart was racing, frightened of every word that came out of Geofrey Davis's mouth. Geofrey Davis began speaking again, "I really think that this plea deal is your best way to go. Just to bring this whole nightmare to an end for the sake of your family."

But what Richard didn't know was that his court-appointed lawyer didn't have Richard's best interest at heart at all. Not in the least way.

Geofrey Davis wanted to hurry up and get this no-money-to-be-made case of Richard Ginn over and done with so that he could spend a week out hunting and drinking beer with all of his old law school buddies. And the only thing in Geofrey Davis's way of getting there any quicker was Richard.

Geofrey Davis thought, *Instead of wasting my valuable hours defending some broke son of a bitch at trial that I'm not getting paid for, I could be out with my buddies getting drunk and hunting deer.*

Richard, sounding obviously concerned, asked, "What type of deal are you talking about, Mr. Davis? And got me a deal for what? I didn't do anything…what do I need a deal for? You don't even believe me, do you?"

Geofrey Davis answered, "Calm down, Richard. Don't get all bent out of shape and worked up on me. For Chrissakes, it was merely just a suggestion. Of course I believe you."

But all along, Geofrey Davis didn't believe one word of what Richard was saying out of his mouth. Geofrey Davis was thinking, *Yeah, sure, everybody that gets charged with a crime is innocent. Get the fuck out of here.* Geofrey Davis was thinking to himself, *You're all guilty. Especially if you don't have any money.*

Geofrey Davis continued, *I'm definitely not wasting my time on you! And you're definitely guilty in my eyes. But if you got that money...I will* find *a way to care! Yeah, that's right, pay me to care, or it's pretty much a wrap. Just put your head between your legs and kiss your pretty little ass goodbye.*

Geofrey Davis began talking to Richard again. He said, "The deal that she had offered you was ten to fifteen years in prison. And all you have to do is plead no contest to one count of sexual assault, and 'no contest' means that you are not actually admitting guilt. I mean...you are...but...you're kinda not."

Geofrey Davis went on, saying, "No contest...is just looked at as a guilty plea. Although you're not actually admitting guilt." Richard was quietly and intensely listening but still unhappy, basically frustrated at the fact that his court-appointed lawyer was still trying to justify his roundabout way of convincing Richard of pleading guilty, even though Richard had adamantly told him that he was not guilty.

Geofrey Davis went on, saying, "The prosecutor agreed to drop the false imprisonment charge. I think that this is an excellent deal, Richard. I mean...in my humble and honest opinion. I really do."

Richard snapped on Geofrey Davis and quickly replied, "A good deal! Good deal? For something that I didn't even do! Are you serious! No! No, no, no, that is definitely out of the question! I am not pleading to that. I will take my chances at trial. Now go and tell the prosecutor that! You make sure you tell her we will see her at trial!"

Richard stood firm and was adamant about his innocence. His mind was made up, and he was willing to take his chance at trial. Richard was willing to risk possibly losing and going to prison. But Richard was thinking, *Prison is better than me pleading to some shit that I didn't do! That's bullshit!*

Geofrey Davis was allowing Richard to vent momentarily while stating his position on the plea agreement before he gave Richard the other news. Geofrey Davis said, "Okay, Richy, but if that's your decision, I just really think that you're making a huge, huge mistake. A mistake that you're going to end up regretting later. It's a lot of should've, would've, and could've people locked up in prison for going to trial and refusing a plea deal for a crime that they thought they could beat. Instead of taking that deal, especially if they are guilty anyway. I'm not insinuating that you are, I'm just saying. But at the end of the day, Richy, you are the one that is going to have to do the time so…"

By Richard not knowing the law, the prosecutor threw a big prison sentence number out there—ten to fifteen years—just to scare Richard. And Geofrey Davis knew that the prosecutor was trying to use a scare tactic on Richard. But Richard's lawyer, Geofrey Davis, didn't care. He just wanted a case that he wasn't making any money on out of his way. So Geofrey Davis was in on it too, in a way, without Richard's knowledge of him doing so.

All Geofrey Davis wanted was to go hunting with his buddies as soon as possible before they started the trip without him.

Geofrey Davis knew that if Richard did get found guilty, by him being a first-time offender, his flawless career history, and his educational background, Richard would get sentenced to no more than seven years in prison.

Geofrey Davis had already calculated Richard's guidelines that would determine his estimated prison sentence, and it was no more than five years. And that was on the extremely high end of his guidelines. So Geofrey Davis knew that the ten to fifteen years that the prosecutor offered Richard was a lie. But again, Geofrey Davis was in on it too just to scare Richard into pleading guilty and get him out of the way as soon as possible.

The estimated calculation of Richard's guideline prison sentence was five years. A long way from the ten years that the prosecutor and his court-appointed lawyer, Geofrey Davis, was trying to scare him with.

Geofrey Davis went on to say to Richard, "The other news that I needed to tell you was that, if you didn't want to accept the ten, the prosecutor is willing to let you take a polygraph test. And if you pass, they agree to drop all charges against you. So this is the million-dollar question that I need to ask you. And I really need you to be honest with me, Richard."

Geofrey Davis took a brief pause, looked Richard into his eyes, and asked, "Can you pass the test, Richard? Because if not, I'm telling you right now, I'm not going to be too happy about you wasting my time when you knew that it was no way in hell that you could pass the test. I'm going to ask you again…Now take your time and answer carefully. Can you pass the test, Richy?"

Richard paused for a brief moment, looking down to the floor. And then Richard lifted his head up with confidence and conviction as he answered, "I told you for the hundredth time, I…DID…NOT… DO IT! And hell yes, yes, if they let me take the test, guaranteed I can and will pass it! Give me the test, dammit! I will take it right now! Let's get this over with! Can we go today?" anxiously asked Richard. "Right now!"

Geofrey Davis answered, "You sound pretty sure of yourself, Richard. And I like that, good. But we can't go today, Richy. Not today. And I really wish that we could. Believe me. I'm going to contact the prosecutor, and hopefully we can set something up for the next couple of days to come because trial is this Tuesday. So I'll give them a holler, and I will let you know something this evening, the time and the location. All right, Richy? Sounds good?"

Richard answered, "All right, I'll be waiting on your call, Mr. Davis." Then Richard and Geofrey Davis both hung their telephones up.

Richard finished putting on the rest of his clothes after getting out of the shower. And then Richard left his apartment to go check up on a couple of job applications that he had been waiting for a callback on. But still, it was either they weren't hiring, or it was just no reply back at all.

All of the jobs that Richard had applied for were all at automotive mechanic shops. The very field of profession that Richard felt most comfortable and at his best in. That was the very field of work that helped Richard to own his own business that was once a very successful business, at one point in time.

Richard returned to his motel room after searching, but still no jobs. Richard changed his clothes and got ready to go to his construction job. Richard's supervisor needed him to work a little bit of overtime today because they were short a man on their work crew. A crew member had broken his leg a week prior.

Richard didn't mind working the overtime as usual. He could use the extra money for his motel room fee, his food, and his gas. Richard didn't get back from working until late that night. And Richard had been waiting on his lawyer, Geofrey Davis, to call all day but still haven't heard from him yet. Richard was beginning to think and wonder if his lawyer might have forgotten about him. So Richard decided to call Mr. Davis himself.

Richard picked his telephone up and began to dial Mr. Davis's telephone number. Geofrey Davis answered his telephone after looking at his caller ID. He saw it was Richard on his phone display before he could even answer. Geofrey Davis answered, "Hey, Richard, how you doing? I just tried to call you about a half an hour ago."

Richard's lawyer, Geofrey Davis, was lying. And Richard knew that he was lying also because he had his cell phone in his pocket all day, from the time that they had spoken much earlier in the day. But Richard let Mr. Davis tell his lie. Richard feared that a confrontation with his lawyer might cause his lawyer not to care about Richard's outcome.

Richard didn't know that Geofrey Davis could care less if Richard ended up in prison or not from the very first day that they met because Geofrey Davis wasn't seeing any money off Richard.

Richard was desperately trying not to show any signs of the way that he was thinking. Richard responded, "Oh, you did try to call me? I must have missed your call or something. I'm sorry about that." And then Richard got right to the question that he wanted to know the most.

Richard asked Geofrey Davis, "So where do we stand on this polygraph thing? I'm ready right now."

Geofrey Davis answered, "Ha ha ha, I know, I know you are, Richard." Geofrey Davis answered Richard in between his swigs of his wine bottle. Richard could tell that his lawyer was drinking something. Richard just didn't think that his lawyer was drinking out of a big wine bottle while talking to him.

Geofrey Davis turned the big wine bottle up again as he took another big gulp of wine. Then he began talking to Richard again after downing a big swallow. Geofrey Davis said, "I know that you are ready to get this over with, Richy. And I don't blame you one single bit. I talked with the chief prosecutor herself, she agreed that if you take the polygraph exam aaaaaaaaaand pass, that she would indeed dismiss all charges against you. I mean this is what you wanted to do, right? I just want to be perfectly clear."

Richard answered, "Hell yes! That's exactly what I want to do! Because that is the only way that people are going to believe me and know that my wife, Kim, has been lying on me! And then I can get my life back!" Richard said with the deepest emotional exhaustion in his voice.

Mr. Davis responded, "Okay…here's the deal, Richy. You have a 10:00 a.m. appointment with the polygraph technician. And it will be at the downtown municipal building. All you have to do is ask for Mr. Vanreen. His office is located on the fourth floor. Now for this phase of the court proceedings, you don't need me there with you. So I won't be there with you tomorrow. You're a big boy, and you should pass with flying colors from what I hear from you. So this case should be dismissed, over and done with tomorrow. Huh, Richy? I'll pick up your results Monday morning."

Geofrey Davis went on, "I'll give you a call sometime Monday afternoon, and…we'll go from there. Okay?"

Richard replied, "The name that you said was what again? Mr. Vanreen, right? And he's on the fourth floor? At ten o'clock?" Richard was jotting the name, the floor, and the time down on a little yellow sticky paper. That was so he made sure that he wouldn't forget it.

Mr. Davis answered, "That's correct. Vanreen, fourth floor, at ten o'clock, Richy."

Richard replied, "And when they send you the results and dismiss this nightmare, drinks are all on me, Mr. Davis. We'll celebrate me getting my life back. Huh?" As Richard thought about it, the voice echoed in his head, *MY LIFE BACK…LIFE BACK, LIFE BACK.*

Mr. Davis gave a little laugh and said, "Sounds good to me, Richy. Vodka on the rocks." Then Mr. Davis took another big gulp out of his wine bottle. He downed the last of what was left. Then he said, "All right, Richy, I will talk to you on Monday." Then they both hung their telephones up.

Richard woke up the next morning feeling like one thousand pounds was about to be lifted from off of his shoulders. And he could finally get his life back. Richard thought, *That's aaaaall I want. To prove my innocence and get my life back.* The voice echoed again, *MY LIFE BACK, LIFE BACK, LIFE BACK.*

Chapter 10

Richard could hardly sleep the night before. So he finally rolled out of his bed and got himself dressed. He was watching the clock tick with each second that had passed. *Click, click, click.* Richard was anxiously waiting to go take his polygraph test. He sat on the edge of his bed, looking around his motel room. He was observing his clothes and his other belongings lying around.

Richard was thinking, *Damn, I turned this cheap little motel room into my home...literally. How did I, of all people, go from almost nearly half million dollar beautiful home, a high-ranking automotive engineer position, and a successful business owner to this? My life? It's a helluva flip. Drastic change.*

Richard continued on, *This is unreal...unbelievable. I feel like an alien or some type of weird shit. Me, me? Of aaaaaaall people, actually living out of a rundown, drug-infested, gun-toting, and maaaaaaaaad pussy-slinging motel room. Never in a million years would I believe this would ever be my life!*

Richard sat paralyzed at the end of his bed. He went on thinking, *I'm working at a construction site for almost pennies. And worst of all, I went from a beautiful wife preparing a nice hot dinner and eating at the dining room table, to not knowing exactly how or even what I would eat from day to day. And when and if I do eat, I have to constantly kill creepy-crawlies trying to eat my food before I do!*

Richard asked himself, "And this is my life?" Richard was beyond ready for this whole nightmare to end and be over with. That's all Richard was thinking about, as he quietly sat still at the foot of his bed before he stood up and began packing all of his belongings to finally leave that motel room and that nightmare behind, once and for all.

Richard was anxious to leave. He had grown tired of hearing all the gunshots every night—*pop! Pow! Pow! Pop*—just outside of his motel room window. But the gunshots that Richard heard last night were entirely different.

It had to be a drug deal gone terribly bad from what Richard had seen as he pulled the curtain covering his window shut. Richard was trying his best not to be noticed by all of the people standing around in the motel parking lot, as they did every night, drinking alcohol, smoking pot, bragging about their guns and the massive holes that the bullets leave in bodies, the drug dealers selling crack, and the women selling sex.

Richard was peeking out of his motel room window, trying not to be seen as he observed the rather large group of different people doing their daily routine, hustling. Some hustling to get money and others hustling to get high.

Richard peeked outside of his motel room door, trying to see what was all of the loud noise that he had overheard. He really couldn't tell what the loud noise was, but it sounded like people arguing. And that's when Richard saw it!

A dark-skinned black male wearing a ski mask, concealing the identity of his face, and in his hands, he had a big black square-face-shaped semiautomatic pistol. The dark-skinned male was pointing the gun directly at the face of a Mexican male.

The night was completely pitch-black, and most of the motel parking lot lights had all been shot out with bullets. So Richard could barely see what people were doing in the darkness of the night. But Richard could clearly see that the male with the gun pointing in his face was a Hispanic male. Also Richard overheard the Hispanic male's thick Hispanic accent.

Richard couldn't understand what the Hispanic male was saying, but it looked and sounded as if he was begging and pleading for his life. The Hispanic male was crying. "*Por favor, hombre! Por favor, hombre!*" His head was bowed, too terrified to look the big black square gun eye to eye. The man had both of his hands covering the front of his face. And the next thing that Richard had witnessed, he could not believe his eyes.

It was loud pops, gunfire, and big sparks coming from the muzzle of that big black square gun. *Blow! Blow! Blow!* Extremely loud gunshots echoed through the motel's parking lot. The black male in the ski mask had shot the Hispanic male three times, point-blank range, as he was begging.

The Hispanic male got shot once in the top of the head. And when he fell to the pavement onto his face, the black male had shot him two more times in his back. *Blow! Blow!*

Then the black male picked the large gym bag up from the Hispanic male's feet. He threw the gym bag strap over his shoulder, and then the black male ran through the trail behind the motel that led through the back of the projects while the Hispanic male that got shot lay bleeding in a puddle of his own blood on the pavement. After gunshots rang out, it was instant chaos with all of the prostitutes and dope fiends running and screaming.

That was the first time that Richard had ever witnessed something like that in his entire life. Richard thought that those type of crazy crimes only happened in the movies. Richard was completely frozen at a standstill until the ambulance and the Minnesota Police Department arrived at the crime scene. They arrived, taped the area off with yellow caution tape everywhere.

After several hours had passed, the ambulance picked the Hispanic male up off of the pavement. They placed his lifeless body, that was covered with a white sheet, onto the stretcher and quickly sped off into the darkness of the night, with their emergency lights still flashing and their sirens blaring.

Richard peeked out of his window into the parking lot. He was looking at all the leftover yellow tape that was left tied onto cars in the motel parking lot and wrapped around light poles. Richard stared out his window until he could no longer hear the sirens from the ambulance. They were now fading away at a faint distance, the further that the ambulance made its way down the street.

Richard was reflecting, looking back on that very night, that gruesome night that took place just a couple of days ago. As he was finishing packing his belongings up, Richard thought to himself, *Yeah...It's definitely time for me to go.* Richard was preparing to move back into his home with his wife. The house was in his name, but the hot rod automotive business was in his wife, Kim's, name. That was just one of the many gifts that Richard had given his wife, Kim, because Kim was into hot rods too.

Richard had huge plans of going home in the next couple of days. And he didn't mind if Kim still wanted to live there. Richard was still madly in love with his wife, Kim. He understood why she did what she was doing—because he cheated on her. Plain and simple. Richard had already forgiven Kim for this and hoped they could work through their differences. Richard just wanted his life back. That's it.

The time was now approximately 9:23 a.m. Richard left his apartment and made his way downtown to his polygraph examination appointment with Mr. Vanreen. Richard left a little early to give himself some time to find Mr. Vanreen's office. Richard was in his car driving and headed toward the municipal building. Richard went to the front desk as soon as he stepped into the building.

Richard stepped inside the municipal building and approached a young receptionist. She was sitting at the front desk talking on the telephone. The young lady held the telephone that she was talking on to the side, trying not to let the other person that was on the other end hear her helping Richard.

The young receptionist said, "I will be right with you, sir."

Richard nodded his head, saying, "Sure." Richard was in awe of all the police officers walking back and forth throughout the building.

The receptionist told Richard to "hold on a second." And Richard took that as an opportunity to let his eyes wander a bit.

Richard was looking up at the municipal's building ceiling, the floor, and the walls, with all of the police officers. They were all police officers who lost their lives in the line of duty. Richard instantly got cold chills running through his body just from the thought of how the police officers violently lost their lives.

Richard felt an eerie feeling because up until this point in his life, he has never felt uncomfortable being around police officers. But this time it was very different. His wife, Kim, was falsely accusing him of rape. And he was potentially facing ten years in prison, according to the prosecutor.

And it didn't make Richard feel a little less uneasy when he saw two police officers escorting a handcuffed man that seemed to be struggling with and resisting the police officers until the officers forcefully lifted the man up onto his tiptoes. They lifted him by grabbing his arms that were cuffed behind his back, inflicting an extremely sharp pain in the man's shoulder joint. And whatever that training technique was supposed to accomplish, it worked because the man instantly calmed down, followed the officers' orders, and walked without resistance.

And that's when the receptionist at the desk said, "Yes, I'm sorry for the wait, sir. Can I help you?"

Richard looked up at the clock hanging on the wall behind the lady. It was now 9:52 a.m. Richard had eight minutes before he had an appointment with his freedom. But if he was to be late, it would be a no-show appointment. And that potentially meant spending ten years in prison.

Richard panicked, nervously answering the lady, "Ah, yes, I have a ten o'clock appointment with Mr. Vanreen." He nervously spoke with both of his hands on top of the desk and leaned his momentum toward the closest doors to him, whether the doors were the right doors or not, he was hoping. Richard was anxiously waiting on the lady's answer and hoping that the doors that he was leaning toward was the direction that the lady was going to point him in. And Richard was right, those were the doors.

Richard let out a sigh of relief when the receptionist replied, "Mr. Vanreen's office is through those doors. Take the elevator to the fourth floor, and when you get off of the elevator, make a right. His door is the fifth door on the left."

Richard was closely listening to every single word of the receptionist's directions. And then he said thank you as he took off flying through the doors.

Richard made it to Mr. Vanreen's door. And when he looked in through the small window, he saw a thin build tall-looking gentleman sitting at a desk. The gentleman was typing on a laptop computer while he was looking over some grid-sheet papers. The grid-sheet papers were all connected together. They were all unfolding as the man lifted each paper higher and higher.

Richard thought, *All of those papers must be lie detector scores that he's looking over.* Richard stood at Mr. Vanreen's door for a second before he let out a deep exhale to gather himself and shake the jitters. Richard thought, *What am I nervous for? I'm ready.*

But before Richard knocked on Mr. Vanreen's door, he read the gold nameplate that was screwed into his door. The gold nameplate read, "Detective Vanreen, Polygraph Examination Specialist." Richard said to himself, "Wow! This must be some serious high-tech stuff going on here..." And that's when the man that had to be Mr. Vanreen turned around like he had eyes in the back of his head and said in a snapping drill sergeant's tone, "Who are you, sir?"

The tone and the aggressiveness of the man's voice caught Richard off guard and startled him. "Oh! Ummmm, ahhhh, yes... I'm Richard Ginn, sir. I have a—"

The man cut Richard off before he could finish. Mr. Vanreen sharply said, "You have a ten o'clock appointment that you are thirty seconds late for!" Then Mr. Vanreen turned back around to his computer and said almost at a whisper, "Yeah...And you're guilty too!" Mr. Vanreen thought that Richard couldn't hear him. But Richard did hear him. And he heard every word that Mr. Vanreen had said under his breath.

But Richard just acted like he didn't hear Mr. Vanreen. Richard was feeling that if he tried to dispute Mr. Vanreen's opinion, like so many other people's opinion about him being guilty, he would really be just wasting unnecessary breath and energy. Richard just thought to himself, *I'll just take this little lie detector BS and prove my innocence once and for all.*

Richard responded to Mr. Vanreen's comments of him being late by saying, "I didn't realize that I was late, sir. The clock downstairs is a little behind."

Mr. Vanreen acted as if he didn't hear a word that Richard had just said. Instead with verbal and frustrated biased prejudice against criminals, Mr. Vanreen replied, "Follow me, Mr. Ginn," while rolling his eyes.

Mr. Vanreen stood up, then escorted Richard through several different offices. They were making endless twists and turns and left and right turns at numerous corners. They finally ended up in a small room. "Have a seat," said Mr. Vanreen. Richard sat down in a big butterscotch leather chair. The chair was so huge that Richard sat down and sunk deep into the chair. Richard was looking and feeling like a little child strapped into a human life-size big baby car seat.

Richard looked around at everything inside of the office while Mr. Vanreen was seating himself at another laptop that was printing out a grid sheet of someone else's test results. Richard was looking at all of the long connected sheets of paper. They were all spilling out nonstop from the printer onto the floor.

After observing all of the grid sheets of paper with what looked like heartbeat lines all over them, going up and down, Richard said to himself, "Damn…those are a lot of questions!" His mind was starting to race, thinking, wondering. Richard started to get a little jittery. But he thought again, *What the hell am I thinking! I'm all right! I'm an innocent man. And I'm finally about to prove it!*

Richard immediately went from a slumping and self-defeated position in a sinking chair to his back straight as a board, sticking his chest out and holding his head up high. He was looking extremely confident and ready to prove his innocence to everyone who thought that he was guilty.

Mr. Vanreen said to Richard, "Just a couple more, Mr. Ginn."

Richard replied, "Oh, take your time. I don't have anywhere to be." But really, Richard was actually growing anxiously impatient as each second went by. Richard wanted to finally get it over with. But Richard just wanted to look calm and maintain his composure in front of Mr. Vanreen before Mr. Vanreen got the wrong impression of him.

Richard looked calm and worry-free as the grid papers continued falling to the floor. Richard just kept looking around the office a little more.

And that's when Richard noticed the numerous gold plaques and awards covering the walls throughout Mr. Vanreen's office. There were even several more on Mr. Vanreen's desk that seemed as if the plaques couldn't fit onto the wall. All of Mr. Vanreen's awards were for winning polygraph examiner.

Also some of Mr. Vanreen's awards were for breaking big high-profile criminal cases month after month and year after year, throughout the entire state. And more often than not, most of Mr. Vanreen's awards were consecutive, back to back.

Chapter 11

Richard was completely flabbergasted, curiously admiring in awe of Mr. Vanreen's numerous acknowledgments. *They sent me to the best examiner in the state of Minnesota! Maybe the best in the country? Wowww!* thought Richard. And the more Richard thought about it, he vaguely remembered hearing Mr. Vanreen's name on a few police investigative shows on television.

Mr. Vanreen's name is notorious for cracking solved and unsolved high-profile homicides and sexual assault cases. Mr. Vanreen solved cases in the state of Minnesota, Wisconsin, Indianapolis, and Chicago—the entire Midwest region of the country. Richard thought, *This man really knows his stuff!*

Richard was also thinking, *Mr. Vanreen could be the very person that sets me free! Maybe he'll win an award for solving my case? His first award for proving someone's innocence!* So it wasn't such a bad thing after all to have the best of the best to test Richard. At least that's what Richard was thinking anyway.

Then Richard just happened to look up at the ceiling of the office. He noticed several little black hidden bulbs strategically placed throughout the office. A person wouldn't easily notice or recognize what the black bulbs were. But watching all of the police investigative shows had given Richard an advantage. There were three little black bulbs that Richard could see out in the open. But there was no telling how many more were hidden throughout the office.

Richard thought to himself, *Ohhh, those must be hidden cameras. To monitor whoever sits in the chair, their body language and how they react to certain questions. That must be another way how they determine if you're being honest or if your answers are lies.*

Mr. Vanreen tore the last paper from the printout. And then he picked all of the rest of the papers up that were neatly folded on the floor as they came out of the printer. Mr. Vanreen was looking down through his glasses, that were at the very tip of his nose, looking at the grid sheet. He let out a subtle sigh. "Hmm." Then he placed it in the metal basket on top of his desk. Then Mr. Vanreen began grabbing all sorts of black cords from the back of the computer.

After grabbing several cords from the back of the computer, Mr. Vanreen looked up at Richard while he was desperately trying to conceal his scientist at work, sinister smirk on his face. It took everything that Mr. Vanreen had in him not to smile.

Richard could tell that Mr. Vanreen really loved his job with a strong passion, which actually meant that he loved to prove that almost everybody that sat in his butterscotch leather chair, they were most certainly liars.

Mr. Vanreen looked up at Richard with each hand holding maybe two or three different black cords. And a few more cords were still lying on the desk. And with that same ridiculous expression on his face, as if he was still desperately trying his best not to smile, Mr. Vanreen said, "These little cords right here, they help my computer recognize if the person that is sitting in my chair is being deceptive. *Deceptive* is just another fancy word for if you're a lying sack of shit. And this little black cord right here…I wrap it around your chest and your back. It keeps a consistent pace and consistent reading on your heart rate."

Richard was just staring at each cord that Mr. Vanreen held up in his hands and described each particular function of each cord. Mr. Vanreen continued, "And these little black cords with Velcro on the ends…I place those around your fingertips. That gives me an accurate reading on your skin conductivity." Mr. Vanreen paused, fumbling with the cords briefly.

After untangling the black cords, Mr. Vanreen went on explaining, "And your skin conductivity, it is measured through electrodes. I can tell if your heart rate speeds up or palms begin sweating, Mr. Ginn. Which indicates to me that you are being deceptive. Again, Mr. Ginn…which basically tells me that you are a lying sack of shit." Mr. Vanreen was nodding his head up and down and smiling sarcastically. "Nahhhht that I'm juhhhhdging you or anything, Mr. Ginn."

Richard was tired of hearing Mr. Vanreen's long speech about what each black cord did. Richard was thinking, *That's probably how this clown got all of those award trophies. He talks you to death! Trying to scare you about what each cord does, and then he wants to hook you up to all of that crap!*

But still, Richard knew that he would pass the test because he didn't rape his wife. And he had nothing to lie about, and he didn't have anything to fear.

Mr. Vanreen said to Richard, "Okay, you know how this works, Mr. Ginn. And I am quite sure you have seen *The Maury Show.*" Richard was looking confused, thinking, *Huh? Maury Show?* as Mr. Vanreen paused for a second, looked over at Richard, and jokingly said, "You are...NOT THE FATHER!"

Richard politely smiled, not thinking that the joke was nearly as funny as Mr. Vanreen did, who was laughing hysterically, as if he was the only one that caught onto his own dry joke. "Ha ha, ooohhh, oh!" Mr. Vanreen's head snapped back as he slapped his knee, in his own world of humorous laughter.

Mr. Vanreen had finally accomplished his mission of strategically hooking Richard up to all of the black cords with flawless precision. Then Mr. Vanreen stared at his laptop screen. He was making sure that it was receiving an accurate reading of Richard's vital activity.

Then Mr. Vanreen said to Richard, "I'm going to ask you a series of questions that you and I know to be actual and accurate true facts. Just to be absolutely positively certain that you and I are getting an accurate reading. Okay, Mr. Ginn?"

Richard agreed, thinking, *The sooner the better*, as he answered, "Yes, sir." Richard was ready for it all to be over with.

Mr. Vanreen said, "The first question that I am going to ask you, Mr. Ginn is, is your name Richard Blake Ginn?" Richard paused patiently and calmly to make sure the reading didn't make any unwanted jeopardizing crucial errors. Richard slowly and clearly answered yes.

Richard had the same approach to all of the polygraph questions throughout until the end. Mr. Vanreen asked the next questions, followed by Richard's slow and clear answers. "Is your birthday January 2, 1977? Were you born in Minneapolis, Minnesota? Do you have any children? Are you married?"

Every question that Mr. Vanreen asked Richard, they both knew the answers to. And Richard answered all of them as Mr. Vanreen carefully observed his laptop screen while looking over the grid sheet's reading. Mr. Vanreen was looking back and forth from the laptop to the paper printout, carefully observing with flawless precision.

Mr. Vanreen was nodding his head up and down while saying, "Okay, excellent, everything looks great. Game time!" Rubbing his hands together, salivating with contained anxious eagerness, Mr. Vanreen's eyes were glowing with anticipation as he said, "Here we go, Mr. Ginn."

Richard sat up in the butterscotch chair as straight as he possibly could to clear air to his lungs. He wanted to speak as clearly as possible. And he didn't want anything interfering with his answers. Richard wasn't taking any chances on the computer or the grid-sheet graph being confused. Or it not accurately being able to read what his answers were.

Mr. Vanreen asked Richard once more with direct eye contact without batting an eye, "Are you ready, Mr. Ginn?" Richard nodded his head up and down and softly answered yes, as if he had a large lump in his throat that he couldn't swallow.

Mr. Vanreen got straight to the questions, the real money ball questions, the questions that mattered the most and would clearly, without a doubt, be an indicator if it was a possibility that Richard committed the sexual assault or not.

The fourth or the fifth question that Mr. Vanreen had asked Richard was, "Did you have sexual intercourse with your wife on the alleged day in question?" Richard confidently answered yes, being truthful because he did have sex with his wife, Kim.

But then the next question would be the question that would ultimately seal Richard's fate. Mr. Vanreen asked, "At any time...did you hold down or restrain your wife during that time frame?"

Richard paused for a second, very carefully trying to choose his words wisely for his answer. Richard was thinking, *That's kind of a trick question…like a no but a yes question.* Richard finally answered the question after a couple of seconds, "Yes…but no…I mean, I did…buut I didn't—"

Mr. Vanreen replied, "Again, Richard, this is a yes or no question, Mr. Ginn. And I'm asking you to choose one answer, sir. One. Either you did or you didn't." Mr. Vanreen was sounding extremely stern in his order, repeating the question once more but, only this time, dramatically slow so that Richard understood the severity of the question that he was asking.

Mr. Vanreen asked, "At any time, did you hold down or restrain your wife…during that time frame?"

Richard's lips were quivering while forming to say the word *yes*. But Richard knew that saying the word *yes* would surely send him to trial. Or better yet, even worse, send him to prison. Richard thought that saying no would show that he was lying. Because he did hold his wife down but only to restrain her from wildly hitting him.

Richard didn't know whether to say yes or no. So Richard's instincts took over, and it was a mere impulse reaction when he took a chance and blurted out, "No!"

Mr. Vanreen was closely observing his laptop screen and the grid sheet with laser-sharp precision. Again Mr. Vanreen was looking back and forth from the laptop to the grid sheets nonstop. Richard leaned forward nonchalantly to see if he could see exactly what the reading was saying.

After unsuccessfully attempting to see what the laptop screen was reading, all Richard could see was a red line like a heart-rate monitor going up and down on the paper. Richard didn't know how to read the graph. All he knew was that his heart rate was racing faster than it was in the beginning of the questioning. And Richard's forehead was beginning to form beads of small sweat.

Mr. Vanreen could see the dampness from the sweat through Richard's shirt. Two large visible sweat rings were forming up under Richard's underarms. Richard quickly looked down, hoping that Mr. Vanreen didn't catch him. Richard couldn't help but notice the sweat forming in his palms as well.

Before Mr. Vanreen could notice it, Richard slowly removed his hands from off of the armrest, trying not to disconnect the black cords with the Velcro wrapped around his fingertips.

Richard eased his hands down to his knees and quickly wiped his hands on the knees of his slacks. Then he quickly placed his hands back onto the armrest. Mr. Vanreen was too consumed with looking over the test results to even notice Richard's movement. But that's when Richard thought, *Damn... That must be why they have hidden cameras all around in here—to catch nervous people doing exactly what I did. Damn!* Richard even felt like he was being watched. Richard was waiting anxiously to hear his test results. Mr. Vanreen stared at the sheet of paper with the grid on it for a couple seconds more.

Mr. Vanreen leaned back into his chair with his fingers interlocked on his lap. He was slightly rocking his chair forward and backward. It seemed as if Mr. Vanreen was in a deep train of thought about something. But Richard wasn't worried, though.

Why should Richard be? He was totally honest from the beginning. But Richard was uncertain about that one trick question. And he couldn't stop thinking about it. All Richard kept hearing in his head were the words repeating, *Did you restrain your wife?* Richard knew with undoubted certainty that he had passed the polygraph test. Hands down.

Mr. Vanreen unlaced his fingers, then he stood up and proceeded to walk toward Richard's direction. Mr. Vanreen began unhooking Richard from all of the black cords one by one. Richard was quietly staring at Mr. Vanreen, as if he was asking or anticipating what the results were. Richard was obliviously frozen in wonder.

But Mr. Vanreen, being as stern as he usually is, was leaving Richard stuck frozen in oblivious anticipation purposely. He was a prick, and he knew it and he loved it! He felt like a mad scientist to anyone who sat in his leather butterscotch chair because they were his science project, at his mercy and his will. Mr. Vanreen was acting as if he didn't even notice Richard staring at him for the test results. Mr. Vanreen just continued unhooking the equipment.

Richard, growing tired of the passive-aggressive torture from Mr. Vanreen, finally asked, "So...Mr. Vanreen, what are, what are the results? I mean…my results? How did I do?" asked Richard nervously.

Mr. Vanreen replied, "I don't know yet." Even though he actually did. Further passive-aggressive torture. A product of the leather butterscotch chair which reminds its visitors of the electric chair.

Mr. Vanreen continued, "Yep! Don't know yet…but I'll look over your results sometime today. Then I will send them to your lawyer early Monday morning. So as of right now, Mr. Ginn…I don't know."

Richard immediately dropped his head low, feeling defeated. Like all of the life had just literally been sucked out of him. Richard's body weight just dropped as he flopped back down into the polygraph chair. Richard lifted his head back up, looking at Mr. Vanreen, who was towering over Richard and said, "So I have to get my test results from my lawyer? On Monday?"

Mr. Vanreen replied, "Yep, your lawyer should contact you with the results."

Richard responded, "But I'm supposed to start trial Wednesday morning!"

But Mr. Vanreen replied, "I'm sorry, Mr. Ginn, but I have no knowledge of or control over when or if you have trial. So…our business dealings are done. Good day to you, sir. You are free to leave now."

Mr. Vanreen grabbed the grid-sheet papers, then he completely turned his back to Richard. And he finished going over all the grid sheets. Richard stood back up, and with a disappointed and sarcastic tone, Richard said to Mr. Vanreen, "You have a nice day too." And as Richard was walking out of Mr. Vanreen's door, Richard said at a whisper under his breath, "Asshole."

Richard was thinking that Mr. Vanreen couldn't hear what he had just said. But he indeed heard every word that Richard had said at a whisper. And Mr. Vanreen heard it clearly at that. Mr. Vanreen just calmly replied, "Please close the door behind you. Thank you."

Richard reached back, grabbed the doorknob, and slammed Mr. Vanreen's door. *Bam!*

Chapter 12

It was now early Monday morning. And Richard had just made it back to the motel room from seeing his daughter, Jessica. Richard went up to her school and did his little ritual of writing *I love you, Jessie* into the outside frost of her classroom window while he blew her kisses from the palms of his hands.

Richard thought about his daughter, Jessica, quite often. He loved and missed her more than life itself. And this time of separation was really wearing and taking a toll on Richard. He wasn't used to this new feeling of emptiness and loneliness which was causing to build a little anger and a little bitterness.

It saddened Richard that he couldn't be there with his baby girl. So Richard, going to Jessie's classroom and to her bedroom window and writing those words and blowing those kisses, at least made Richard feel close to his daughter, Jessie, again as he was flooded with a roller coaster of mixed emotions.

The time was almost noon, and Richard was still waiting to hear from his lawyer, Mr. Davis, about the results of his polygraph test. The polygraph test that he had taken last Friday. Richard was really feeling optimistic about it. But he was still disappointed and angry about that trick question that Mr. Vanreen had asked him.

Mr. Vanreen had asked Richard if he had held his wife down at any time during the day in question. And Richard did hold his wife down but not to *rape* her! Richard held his wife, Kim, down, trying to stop her from wildly swinging on him and hitting him.

Richard was now beginning to think that he didn't pass the lie detector test just on that very question alone. And the fact that he fumbled the answer when he was asked that question while his heart rate began beating extremely fast, and he began to sweat. But even then, still Richard really liked his chances. He liked his chances because he didn't rape his wife. He was an innocent man 100 percent!

Richard was back sitting on his motel room bed, watching television. He was sitting there, dozing in and out of sleep.

Richard's construction job foreman had given him the day off earlier, telling him, "Focus on your freedom, Richy! I want you to go back to your motel room and wait for that call. Get your life back. I call those public defenders public pretenders. Look…" The foreman paused and pulled his sock down, then showed Richard his ankle, which had an electronic monitor ankle bracelet device. The foreman paused and said, "Public pretenders, man." Then he pulled his sock back up.

The foreman went on to say, "Your focus is important right now. Then if you need us, you can always come back and work anytime."

Richard really appreciated the support from his boss at such a vulnerable time in his life. Richard didn't have many friends left once they had heard what he had done to his wife, Kim. Richard was faced with losing everything that he had worked so diligently to build from nothing. *And* it was a great possibility that he could end up going to prison.

Richard thought, *Yeah, maybe it's best that I get a little rest from my job today and focus on regaining my freedom.*

Richard fell asleep, finally getting a chance to relax for a moment. Richard slept for about an hour. His cell phone, which was in his hand, laid on his chest, had slipped out of his hands. The phone slid off of Richard's chest and onto the bed right beside him. Richard rolled over right on top of his cell phone in the midst of him sleeping.

Then suddenly Richard heard the phone ringing in his sleep. *Ring. Ring. Ring.* Half asleep, he reached up under the back of his right shoulder, grabbed his cell phone, then answered it. It was Richard's lawyer, Mr. Davis. Richard answered his phone, and Mr. Davis said, "Hey, Richard, it's Mr. Davis here."

Richard anxiously replied, "Oh! How are you, Mr. Davis? I was really hoping it was you! Did you get my results yet? Please tell me you did!"

Mr. Davis replied, "As a matter of fact, Richard, I did, yes, I did. I went and picked them up this morning. And the prosecutor left a sticky note on top of them saying that your trial date is set for March 5, which is Wednesday at 9:30 a.m. And we will be in front of Judge Burquette."

Richard, sounding extremely confused, replied, "Huh? No, no, no! Wait a minute! Wait a second! Let me think! Let me collect my thoughts! I don't understand! I don't think I heard you exactly correctly or correctly exactly right." Both of Richard's hands were on top of his head in a confused state of panic as his words were misfiring and stuttering out.

Mr. Davis nonchalantly, and seemingly without the slightest of concern, responded, "What do you mean that you don't understand? Trial is Wednesday." Mr. Davis paused to make sure Richard was clearly understanding. "Wednesday, Wednesday at 9:30 a.m. You lied, Richard. You failed. Just that simple. And all we can do now is prepare for your trial."

Richard, still sounding confused and in disbelief, replied, "No, I DIDN'T LIE! It was a trick question! He asked me if I held my wife down. And I answered I did, but I didn't!"

Richard went on, explaining to Mr. Davis, "I mean…Yes, I held my wife down, but not for that reason. Not to RAPE her! I held my selfish wife down to prevent her from hitting me!"

Richard stood up by now while explaining on his cell phone and pacing back and forth across the floor, trying desperately to explain. But Mr. Davis replied, "I don't know, Richard…the prosecutor said that you failed miserably. Hands down. She's convinced. No questions asked. And it was one question in particular, the most important question of them all where you showed an alarming amount of deception."

Mr. Davis went on, "So all I can do as your attorney is prepare you for trial. But if I would've known that you couldn't pass the test, I would not have allowed you to take the polygraph. Or at least advised you to decline."

Mr. Davis continued, "I really think that you knew you were lying to begin with, Richard. As your lawyer, I think that you should really consider taking that ten-year-plea agreement that the prosecutor's office still has on the table for you right now. I mean look at it this way, at least you'll still be fairly young when you get out."

Richard envisioned a quick flash of him in prison getting older, daughter a young lady, wife moved on, business up in flames. Everything gone. Done? Over? He snapped out of it.

Richard replied passionately, "Are you serious! You're supposed to be my lawyer, Mr. Davis! I thought as my lawyer, you are supposed to defend me and prove my innocence! Not talk me into doing ten years in prison for a crime against my wife that I didn't do!"

Mr. Davis responded, "Just right now, Richard…I think that's what's best for you in the long run. You can get out early for good behavior and build you a fresh new life."

Richard, in frustration, replied, "I DON'T WANT A FRESH NEW LIFE! I WANT MY LIFE! MY LIFE BACK! MY FAMILY BACK! MY WIFE AND DAUGHTER! I WAS WRONG! NOT THEM! MY STUPIDITY! THEY DID NOTHING WRONG! Look…I am an innocent man, Mr. Davis. I don't think you are hearing me clearly! IN-NO-CENT!"

But Mr. Davis, not wanting Richard to feel like he didn't have his best interest at hand—which he really didn't—he was selfishly trying to convince Richard without feeling forceful but as if he cared. Even though Mr. Davis could care less because he wasn't making a dime off of Richard. Win or lose.

Mr. Davis calmed Richard down by saying, "I'm going to fight for you and get your life back, Richy! If you want to go to trial, then trial it is. I'm with you, not against you, Richy." Mr. Davis was hoping that his reassurance to Richard, that he would fight and prove his innocence, had indeed gained Richard's trust. Mr. Davis didn't want any confrontation from Richard because Mr. Davis knew that would slow him down and could possibly delay him from going on that hunting trip with his buddies.

Mr. Davis wanted this whole—as he called it—Richard Ginn soap opera to be over with as soon as possible. So once Mr. Davis gained Richard's trust back again, he told Richard, "So I will see you Wednesday at 930 a.m. in Judge Burquette's courtroom." They both hung their telephones up.

Normally Mr. Davis would meet a client and prep him for trial as far as questions from the prosecutor to anticipate, the judge's tendencies, and meanings of certain words that his client may hear during court proceedings. Mr. Davis is usually detailed and very thorough.

Mr. Davis, a student of law consistently trying to find that hidden treasure, that hidden key, that edge, for his client to leave the courtroom victoriously. Prosecutor's respect his acumen, strategy, and legal tactics for law. But they only respected it with his paying clients. His body language was subtly different with paying clients.

Mr. Davis would prep paying clients that he represented for trial many times; it would be repetitive and consistent days prior to the trial. So it would be fresh in his client's mind. And they would be sharp. And Mr. Davis would also prep paying clients an hour just before trial was actually scheduled to begin.

But this case was a little different. Actually enormously different. Richard wasn't a paying client. So Mr. Davis skipped all of the trial prepping and would just show up directly in the courtroom for trial without telling Richard what to expect throughout the proceedings. He would talk to Richard if they bumped into each other randomly in the hall before proceedings. But that was rare.

One of Geofrey Davis's favorite pillar quotes was, "If you ain't got a dime, then Jeff ain't got the time." His buddies called him no-dime-no-time Jeff. And his lifestyle and his ego exemplified just that.

It was final; Richard's trial was set for Wednesday. And Richard was more than ready to prove his innocence! Wednesday crept up on Richard and had arrived sooner than he had expected. It was now Wednesday, and Richard had awakened with nervous butterflies inside of his stomach. So he read a quick passage from out of the Bible. He was trying to calm and settle his nerves. The verse from out of the Bible read, "With God with me, then who can be against me?" Then Richard said a quick prayer, never believing or relying on God as strongly as he needed him now.

Richard then grabbed his list of questions that he had stayed up most of the night thinking of and jotting down in between him nodding in and out of sleep.

The questions that Richard had wrote down were for his lawyer to ask his wife during the trial. Richard poured every ounce of brain-busting thinking into those questions, almost to the point of a severe migraine headache.

As Richard was reading over the questions, Richard thought, *Yeah, these questions will definitely prove my innocence right here!* Richard smiled as if he was certain that he would be found not guilty.

Richard felt like a lie detector machine couldn't understand him like a jury would.

Richard went on, saying, "Juries are everyday people that understand and have feelings and emotions." Richard really liked his chance with a jury.

Richard got into his car and drove to downtown Minneapolis, to the municipal building. He was scheduled to begin his trial. Richard made it to the judge's courtroom that would be over his trial. The name on the front of the huge double doors read, "The Honorable Judge William Burquette."

Richard stood on the outside of the doors reading the name. Richard thought, *Wow... This is just like all of the TV shows that I watch.* Richard really got butterflies in his stomach when he thought, *Damn, my wife, Kim, could possibly be on the other side of those doors.*

Richard hadn't seen his wife, Kim, in such a long time. And it felt like forever. And he was still madly in love with her today. Richard's feelings didn't change. If anything, his love for her had grown even stronger from being separated from his wife, Kim, especially for that long of a period of time. Richard and Kim had never been apart since they met as teenagers in high school.

Richard had to build up the courage to walk into the courtroom just on the other side of those big doors. As he stood there, Richard's legs were becoming weaker and weaker, almost giving out, the longer he stood there. The very thought of seeing his wife for the first time since that day that they made love, and she falsely accused him of raping her.

Richard looked down at his watch to see what time it was. The time was 9:23 a.m., seven minutes before trial. Richard thought, *Maybe I should be making my way into the courtroom before I possibly upset the judge and the prosecutor, and they try to lock me up for contempt.* Richard didn't want to get on their bad side any further than he already was.

Richard thought that mostly everyone looked at rape as more of a heinous crime than murder because rape leaves its victim emotionally scarred for the rest of the victim's life. Rape is a crime that most people look down on and consider inexcusable and unforgivable.

Richard lifted his hand to grab the doorknob of Judge Burquette's door, and without warning, the door suddenly flew open—*whosh!* With a quick reaction, Richard quickly snatched his hand back. "Whoa!"

And the female's voice on the other side of the door said, "Oh, excuse me! I'm terribly sorry!" The door was still opening up, until the door was finally fully open, and to Richard's surprise, it was his wife, Kim.

Kim was on her way out of the courtroom to smoke a cigarette real quick. Richard and Kim locked eyes and stared at each other, completely speechless. Richard gave Kim that look that said, *How could you do me like this? The father of our daughter? Your husband? I thought you loved me...*

This was the first time that Richard had seen his wife, Kim, since that day they had made love. The day that she had accused him of raping her. All of those deep and strong feelings of love for his high school sweetheart had seemingly stirred up again for Richard.

But before Kim gave in to the temptation or the weakness of allowing hers to stir, she quickly took her eyes from off of Richard and looked down to the floor. Kim couldn't even look Richard in his eyes. She knew that she was wrong, but she justified her getting even because Richard lost his job and cheated on her. That was Kim's way of not feeling guilty and showing a stone-cold heart of no remorse.

Kim felt like she could finally own it all. Everything that Richard had worked so diligently hard for would all be hers and only hers. Kim thought, *Now I'll have all the money, the house, and the hot rod business.* The hot rod business Richard worked blood, sweat, and tears for, day in and day out, to gross over $100,000-plus annually for his wife, Kim.

Kim quickly took her eyes off of Richard and said, "Excuse me." Kim hurriedly walked off, as if Richard was a stranger that she had never known. And Richard didn't even turn around to watch his wife walking off. All Richard heard was the sound of Kim's heels hitting the floor with each step that she took. *Tap, tap, tap, tap.*

After listening to his wife, Kim's, heels hitting the floor as she was walking off behind Richard to smoke a cigarette, Richard exhaled a deep breath and was about to finally make his way into the courtroom.

Just then Richard's lawyer, Mr. Davis, was leaving out of the courtroom. Mr. Davis said to Richard, "Come on, Mr. Ginn. And take a seat at the table on the left." Richard stepped into the courtroom, and the very first person that he sees is who? None other than his beautiful daughter, Jessica. She was sitting in the courtroom. Richard made eye contact with Jessie, and when she saw Richard, she instantly became excited to finally see her daddy up close and within hugging distance.

Kim had made her way back into the courtroom by this time. She came and sat down right beside Jessie. Kim tried to grab Jessie, but Jessie pulled away and ran to Richard's arms for a big hug. Richard picked Jessie up and hugged her as tight as he has ever hugged her his entire life.

Richard held her high up into the air, stared at her, and formed his lips to say at a whisper, "I love you, Jessie." Tears formed in Richard's eyes and slowly streamed down his cheeks.

Richard loved his daughter, Jessie, so much! And just as Richard was about to give her a big kiss on the top of her head, Kim came over and snatched Jessie away from out of Richard's arms. Jessie looked helplessly back at her dad as Kim tightly gripped her hand and was pulling Jessie back to where they were originally seated.

Richard took a seat next to his lawyer, Mr. Davis, who was already sitting at their defense table with a large stack of papers directly in front of him. Mr. Davis was leaning back from the table with his legs crossed and looking as if he didn't have one single worry in the world.

Judge Burquette's bailiff announced, "All rise! Judge Burquette residing in the case of the *People of the State of Minnesota v. Richard Blake Ginn*. Court is now in session!"

Judge Burquette entered into the courtroom and took a seat in his gigantic luxurious all-black Italian leather headrest cushioned chair. Judge Burquette arrogantly took a small whistle-wetting sip out of his glass of water. Then he thumbed through a small stack of papers sitting in front of him, all the while leaving the courtroom still standing up, waiting to be seated.

After a few seconds had passed, Judge Burquette finally said, "You all may be seated." And it was easily visible that the family and friends in the courtroom were somewhat frustrated at Judge Burquette's arrogance and inconsideration that left them standing for an unusual exaggerated period of time.

Judge Burquette announced, "This case is the *People of Minneapolis, Minnesota, v. Richard Blake Ginn*...Mr. Ginn is charged with sexual assault and false imprisonment. The victim in this... unusual circumstance is the wife of the accused, Mrs. Kimberly Ginn."

Judge Burquette looked over at the prosecutor's table and asked, "Mrs. Rollins, I see here where it was noted that the prosecutor's office had approached Mr. Ginn and his lawyer, Mr. Davis, with a plea agreement?"

Mrs. Rollins stood up and answered, "Yes, we did, Your Honor. It was a plea agreement that we felt was a fair offer, considering the unusual circumstances, to save the family some grief of having to relive this nightmare all over again, Your Honor. It was a ten-year plea offer. If Mr. Ginn pleads guilty to sexual assault, we would, in turn, dismiss the false imprisonment charge."

Judge Burquette asked, "Is this offer still an open agreement of consideration?"

Mrs. Rollins quickly leaned over to the assistant prosecutor and whispered something. Then the male assistant prosecutor leaned back over to Mrs. Rollins and whispered something into her ear.

Then Mrs. Rollins answered, "No, Your Honor, it is no longer on the table for the defendant. We talked to Mr. Davis, who is Mr. Ginn's attorney. And we were informed that Mr. Ginn would not be interested in any plea agreement that we may have. So, therefore, Your Honor, the ten years is no longer an option for Mr. Ginn."

Judge Burquette tried to hide the snarl on his face which was barely noticeable—very subtle—as he looked over at the defense table. After trying his best to hide his look of disgust, Judge Burquette asked Richard's attorney, Mr. Davis, "Is this an accurate account, Mr. Davis?"

Mr. Davis answered, "Yes, it is, Your Honor. My client, Mr. Ginn, is not interested in any plea agreement and wish to proceed to have his day in court."

Judge Burquette's writing pen was swiftly moving, jotting down every word that the prosecutor and Mr. Davis said. And the court's recorder was swiftly typing every word that both parties were saying. The courtroom was completely silent as Judge Burquette continued jotting down his notes.

Richard stared around the courtroom. He was looking at the judge's big shiny stainless steel pen swiftly moving down the paper. And then Richard looked at the bailiff and the bailiff's gun snapped into his holster on the side of his waist.

Richard suddenly envisioned himself going for the bailiff's handgun, shooting the courtroom up, and making his great escape. Richard thought, *Then I wouldn't have to face these false allegations of rape ever again!* Richard quickly snapped out of it.

Then Richard continued looking over the courtroom. And then he looked into the jury box as they sat staring at Richard. Some of the jury looked as if they were angry. And some looked at Richard with fear in their eyes as if he was a serial rapist or something.

Richard didn't really notice them staring at him until they made direct eye contact and locked eyes. Richard thought about when he and his lawyer had picked that particular group of jurors.

Richard hoped that the group that they had assembled would ultimately get him acquitted so that he could get his life back. The jury was mostly all men with an exception of three women. Richard really didn't know how to read the women. Couldn't quite figure them out. And it was a definite challenge picking them, especially picking the women to be jurors for a rape case. Richard just basically followed his gut feeling.

Richard took his eyes off of the jury and looked toward where his daughter was seated, but Jessie was no longer sitting there. Richard thought that Jessie must have gone to the restroom and should return shortly. Judge Burquette finally quit writing and made his pen into a motion, as if he were crossing the letter *T* and dotting the letter *I* overdramatically.

Judge Burquette leaned back into his big black leather chair, as if he was thinking about something. And he twirled the pen in the corner of his mouth and was lightly chomping down on the pen, thinking. He then removed his glasses.

Judge Burquette looked over at Mrs. Rollins, then he looked over at Mr. Davis and said, "Let's get this trial underway. Are we ready to proceed, Mrs. Rollins and Mr. Davis?"

They both answered simultaneously, "Yes, we are, Your Honor."

Judge Burquette replied, "Please stand and state your name for the record."

Mrs. Rollins stood up first and said, "Good morning, Your Honor. My name is Joyce Rollins, representing for the People of the State of Minnesota vs. Richard Blake Ginn in the sexual assault and false imprisonment trial."

Then Richard's lawyer, Mr. Davis, stood up and said, "Good morning, Your Honor. We really appreciate your patience this morning. Uhhhhh, I'm Geofrey Davis, attorney representing the defendant, Mr. Richard Ginn, here before you today, Your Honor. Thank you."

Judge Burquette told Mrs. Rollins to begin with her opening arguments. Mrs. Rollins stood up and cleared her throat as she was buttoning up her dress suit. Mrs. Rollins approached the jury box, and she had every juror's complete and undivided attention as she aggressively set the tone with her opening arguments.

Mrs. Rollins said, "Here…today, people, we have a clear and cut case of flat out rape! And flat out outright kidnapping!" Mrs. Rollins sarcastically went on, "See, sexual assault and false imprisonment is just how the state categorized this heinous crime! But…at the end of the day, we aaaaaaaaall know it as rape and kidnapping! And, ladies and gentlemen of the jury, I am going to convincingly prove it with factual evidence. Undisputable evidence. Right here and right now, today!"

Mrs. Rollins went on with her opening arguments, "I'm going to prove that the defendant, Mr. Ginn, sitting like some innocent and little choir boy, who, in his own twisted little eyes, somehow feels like that is hiiiiis wife. And since Mrs. Ginn is hiiiiis wife, he has the entitlement to take the sex from his wife and force her to have sex and give him oral sex whenever he's drunk and his little teeny weeny pecker gets hard!"

Mrs. Rollins saw that she had the jury's attention focused on her every word. So she went even further, saying, "But I bet if you ask the defendant, he'll tell you that it's nothing wrong with what he had done! And that his wife, Mrs. Ginn, is his property!"

Mrs. Rollins continued, "But I'm here to tell you and prove to you today that FINANCIALLY well-off Mr. Ginn, sitting beside his high-powered attorney, is 100 percent guilty as charged!"

Mrs. Rollins ended her opening arguments with both of her palms pressed down flat onto the defense table and looking Richard square into his eyes, without blinking or batting an eye once.

Then Mrs. Rollins looked up at the jury, seated to the left of her, who she could instantly tell that they had felt every single word that came out of her mouth.

Mrs. Rollins was frowned up in disgust and anger. But that was just the show that she was putting on for the jury, and underneath that angered frown, Mrs. Rollins was smiling from ear to ear. She thought, *Point taken. That's one point for me!*

Mrs. Rollins was feeling as if she had the case won already. She thought, And I haven't even pulled out my ace-in-the-hole evidence yet." Mrs. Rollins stood upright from the defense table, straightened her dress suit, and confidently said, "Thank you, Your Honor."

Mrs. Rollins didn't waste any time, coming straight out, blinders on and swinging! Setting up that knock-out blow that'll get Richard out of there! And the quicker the better.

But little did Richard know, his attorney, Mr. Davis felt the same exact way as Mrs. Rollins did—getting Richard out of there, and the sooner the better.

Richard's lawyer, Mr. Davis, was very familiar with the leading prosecutor, Mrs. Rollins', legendary prosecutorial history, of her going straight for the defense's jugular. Mrs. Rollins was infamous all through the state of Minnesota for getting cases over with before they had even really begun.

But that was a good thing in Mr. Davis's eyes. Mrs. Rollins' style of getting cases over with as soon as possible worked in Mr. Davis's favor. All during her opening arguments, Mr. Davis couldn't stop thinking about going on that hunting trip with his buddies. That's probably why he didn't hear Richard when Richard kept tapping him and whispering for him to object. "Object that. Object to that too..." during almost all of Mrs. Rollins' entire opening arguments.

Richard was trying to tell Mr. Davis to object to the accusations that Mrs. Rollins were making against him that weren't true. Richard felt like Mrs. Rollins was slandering his character to the jury by lying on him.

But all Richard could do was look at his lawyer, Geofrey Davis, then Richard looked at the judge, then he looked at Mrs. Rollins. And lastly he looked at the jury, feeling helpless as he saw that, by the jury's facial expressions, they were believing every word that came out of Mrs. Rollins' mouth. And Richard's attorney didn't object to anything!

Judge Burquette looked over at Mr. Davis and said, "Your rebuttal, Counsel."

Mr. Davis stood up and said, "Thank you, Your Honor." And then he proceeded toward the jury as every one of them stared at him intensely with anticipation, eagerly anxious to hear how he could possibly dispute the razor-sharp opening arguments that Mrs. Rollins had just convincingly displayed.

The jurors stared at Mr. Davis as he approached closer and closer to the jury box. The jurors were anticipating Richard's lawyer's mouth to open up, and the words that would come out to hit hard and have as much, or even more of a vicious, damaging bite, countering Mrs. Rollins' bitter words. And to the jurors' disappointment, as well as Richard's, as he watched, listened, and waited, just as intense as the jurors, or maybe even more, since it was his life hanging in the balance.

As Mr. Davis approached the jurors, he stood up and all he said was, "Ladies and gentlemen of the jury, my client, Mr. Ginn, is not guilty! And we shall prove it! The prosecutor's arguments are more opinionated than facts of evidence against my client."

Then Mr. Davis returned back to his seat next to Richard. All the jurors could do was let out a sigh, like someone had just let all of the air out of them. The jury quickly deflated, like a popped balloon!

Geofrey Davis didn't want to put up much of a fight. He was thinking about that trip and didn't want to be held up by an indecisive jury when it came to deliberations. He also had to make the fight feel like it was real for Richard.

Richard looked over at Mr. Davis and said, "That's it! That's really all you could think of to defend me!"

Mr. Davis responded to Richard, saying, "This is not the most important phase of the trial right now, Richard. I'm your lawyer, which means—at least the last time I checked—I'm the one that KNOWS LAW! So just sit back, relax, and let someone who KNOWS law handle this...that's only if you don't mind?" Mr. Davis paused. "Geez!" An aggressive whisper.

Richard felt as if Mr. Davis did have a valid point because he was his lawyer. Richard thought, *Yeah, maybe I am worrying for nothing...I don't know law. I'll just sit back, relax a little, and allow my lawyer to do his thing.*

Richard sat back in his chair, feeling enough at ease to agree with Mr. Davis, partly because Richard didn't know the law or anything about the judicial system. So Richard trusted Mr. Davis from that point forward.

Next Mrs. Rollins began calling witnesses for the prosecution. Mrs. Rollins stood back up and said, "Your Honor, I would like to call my first witness to the stand for the prosecution...Officer Trau."

Richard didn't even know that Officer Trau was seated in the courtroom until Officer Trau stood up in a dress shirt and a tie. He was clean-shaven and had a fresh buzz cut. Officer Trau looked as if he just recently left the barbershop. Officer Trau began to make his way from the back of the courtroom. He nodded his head, speaking to Richard as he walked past him.

Richard had a blank numb look on his face. Richard was thinking, *What type of person speaks to you just before they lie on you? And try to send you to prison? And secondly, what type of witness could this guy possibly be for the prosecution? He wasn't there* witnessing *my wife smacking, scratching, kicking, and hitting me because I lost my job! And me trying to get her to stop by holding her down!*

Officer Trau took the witness stand, raised his right hand to be sworn in, and then Officer Trau said, "Good morning, Your Honor."

Judge Burquette responded, "Good morning to you, Officer Trau, as well."

Then Mrs. Rollins began her questioning. "Officer Trau, were you called to the defendant's home on or about November 20?"

Officer Trau replied, "Yes, ma'am, I was. My partner and I received a call from dispatch. It was a report of a domestic dispute and sexual assault."

Mrs. Rollins replied, "And, Officer Trau, did you make an arrest that day as well?"

Officer Trau answered, "Yes, ma'am, I did."

Mrs. Rollins continued on with her questioning, "Is the person you arrested that day for sexual assault—better known as rape—is that person present in the courtroom today?"

Officer Trau replied, "Yes, ma'am, he is. It was Mr. Ginn, sitting right there." Officer Trau raised his right hand to point at Richard. Mrs. Rollins said, "Your Honor, note that Officer Trau made a positive identification of the defendant, Mr. Richard Ginn, for the record."

Judge Burquette replied, "Note taken, Mrs. Rollins."

Richard was looking at Mr. Davis with a look of disgust from out the corner of his eye. Richard was still sitting back, waiting for his lawyer to *say something*!

To Richard, it seemed as if Mr. Davis, his lawyer, the judge, the police officer, and the prosecutor were all working together. Mrs.

Rollins said, "That will be all for now, Your Honor. Thank you." Then she confidently walked away, taking her seat once more.

Judge Burquette looked at Mr. Davis and said, "Your cross, Mr. Davis."

Mr. Davis stood up, buttoned his sport coat, and said, "Officer Trau, when you arrived at the defendant's home, did his wife, Mrs. Kim Ginn, act like a typical sexual assault victim? Or did she act like a typical spoiled wife, throwing a temper tantrum? Because she couldn't seem to get her little way? For the first time in her ungrateful life?"

But before Officer Trau could answer, Mrs. Rollins jumped to her feet and hollered, "Objection, Your Honor! Counsel is being insensitive and making light of how the victim was sexually assaulted!"

After Mrs. Rollins stood up and hollered her objection to Richard's lawyer, Mr. Davis, being insensitive, Mr. Davis looked at Judge Burquette and said, "Your Honor, I am just merely asking a simple question. A question to differentiate between the two. I'm just looking for a little clarity here."

Richard was feeling his lawyer, Mr. Davis, was at least trying to defend him now. Judge Burquette looked at Mr. Davis and sternly replied, "Let's not sarcastically try to ask questions, Mr. Davis. It is rather somewhat insensitive to the victim. Just ask your question please, Mr. Davis, minus the unwarranted shenanigans."

Judge Burquette looked at Officer Trau who, by now, had a look on his face that said he didn't know if he should answer the question or not. Judge Burquette replied, "Please answer the question, Officer Trau. Did Mrs. Ginn act like a typical sexual assault victim, I believe, was the question by the defense. Correct, Counsel?"

Officer Trau answered, "No, Mrs. Ginn did not have the typical hysterical characteristics of a victim of sexual assault. In my humble but very honest opinion. So…I guess my answer would be no."

Officer Trau continued on, "But Mrs. Ginn did have some visible bruises on her wrists. Which was a strong indicator to me and my partner that, at some point, Mrs. Gin, was held down or restrained tightly by her wrists."

Richard was thinking to himself, *That's because I held my wife down to stop her from going crazy on me!*

Then Mr. Davis walked over to the defense table and asked, "Can I have just a moment, Your Honor?" Mr. Davis leaned over the table, thumbed through a couple of papers, he stood back up, then approached Officer Trau, who was still seated in the witness stand.

Mr. Davis asked, "I see in the medical report aaaaaand in the booking report that you have pictures of Mrs. Ginn's bruises on her wrist." Mr. Davis had the pictures that the prosecution had given him in his hands. Mr. Davis gave the pictures to the first juror sitting in the jury box, then he said, "Please pass those around, would you?"

Officer Trau responded, "Yes, another patrol car had taken Mrs. Ginn immediately to the hospital for an examination. Just like we do in all sexual assault offenses. And all of the evidence is documented."

Mr. Davis went on questioning Officer Trau. "And I also see that the victim even had a sexual assault kit physical examination performed on her?"

Officer Trau responded, "Yes, she did. That is also our typical protocol as well. Again with all sexual assault offenses."

Richard was looking at Geofrey Davis and thinking, *What are you doing! You're proving their case for them! And making me look guilty! How in the hell could you give the jury all of the evidence against me! And you call that helping me out!*

Even the prosecutor, Mrs. Rollins, was surprised by Mr. Davis's move. But she didn't act like it. Mrs. Rollins kept her composure while thinking the same exact thoughts as Richard. That actually was the next phase of her strategy, using the sexual assault pictures to prove Richard was guilty. But Richard's lawyer, Mr. Davis, was making Mrs. Rollins' case easy for the prosecution. And Mrs. Rollins didn't mind it at all either.

Mrs. Rollins didn't object to Mr. Davis either, not one time during his presentation. Richard didn't know law, but the whole thing just didn't seem right to him. Richard thought, *No, I don't know law. But I have good goddamn sense!* But Richard was thinking about what his lawyer had said to him earlier, "I'm the lawyer, I know law. You don't. So just sit back and trust me to defend you!"

So Richard began thinking that his lawyer, Mr. Davis, was putting on a classic reverse psychology strategy. That Mr. Davis had done and won so many cases in the past. Richard was uncertain about Mr. Davis's strategy, but he decided to trust in his lawyer's strategy anyway.

So Richard just let it all unfold and play out. Richard was hoping that it all would make sense in the end. While Richard was listening to his lawyer, Mr. Davis, question Officer Trau, Richard looked up and saw all of the expressions on the jurors' faces. And Richard could tell by their facial expressions that things weren't looking to be in his favor. Or even going his way.

Richard observed each juror take long hard stares at each photo of Richard's wife, Kim's, bruises on her wrist. That for one, Richard didn't think he had held her wrist tight enough to leave bruises.

Richard was just trying to stop his wife from wildly hitting him. But he was caught up in the heat of the moment. And secondly, Richard didn't know that pictures of his wife's bruises even existed. His lawyer, Mr. Davis, failed to mention it to him. He wasn't a paid lawyer, so he didn't feel it was that important. And quite frankly wasn't going to do anything extra. Just the bare basics and minimum requirements within his sworn attorney's bar.

But any decent lawyer—not even a good lawyer, just any halfway decent lawyer—that has integrity about his profession would have informed his client whether if the lawyer was paid or not. But not all lawyers place decency or integrity before that almighty dollar/dead presidents. The love of the American dollar, since the beginning of time, has been the root of all evil. And Richard's life right now was living proof of this evil.

Mr. Davis was different. He has always said, "If you ain't got a dime, I ain't got the time!"

Richard couldn't help but stare at each juror's face. Especially the three women jurors that he and Mr. Davis had handpicked themselves. Richard wanted to get a reading of their faces as his lawyer and the prosecutor were going back and forth.

To Richard, the look on the jurors' faces was an indicator. And it didn't look good. Richard thought, *I need this clown to clean up this mess that he created. And the sooner the better!*

Mr. Davis went on with his questioning of Officer Trau. Mr. Davis asked, "Officer Trau, I also have documents and photos here... of my client, Mr. Ginn's bruises and scratches to his neck, chest, arms, and face." Officer Trau was listening and patiently waiting for the question as he stared at Mr. Davis without batting an eye.

Mr. Davis went on with his questioning of Officer Trau. "Now...did you get a chance to look over the documents and photos of Mr. Ginn, sir?"

Officer Trau replied, "No, I didn't, sir. I didn't know photos of Mr. Ginn's wounds existed, sir. And I can't say definitively that...I noticed any wounds either. I—" Mr. Davis abruptly cut Officer Trau off in the middle of his explanation before he could finish his sentence.

Mr. Davis interjected aggressively and rudely, "I know, I know, you somehow mysteriously failed to see or notice the defendant's cuts, bruises, and scratches that a frickin' blind man would've seen!"

Mrs. Rollins stood up and hollered, "Objection! Objection, Your Honor!"

Judge Burquette looked at Mrs. Rollins as if to say he's not going to spend the entire day listening to her object to every little thing that Mr. Davis says. Judge Burquette looked at Officer Trau and said, "Please answer the question, Officer Trau."

Officer Trau answered Mr. Davis, "Like I said, sir, no. I did not notice any of Mr. Ginn's cuts or scratches."

Mr. Davis replied, "So...Officer Trau, is it a possibility to say that Mrs. Ginn could have gotten those bruises to her wrist, while Mr. Ginn was restraining her? From further scratching and hitting him? When he suddenly told her that he had lost his job?"

Officer Trau answered, "Yes, it's a possibility, sir."

Then Mr. Davis pulled out Richard's mug shot of the day that he got arrested, fingerprinted, and booked. Richard's mug shot clearly showed fresh scratches to his neck, chest, face, and arms. Minimal, tiny little scratches yet still scratches.

Richard's lawyer, Mr. Davis, gave his mug shot to the first juror closest to him and said, "Please pass that around, ma'am." The lady juror took the photo of Richard, looked at it, and passed it to the juror sitting next to her. They passed the photo around the jury box until it made its way back around to the first juror who originally passed the mug shot of Richard.

After every juror looked at the mug shot of Richard with scratches, Mr. Davis replied, "No more questions, Your Honor! Thank you."

Judge Burquette looked at Mrs. Rollins and said, "Your cross, Mrs. Rollins."

Mrs. Rollins, who was feverishly taking notes during Geofrey Davis's questioning of Officer Trau, quickly stood up. And she couldn't have waited one second longer. She was eagerly anticipating her turn to counter what Mr. Davis had just said.

Because up until that point, Mrs. Rollins enjoyed the so-called "defense" that Mr. Davis was putting on. Richard's lawyer, Mr. Davis, was making Mrs. Rollins' job that much easier. And he was actually proving her case against Richard.

Mrs. Rollins stood up and said, "Ladies and gentlemen of the jury, these cuts and scratches on Mr. Ginn aren't from stopping his wife from hitting him! These cuts and scratches are from his wife, Mrs. Ginn, defending and trying to protect herself from her husband, Richard Ginn, holding her down and raping her!"

Mrs. Rollins voice was getting louder and louder with each word that she said. And her last word was the loudest, making everyone in the courtroom jump when she startled them, emphasizing her last word, almost at the top of her lungs.

Mrs. Rollins had instantly regained the jurors' complete and undivided attention, as if they had just forgotten every word that Richard's lawyer, Mr. Davis, had just said to them. But Richard was finally beginning to feel confident of his lawyer's ability and strategy. Richard was finally feeling like Mr. Davis was defending him.

Mrs. Rollins had made her final statement with emphasis. And she ended with, "That's it. That'll be all, Your Honor. Thank you."

It was approximately 4:00 p.m. after all of the questioning. Judge Burquette looked at his watch and said, "We'll take a recess and resume trial tomorrow. We'll begin at 9:00 a.m., and I am requesting that everyone be present and prepared to begin in a timely fashion."

Judge Burquette picked his oak gavel up, then he hit the judge's bench—*boom! boom!*—and then he said, "Court is now in recess." Everyone left the courtroom with plans to come back.

The next morning arrived, and everyone was indeed present.

Judge Burquette's bailiff hollered, "All rise! Judge Burquette's courtroom is now in session!"

Judge Burquette replied, "You all may now be seated." Trial was underway. The jury was scheduled to deliberate in the later part of the day. Judge burquette looked at Mrs. Rollins and said, "Your witness, Mrs. Rollins."

From all of the questioning and opening arguments, Richard thought that the prosecution presented a strong-enough case to have an advantage. Richard said, "It's lopsided. I just know it is. Because it was so much more that my lawyer could have said in my defense to convince the jury of my innocence. Instead of allowing Mrs. Rollins to say and do whatever it was that she wanted to do to prove her case."

Richard was pointing to the questions that he was up all night the day before trial, writing down for his lawyer to ask. For the majority of Richard's trial, Mr. Davis ignored Richard's plea for him to ask the questions.

As a matter of fact, Mr. Davis didn't ask any of the questions that Richard had written down for Mr. Davis to ask all of the witnesses. So far, the trial wasn't looking to be in Richard's favor.

Mrs. Rollins was proving her case and winning by default with more help than usual from Richard's lawyer whether Mr. Davis knew it or not. Richard had felt like the jury was really beginning to believe that he was a guilty man. And Richard was really beginning to blame his lawyer, Mr. Davis.

Judge Burquette said to Mrs. Rollins, "Your witness, Mrs. Rollins."

Mrs. Rollins stood up and said, "Thank you, Your Honor." Mrs. Rollins began closing arguments with calling Richard's wife, Mrs. Kimberly Ginn, to the stand.

Kim walked past Richard from the first row. She came from behind the prosecutor's desk. Kim didn't even think about looking in Richard's direction. She was confidently, without a conscience walking past Richard, as if he actually did sexually assault her and as if he was getting everything that he deserved.

But really Kim justified her motivation for extorting her husband by wanting to clean him out for every dime that he had. And Kimberly Ginn wanted everything! Starting with the automechanic shop, the hot rods that Richard owned, the quarter-million-dollar-plus home that they owned together. Kim also wanted the spousal support, the child support, custody, and anything else that she could think of. She wanted it all!

Kim took the witness stand, raised her right hand while being sworn in. She wore no makeup, which was very unusual for her. She has always worn makeup since high school. But not today. And Kim also wore an innocent plain-looking and very conservative dress, which, Richard thought, was very unusual as well.

Richard said to himself, "Kim always wears provocative clothes that exposes her hips, butt, and her breast. But not today? That's definitely strange."

Kim wanted the jury to look at her like an innocent little schoolgirl so she could be believable as possible that her husband raped her when she takes the stand and testify about how she was raped by her husband.

Kimberly Ginn was playing her role good enough to win an Oscar for best actress award. Kim was focused on taking all of Richard's money that he had worked hard for. And Kim wasn't going to let anybody or anything get in her way!

Mrs. Rollins asked Kim a few questions just to paint a picture of her and Richard's marriage life to the jury. Then Mrs. Rollins proceeded with the questions that meant the most and would get her closer to a guilty conviction.

Mrs. Rollins was a few questions in before she asked Kim, "Mrs. Ginn, just prior to your husband, Richard Ginn, assaulting you and holding you captive inside of your own home, did you and your husband have a temporary separation and falling out?"

Mrs. Rollins didn't want to mention a falling out due to her husband cheating on her because then, the jury might believe that was Mrs. Ginn's motive for possibly lying about her husband raping her. A high-stakes risk that Mrs. Rollins wasn't willing to take. Mrs. Rollins felt as if she was making a strong-enough case thus far and thought against her better judgment not to mention the affair that Richard had outside of his marriage.

Kim answered, "Yes, we were separated and spent some time apart."

Mrs. Rollins asked, "And...was your husband, Mr. Ginn, still living in the home? And if so, were you and your husband still sexually intimate?"

Kim Ginn replied, "Yes, the defendant and I were still living together. But he slept in the basement. And he only came upstairs to eat, shower, and spend a little time with our daughter."

Kim paused and said with an attitude, "But we were NOT sexually intimate. Not even on the day that he RAPED ME!"

Kim looked at Richard and began crying while she gave her damaging testimony. She was putting on a show for the jury. Kim dug deep down inside and mustered up those fake tears.

Richard thought to himself as he watched his wife pouring out fake tears, *Please! You really need an acting Oscar for the show that you're putting on right now!*

Kim reached over and grabbed some Kleenex tissue that Judge Burquette was handing her to dry her tears. Then Kim finished answering the prosecution by saying, "I kept telling Richard stop! 'Please stop! Don't do this to me! Please!' I begged him, and I begged him. But he was too strong. He overpowered me. I looked into his eyes as he was pulling my hair. Something must have gotten into him because he seemed possessed!" Kim paused to sob and shed a few tears while sniffling.

Mrs. Rollins cut Kim off while she was crying uncontrollably during her testimony. Mrs. Rollins asked Kim, "And what else did the defendant do to you, Mrs. Ginn? Take as much time as you need to...I know it's painful."

Kim Ginn went on with her testimony, saying, "He tore my panties off! Just ripped them..." Kim sniffled and sobbed in between pauses. "Then he forced himself inside of me while I cried and begged him to stop..." Kim was crying and reaching for more tissue.

Chapter 13

Kim was smiling inside as she was giving her Oscar-winning testimony. She was peeking through her hands full of Kleenex, looking to see if the judge and the jury were believing the show that she was putting on. And Kim could easily see that the jury was definitely buying her sympathy role.

Two of the three juror ladies requested Kleenex to dry their tears from off of their face. And Richard couldn't do anything but shake his head in disbelief and look on. Kim really knew that the jury was sympathetic to her story of being raped.

Kim saw a male juror sniffling, as if he had been trying to hide his tears. And Kim saw another male juror with a fierce look of anger all in his face, trying to control it. And that same juror was staring at Richard as if he wanted to put his hands on Richard right then and there! But Judge Burquette was completely stone-faced, showing absolutely no emotions!

Mrs. Rollins saw the looks on everyone's faces and capitalized on the moment when she said, "That will be all for now, Your Honor. Thank you."

Richard looked over at Mr. Davis with a puzzled expression all over his face. Richard was thinking, *You just let my wife say all of that! Put on her little show with fake tears? And you didn't say anything!*

Mr. Davis could feel the heat of Richard angrily staring at him from out of the corners of Mr. Davis's eyes. Richard's stare was burning a hole into the side of the head of his lawyer, Mr. Davis's. Richard asked, "Why didn't you object to any of that garbage!"

Mr. Davis instantly snapped back at Richard with his response, "She was believable, Richard! DO NOT piss the judge off! Objecting to EVERYTHING! You'll be found guilty, sure as shit!"

Richard didn't want to get found guilty and sent to prison. So he bit his tongue. Richard remained calm and silent against his better judgment, taking his lawyer's advice and letting him do his job. Even though his strategy didn't make the slightest sense to Richard.

Judge Burquette said to Mr. Davis, "Your cross, Mr. Davis."

Mr. Davis stood up and asked Richard's wife a series of frivolous and insignificant questions. The questions didn't help or prove Richard's innocence at all. Richard felt as if he was sinking deeper into a hole, feeling more and more helpless with each question that his lawyer had asked.

The further that Richard's trial had went on, Mr. Davis was continuously ignoring Richard's request of asking the questions to his wife that he had stayed up writing all night, preparing the day before his trial. Mr. Davis kept ignoring Richard like his questions were insignificant, like he couldn't see or hear Richard's request.

But Richard's questions were actually better questions than the questions that his own lawyer were asking. Richard's questions could at least balance out this one-sided trial that Mrs. Rollins was easily proving Richard's guilt—guilt for a crime that he didn't commit.

After that quick series of frivolous questions that Mr. Davis had asked Kim, he asked his last question which was basically the very same and only question that Mr. Davis had asked every witness that had taken the stand.

Mr. Davis approached Kim on the witness stand. He stood there, quiet and motionless, stared at Kim for a moment as he dramatically sucked his teeth, like some other lawyers that Mr. Davis had seen on other court TV shows. Mr. Davis wanted to make it seem like he was a top-notch serious attorney that was on his job for his client.

But underneath all that, Mr. Davis knew wholeheartedly that he could actually care less about Richard or his trial fate. A lot of lawyers get their client's money and could still care less about their client's fate. It seems there is no integrity on either side of the law these days.

But the pause/stare acting dramatic show that Mr. Davis was putting on in front of Kim was just a move that he saw on TV last night and thought this was the perfect time to practice it and try it out.

Kim Ginn arrogantly stared back at Mr. Davis without blinking, batting an eyelid, or flinching a muscle. Kim was waiting on Mr. Davis to hit her with his best question that he had. And Kim was cocked and loaded, ready to fire back.

But to everybody in the courtroom's dismay and disappointment, Mr. Davis asked the same question that the jury had felt like they were sick of hearing the same nontactical and nonstrategic predictable questions. The jury was waiting on Mr. Davis to ask a different question, just to give Richard the benefit of the doubt. But Mr. Davis disappointed them all because he never did.

Mr. Davis asked Kim, "Mrs. Ginn, is it true that you are making all this up? Accusing your husband of raping you because you want his money! Don't you? Isn't his money your sole motivating factor for making this all up!"

Richard was angry. And it was very apparent all in his face. He was angry that his lawyer basically kept asking the same exact question all through the entire trial. Richard was far from being a lawyer, but he thought, *My questions had a much better chance than my dumbass lawyer's questions!*

Kim calmly, without any pressure whatsoever, answered Mr. Davis' weak question, saying, "Once again, sir, don't want Richard's money. And quite frankly, don't exactly *need* Richard's money." Kim emphasized the word *need* with stressed exaggeration.

Kim continued, "That's my husband, so doesn't that make it *our* money?" Kim again emphasized the word *our* with stressed exaggeration. She continued, "Mine and his? God knows that I loved my husband. That is until he felt like he had the right and the need to rape me! Just because I'm his wife? I told Richard NO! anything he does to me after that is rape! Bottom line!"

Kim was more convincing with each question. Richard thought, *My lawyer should not have asked that question!* The more that Richard thought about it, Kim was even beginning to make him believe. *Maybe I did rape my wife.* That's how convincing the show was that Kim Ginn had put on.

Mr. Davis said, "That will be it for now from Mrs. Ginn, Your Honor, thank you."

Judge Burquette asked Kim Ginn, "You can step down now, Mrs. Ginn. Thank you."

As Kim walked past Richard to walk back to her seat, she tried her best not to make direct eye contact with Richard. But Kim couldn't help but to quickly glance over at her husband, Richard, as she walked by.

Richard looked up at his wife, Kim, hurt by what she was doing to him. But Kim just rolled her eyes and continued walking past Richard, as if she was heartlessly trying to get Richard for every penny that he had till the money was all to herself. And she didn't have a care in the world of possibly sending Richard to prison.

That hurt Richard deeply. Because only those two knew the real truth—that he was innocent and didn't rape her at all. But Kim just kept walking past Richard. She sat down, crossed her legs, and looked straight ahead, emotionless. She was waiting for the trial to continue.

Kim was the only person who could free Richard from out of this tangled web of deceit. Richard glanced back at his wife once more. He was still trying to come to grips with his wife doing the unthinkable—treated him as if he was a total stranger, like they weren't ever married and didn't have a daughter together.

Judge Burquette looked at Mrs. Rollins and said, "Your closing arguments with your final witness, Mrs. Rollins."

Mrs. Rollins stood up and said to Judge Burquette, "Please, can I have just a second to bring the witness in, Your Honor? The witness is safely waiting in another secret room to protect the integrity of the trial, Your Honor, so that the witness would not be threatened or coerced."

Judge Burquette replied, "Make it quick, Mrs. Rollins! The court is waiting on you, Prosecutor…and we don't like to wait!"

Mrs. Rollins replied, "Yes, Your Honor. Sorry, I apologize, Your Honor. Thank you."

Richard instantly began looking puzzled. He was thinking, *Who is this secret witness?* Richard was trying to figure out who the surprise witness could be? And it had to be kept a secret? Richard thought that all the witnesses had been called to the stand and questioned.

Richard just kept staring toward the back of the courtroom, looking to see who would come walking through the big wooden double doors. Richard leaned over to Mr. Davis and whispered, "Who is this mysterious witness for them?"

Mr. Davis replied, "I don't know."

Then Richard asked Mr. Davis, "They didn't tell you before trial who this mysterious star witness is?"

Mr. Davis replied, "Yes, the prosecution did inform me. But I didn't feel it could hurt us. So I never thought twice about it, Richard."

Richard began to become angry and frustrated. And his whole demeanor quickly switched from calm to anger as Richard said to his lawyer, "You didn't think twice about it? What do you mean! This is my freedom and my life on the line! Not yours! I told you in the very beginning that if it's the money that you want, I will try my best to pay you! Just get me out of this! You said that you didn't want the money!"

Richard was growing more and more angry the more he talked to Mr. Davis in an aggressive whisper. And Judge Burquette couldn't help but notice the heated exchange of discussion between Richard and his lawyer, Mr. Davis. Judge Burquette asked, "Is everything all right between you and your client, Counsel?"

Mr. Davis replied, "Yes, Your Honor. Everything is fine. It's just a little misunderstanding. That's all, Your Honor."

But that's when Richard stood up and said, "No, YOUR HONOR! EVERYTHING ISN'T ALL RIGHT! My so-called legal advisor is waaaay too incompetent TO PROPERLY REPRESENT ME AND THE SERIOUS NATURE OF THIS TRIAL!"

Mr. Davis looked up at Richard, then dropped his head down, as if to say that Richard was making a fool out of the both of them and embarrassing the both of them as well. But Richard didn't care enough as he vented more, "Your Honor! I could have really done a better job of defending myself and proving my own innocence!"

But Judge Burquette responded, "I am going to have to ask you to take your seat, Mr. Ginn! Or you will force me to hold you in contempt of my courtroom for your disruptive outburst! That's why

Mr. Davis is a lawyer, Mr. Ginn! Because he KNOWS the law! If you would have been a lawyer, Mr. Ginn, then you would know the law. But since you aren't an attorney, allow your lawyer to do what he is trained to do, Mr. Ginn! Now you may be seated, Mr. Ginn...last request!"

Richard sat back down into his chair, then demanded that Mr. Davis check his papers for all of the witnesses against him. Richard was demanding to know who this mysterious secret witness is.

Mr. Davis frantically went through his rather large pile of papers that listed all of the potential witnesses for the prosecution. Mr. Davis was going through several papers before he realized that he had made a mess. Papers were scattered all over the defense table.

Richard was watching Mr. Davis, wanting an answer in between continued glances behind him over his shoulder to see who this mysterious witness would be walking through the doors. But before Mr. Davis could find the list of witnesses, the doors to the courtroom had opened.

Who came through the door escorted by two police officers? Richard would have never guessed. Richard's mouth dropped in total disbelief. He was speechless and stunned. Who Richard had seen walking past him to take the witness stand had paralyzed him! Richard's whole body was frozen numb from head to toe.

The prosecutor, Mrs. Rollins, said, "I'd like to call Jessica Ginn to the stand, Your Honor."

Richard thought, *My daughter! My baby girl!* just as Jessie walked past Richard, waving hi to her daddy with a big innocent sweet smile from ear to ear on her face.

Mr. Davis finally found the witness list of names. He said, "Oh, here it is! Testifying for the prosecution is...your daughter, Jessie."

Richard angrily looked over at Mr. Davis furiously, with his lips tight, speaking so the judge wouldn't notice his lips moving. He furiously said, "Oh! Now you tell me! My daughter! She is already sitting on the stand for Christ's sakes! You know what? You're a real piece of work! Yeah, you're a real piece of work!"

Richard and his lawyer, Mr. Davis, trying their best not to cause an obvious scene, bickered intensely back and forth. Richard watched his daughter, Jessie, walk past him as she took the witness stand.

Then Richard looked back at Kim, thinking, *That was the lowest and the dirtiest blow that you could have done. Put our daughter in the middle of this fake rape case. How could you allow our daughter to listen to all of these lies that you made up about her daddy?*

Richard went on thinking, *How could a mother even let her daughter be involved? And let our daughter listen to the prosecutor lie and paint her daddy as some sick and crazy psycho that raped her mother? What can you possibly have my daughter be a witness to? She didn't see anything. Me and you were in the bedroom with the door shut.*

Richard sat back and waited to hear what lie Kim had thought up for his daughter to say against him. Richard thought, *Yeah, she's playing dirty and hitting below the belt now.*

Richard's daughter, Jessie, sat down, taking the witness stand. She was looking cute and innocent, just as the day that she was born, and Richard held her in his arms.

Just as Jessie was sitting down in the witness stand, Mrs. Rollins stood up and said, "Your Honor, may I proceed?"

Judge Burquette replied, "Yes, you may, Mrs. Rollins."

Then Mrs. Rollins asked Jessie a couple of questions about how good of a mother is her mother? Mrs. Rollins was just warming up.

Mrs. Rollins was trying to get Jessie comfortable on the witness stand. It was quite a few people staring at Jessie. Mrs. Rollins was about three questions in with Jessica before she asked the killer question. And the answer that Richard's daughter, Jessica, gave would definitely have an great impact and influence, weighing in with the jury.

Mrs. Rollins asked, "Jessie, do you remember that day that your mother and your father got into a loud argument in their bedroom?"

Jessica answered yes, sounding like a sweet and innocent little girl, just like the way she looked. Mrs. Rollins continued with her questioning. She asked Jessica, "Were your parents pretty loud? What did you do when you heard the commotion?"

The jury was intensely focused, listening to little Jessie's every word so far with each answer she gave. But now the jury was listening to the words from her that would prove Richard's guilt or innocence. And Richard was intensely listening to Jessie's every word as well. He was still asking himself, *What can she possibly be a witness to? Yes, Kim and I were arguing... but arguing isn't rape!*

As Jessie was giving her account of what happened between her mother and father on the day in question, a blanket of complete silence was all through the courtroom as everyone was waiting on Jessie's answer of what she did when she heard the commotion. Even Judge Burquette was silent, waiting on Jessie's answer, while staring over the top of his eyeglasses at Richard's reactions to Jessie's answers.

Jessie answered, "When I heard how loud my mom and dad were arguing, it really made me scared. So I walked up to their bedroom door, turned their doorknob, and peeked in..."

Mrs. Rollins asked, "And when you peeked into your mom and dad's bedroom, what did you happen to see, Jessie?"

Jessica answered, "When I looked into their bedroom, I saw my dad sitting on top of my mom and holding her wrist down. While my mom was crying and yelling for my dad to get off of her."

The jury and the courtroom let out a loud sigh. "Oooooohhh!" Little Jessica's testimony was devastatingly damaging to Richard. Richard sat straight up in his chair, and his mouth dropped, crushed in total disbelief.

Richard thought, *Huh? shit! I forgot all about Jessie looking into our bedroom when we were fighting. And Kim and I telling her to get out.*

All Richard could say after hearing his daughter's testimony was "Dammit! I forgot all about Jessie looking in on us! Shit!"

Jessie wasn't lying, but what she had seen that day wasn't her dad raping her mother. When Jessie looked into the bedroom that day, she witnessed the end of what had actually just happened. Jessie saw her father holding her mother down but not to rape her, holding her mother down to stop her from hitting and swinging on him.

Mrs. Rollins said, "Thank you, Jessica. That's it, Your Honor." Mrs. Rollins had a small smirk of victory on her face that she was trying her best to hide as she was returning to her seat at the prosecutor's table. Mr. Davis quickly hopped up to his feet.

Mr. Davis had every intent on drilling Richard's daughter, little Jessie, but grilling her with basically the same questions that Richard, the judge, and the jury had heard all day.

As soon as Mr. Davis stood up, Richard quickly grabbed his arm, pulled him back down to his seat, and said in a furious whisper, "No! Not my daughter! We're not going to stoop to Kim's level and put my daughter through Kim's bullshit! She doesn't deserve to go through it!"

Mr. Davis looked at Richard and asked, "So what do you want, Richard? You don't want me to question your daughter?"

Richard answered, "No, I'll take my chances with the jury. I think you've done enough damage so far. My daughter is off limits!"

Mr. Davis stood up and said, "Your Honor, we do not wish to cross-examine the witness. Thank you."

Judge Burquette looked over at Jessica and said, "You are free to step down, young lady, thank you." Judge burquette was smiling and waving at Jessica as she stepped down and walked past her father, Richard, who purposely put his head down like he was reading a paper just so he wouldn't make eye contact with Jessie as she walked past.

But Richard couldn't help himself, he loved his daughter, Jessie, too much. Richard looked up at Jessie and said, "I love you, sweetie."

Richard wasn't mad at Jessie. He just couldn't believe that his wife, Kim, had coached their daughter into testifying about a rape trial that she was selfishly lying about. Jessie went and sat back down snugly next to her mother.

Judge Burquette gave the jury their instructions. Then he ordered them to deliberate on one count of sexual assault and one count of false imprisonment. The jury deliberated for two hours but still no verdict.

Time had elapsed to almost 5:00 p.m. Judge Burquette adjourned deliberations. And then he ordered the jury, the prosecution, and the defense to "Be present first thing tomorrow morning. Nine o'clock to resume jury deliberations."

Chapter 14

Court was back in session promptly at 9:00 a.m., just as Judge Burquette ordered. Time had elapsed to approximately 10:30 a.m., jury was still deliberating Richard's fate as he nervously awaited on pins and needles. He was worried what the jury's verdict would be. He patiently yet nervously sat down on the stairs from the courtroom in the café, drinking a latte and eating a Danish.

Richard was making a mental account of everything that had taken place and everything that was said during the days of his trial. Richard was playing everything back in his head and was making a mental tally. He was scoring a point for the prosecution versus the defense during all of the highlight moments of his trial.

As Richard was staring down at the paper that he had been writing his tally on, he occasionally glanced over at his lawyer, Mr. Davis, who seemed to be having a good time and enjoying himself without a single care in the world. Mr. Davis was sitting off at a good distance and conversing with a table full of his colleagues and drinking cappuccinos.

Richard thought to himself, *Yeah, I guess you wouldn't have a single care in the world. Because it isn't your life, your freedom, your future, or your family on the line for an absurd crime that you didn't commit and would never think of committing. Oh, and I almost forgot, you're not the one facing going to prison either. It's not you, so I guess you're not supposed to have a care in the world.*

Richard stared at all of the attorneys laughing it up and joking with all of their big expensive designer briefcases and European-cut and tailored suits on. Richard was beginning to feel like they were all laughing and talking about him as he sat, there burning with bitter fury and angered disgust. To Richard they all seemed to be looking at and laughing at him, even though he wasn't the topic of discussion.

Richard was stuck in the moment of overthinking, in mental chaotic oblivion.

They really weren't. That was just Richard's resentment toward all lawyers now. A resentment that was beginning to grow stronger and stronger. This whole experience traumatized and scorned Richard to a deep passion of hate and transformed his mind and spirit in a way that he never thought was possible. Richard's heart was becoming a stone-cold and empty place as he stared lost in thought, with each empty sip and slurping sound of his empty cup of latte.

Richard had a snarl on his face as he occasionally glanced up, looking at a table full of crooked lawyers, at least that's what Richard thought about them.

With a bitter look on his face, Richard said to himself, "They're all a bunch of fucking jokes! Disloyal backstabbers! No integrity. Took an oath to defend? That's all a bunch of bullshit! How can my lawyer laugh and joke at a time like this!"

All of the other attorney's sitting at the table with Richard's lawyer were all having their own separate trials as well. Richard was getting a close-up look at how all lawyers thought.

Richard even overheard occasional lawyer jokes. One lawyer asked another lawyer, "What did the lawyer say to his client just before he got forty years in prison?"

The other lawyer answered, "Uuuhhh…I don't know. What?"

The first lawyer replied, "Just before the judge gave the man forty years…his attorney told his client…Fuck you, pay me!" The table full of attorneys all burst out in hysterical and uncontrollable laughter.

Richard, as well as all the other lawyers' clients, were all currently in the middle of trial or awaiting verdicts. And they all were uncertain if they would be sent to prison. Richard felt like lawyers didn't take their jobs with the seriousness that he thought their clients' life and freedom demands. Laughing, joking, and occasional socializing with the enemy. The prosecutor?

Richard had finally finished writing down his tally. He wrote at the top of the ripped scrap paper "wins vs. losses." Richard estimated the prosecution to have two more tallies than the defense. Richard didn't even know how that was possible, to even be that close because his lawyer, Mr. Davis, barely said a word during the entire trial.

Mr. Davis ignored Richard's list of questions that he had written out the night before trial. Mr. Davis never asked, only to basically repeat the same predictable question that he had asked every witness the entire trial.

The only two questions that Richard thought could actually hurt him, maybe, was his wife lying and putting on that show with those fake tears. All of those scratches that Kim had put on his neck, chest, and arms while they were having sex. And probably the most damaging, his daughter, Jessica, testifying that she witnessed him holding her mother down while she cried and told Richard, "Get off of me!"

Richard had a gut feeling that it didn't look good for himself. Mr. Davis and all of the other lawyers all stood up and parted ways after they all exchanged handshakes, pats on the back, and smiles. Richard stared at the lawyers from afar with even more disdain than ever.

Mr. Davis walked toward Richard, who was still sitting down at the table, chewing on his straw that was still down inside his empty cup of latte. Mr. Davis was trying to see what Richard had been writing down onto the scrap paper. But since he couldn't see what it was, he just asked Richard, "What are you writing, Richard?"

Richard quickly balled the paper up, stood up, and answered, "Oh, nothing. Just some scrap paper."

Mr. Davis looked at his watch and said, "Well…it's time to head back up, Richard. Are you ready?"

Richard replied, "No. Not really. But I really don't have a choice in the matter, do I?"

Mr. Davis shrugged his shoulders, as if to say, *No…not really.*

Richard and Mr. Davis made their way back up to Judge Burquette's courtroom. Richard walked past a waste basket and threw the paper with the tally scores into the trash. They both stepped inside the courtroom and walked toward their defense table. While walking up the aisle, Richard walked past his daughter, Jessie, and his wife, Kim.

Kim stared down at the floor in hopes of not giving Richard eye contact. As bad as she wanted to justify her actions, Kim couldn't.

But Jessie, as she always was, was extremely excited about seeing her daddy. Jessie smiled, waved, and then ran to Richard's arms. Richard picked Jessie up as they stood in the middle of the aisle. Richard kissed her on her cheek and told her he loved her.

Richard couldn't be mad at Jessie for what she said on the witness stand because she didn't know what was going on that night he and Kim fought. Jessie only testified to what she saw take place inside of the bedroom between the two.

Richard felt like Jessie's testimony could actually be the very thing that possibly gets him sent to prison. He just wanted to keep Jessie protected as best as he could and not drag her through this as well.

Judge Burquette entered the courtroom and said, "We will now resume trial as scheduled." The bailiff approached Judge Burquette's bench and handed him a piece of paper.

Judge Burquette instantly sat upright, surprised. He put his glasses on, read the piece of paper, and then he told the bailiff, "Okay," as Judge Burquette was nodding his head. The jury entered the courtroom from out of one of the back rooms. Then they all took their seats inside the jury box. Judge Burquette asked, "Ladies and gentlemen of the jury, have you all reached a verdict?"

The jury foreman, who was a Caucasian woman who seemed to be in her early fifties in age, stood up and answered, "Yes, Your Honor, we have."

Judge Burquette replied, "Prosecutor and defense, would you please stand as the verdict is being read?" Hands interlaced in front of him, Richard confidently stood up, as if to say that his wife's evil intention of lies to hurt and destroy him would not prevail today.

Richard continued thinking that this is a just justice system. That should be strong enough to see the truth and strong enough to withstand the careless flaws of his inadequate and incompetent lawyer. I mean, the court system represents pride and quality of doing the right thing. Richard wholeheartedly believed in the justice system. And not guilty was the correct and only verdict for an innocent man.

Mr. Davis reluctantly stood up, ready and eager to move. He wasn't being paid, thinking, *I didn't get paid to stand up. He needs to be standing up, not me. That's on him.* But Mr. Davis stood up so Richard wouldn't think he was by himself.

Richard thought to himself, *Here we go. The moment we waited for. The moment that everyone had been waiting for. The moment of truth.* Richard was visibly nervous of the unexpected and the unknown. You could almost see his heart beating through his chest. His heart rate was racing just as fast as you could see him breathing.

Beads of sweat were beginning to form on Richard's forehead. Richard began thinking about this whole nightmare, from the very day that it all began up unto this very place where he is at today. He was playing it all out in his mind from the very day that he had made love to his wife, Kim.

Richard said to himself, "How could I have been so stupid to let her put all of those scratches on me! But I couldn't see that coming. Nobody could…Every now and then Kim gets in her overly aggressive sexual moods, highly aroused where the sex is so intense she scratches me. It feels amazing to her. That's not the first time she has done that."

Richard was thinking, *But she was setting me up right from the beginning! Damn! I should've seen that! She knew that the scratches would make her lies more believable! She set me up right from the beginning.*

Richard was also thinking about his lawyer, Mr. Davis, as the judge was preparing to read the verdict. Time felt like it was frozen still as Richard reflected. He thought about his lawyer and how it felt like Mr. Davis was working against him and not for him. Richard also thought about his wife and his daughter taking the stand to testify against him. And now, Richard was waiting on the verdict— guilty or not guilty.

Judge Burquette said, "Jury foreman, could you please read the verdict that you all have reached?" Richard was still standing up and watching his life flash before his very own eyes.

As the jury foreman began reading the verdict, her voice was sounding like a slow recording. In Richard's mind, her voice was dragging in slow motion. To Richard, everything was in slow motion. Even the courtroom seemed like it began spinning fast, round and round.

As Richard began to get dizzy and nauseous, he was feeling like his latte and his Danish that he eaten earlier during court recess was on the verge of coming up. And it was also a huge lump of nervousness in the middle of his throat. Richard couldn't swallow his saliva if he wanted to. The jury foreman began reading the verdict.

She held the large sheet of paper in her hand, reading it, "We, the jury, find the defendant, Richard Blake Ginn, guilty as charged on count one, false imprisonment. We, the jury, find the defendant, Richard Blake Ginn, guilty of sexual assault in the first degree."

Richard stood there, emotionlessly frozen. He couldn't believe what he had just heard the jury say. Richard's legs gave out from underneath him. And he fell back onto his seat. Richard leaned over forward with his face buried into the palms of his hands. He was silently whimpering at what his life would be now and only God knows for however many number of the next years for an innocent man.

Richard's lawyer, Mr. Davis, was gathering up all of his papers to put back into his briefcase. Richard dried his eyes, then confidently held his head up, ready to face his inevitable future.

Richard looked back to see the reaction on Kim's face after the verdict was read. But when Richard looked back, his wife and their daughter, Jessica's, seats were completely empty. And no sign of them anywhere inside of the courtroom until Richard looked back toward the back of the courtroom. And that's when he saw the both of them briskly exiting the courtroom. Kim just wanted to stay long enough to make sure she heard the right verdict. And once she heard *guilty*, it was confirmed. So she left.

Judge Burquette looked over at Richard and said, "Mr. Ginn, you have been found guilty on both counts as charged. Your bond is revoked, and you are remanded to the county jail until your sentencing which is scheduled for April 27, at 10:30 a.m."

Richard sat back in his chair, still trying to make sense of everything that had just taken place. He still couldn't believe that the jury found him guilty. Judge Burquette told his bailiff, "Take Mr. Ginn into custody."

The courtroom bailiff and a Minneapolis police officer walked over and ordered Richard, "Stand up for me, sir." They, with stern authority and firm grip, interlocked one arm around one of Richard's arms and the other put the handcuffs on Richard.

Richard could tell that his lawyer, Mr. Davis, felt guilty and nervous about Richard being found guilty, as they were sitting side by side because Mr. Davis was still nervously scrambling to gather up all of his paperwork to put into his briefcase. Papers were falling to the floor and being crumpled up as Mr. Davis collected them.

Judge Burquette's bailiff and the Minneapolis police officer began to walk Richard off to the back in handcuffs. But before Richard was escorted off, his lawyer, Mr. Davis, patted him on the back and said, "I'm certain that you'll get back on appeal. Good luck to you, Richy."

Mr. Davis told Richard what all court-appointed lawyers tell their clients when they get found guilty. They all say, "You'll get back on appeal."

See, Mr. Davis, like all court-appointed lawyers, don't really believe those words as the words roll off their tongues. Those same lawyers know that the chances of you getting back on appeal are highly unlikely. And on top of Mr. Davis lying to Richard, he called him Richy, as if they have been the closest of friends their entire lives.

But Richard didn't acknowledge anything that Mr. Davis had said to him. Richard just walked off, handcuffed, toward the back with the bailiff and the Minneapolis police officer following close behind.

Richard was the angriest that he has ever been his entire life. And he was disappointed, extremely disappointed in not only the guilty verdict but at his lawyer, Mr. Davis.

*****

Richard slept most of his days away in the county jail, awaiting sentencing. Richard's sentencing date had finally arrived. And he was present in the courtroom with his lawyer, Mr. Davis, at his side, which whom Richard hadn't heard from or seen since he was found guilty at trial where Mr. Davis had made a quick exit out of the courtroom, fearing that Richard might turn violent after his verdict reading.

Before Judge Burquette entered into the courtroom, and while everyone was preparing for Richard's sentencing, Mr. Davis whispered to Richard standing in a county jail one-piece jumpsuit. Mr. Davis whispered, "I misread the prosecutor's plea offer to you before your trial. I stumbled across the agreement last night. The prosecutor was offering you a ten-year maximum, Richy, not minimum. And I am man enough to apologize to you as a man. I accept the blame for that, Richy."

Richard just stared at Mr. Davis, thinking, *How many more mistakes will this idiot make before he mistakenly sends me to prison for thirty, forty years! And all his dumbass will be able to say is, "My mistake? My bad? I apologize—"*

Mr. Davis went on, saying, "But the good thing about finding out, Richy, is that I rescored your guidelines over to re-estimate a potential sentence for you. Since the plea wasn't ten years minimum, that made your score drop dramatically."

Richard looked over at Mr. Davis and anxiously asked, "So what did you come up with?"

Mr. Davis pulled out Richard's guidelines grid sheet and began showing Richard his scores and explaining.

Mr. Davis explained to Richard, "Since this is your first offense ever with the law, and you have been a model citizen—not even a traffic ticket—that helps you out, Richy."

Richard began to feel hopeful again. Richard was hoping that the judge would show him mercy and be lenient toward him. Mr. Davis continued, saying, "And by you owning your own successful hot rod business, being married…You have a lot in your favor here. You have a daughter and strong family support prior to this incident. That all helps you, Richard."

Richard sat straight up in his chair, feeling optimistic and like he was full of life again. Richard could barely control himself, full of excited energy. Richard was feeling like his wife, Kim, still didn't win because he escaped her plan of trying to get him out of the way by sending him to prison.

Richard thought, *Oh...I'm going home today with probation. Then I can fight to get my business, my daughter, then my life back,* still feeling hopeful that he and Kim could possibly work out their differences.

In Richard's mind, he forgave the mother of his child, his high school sweetheart. Richard invested his life and his soul into Kimberly Ginn. And Richard wasn't going to give up that easy. He was still madly in love.

Mr. Davis continued explaining to Richard as Judge Burquette entered into the courtroom. Judge Burquette took his chair, then said, "Today is the sentencing of Richard Blake Ginn."

Richard and Mr. Davis were still standing up when Mr. Davis spoke his last words to Richard. Mr. Davis whispered to Richard, "Just trust me, you have no worries, you're fine. I scored the judge to give you probation." Mr. Davis was confidently smiling at Richard as he winked one eye at him, as if to say congratulations. Mr. Davis was trying not to let the judge see him being rude. Richard heard Mr. Davis say, "Probation?"

Richard was smiling on the inside from ear to ear and saying to himself, "Probation?" Richard kept repeating it in his mind and imagining the judge saying that very word over and over in his head. All Richard could think about was wanting the sentencing to hurry up and be over with so he could leave out with probation, go home, and put his life back together.

Richard was thinking, *Even though I'm not guilty, I at least escaped prison with probation. Still not bad. I can kinda live with that. I guess.*

Judge Burquette went through all of the presentencing formalities and questions as Richard and his lawyer stood at the podium in front of Judge Burquette. Richard was keeping a calm demeanor while anxiously wanting to get it all over with. Richard was growing bored with all of the questions, questions that he had already previously answered with the presentence investigator while he was in the county awaiting sentencing.

Judge Burquette began his allocution, saying, "Mr. Ginn, I think that's a huge problem that most men seem to have in today's world. It's very strange to me."

Richard thought, *Uh-ohhh…this isn't sounding like it's going to turn out good already.*

Judge Burquette went on, saying, "Some men, particularly husbands, feel a sense of entitlement above their wives. Like their wives somehow instantly owes them whatever you demand. Instant gratification. Just because the man or the husband feels like he's the breadwinner or maybe the sole provider that…what the man says goes…"

Richard thought, *What is this damn man trying to say! What is he getting around to!*

Judge Burquette continued on, "Some men feel like their wives or their girlfriends are their property. And whatever the man says he wants done sexually, he wants it done now! Or they take it!" Judge Burquette was staring directly into Richard's eyes while listing his reasoning.

Judge Burquette went on, "And then you hear men say all of the time, 'How can I rape her? It's my girl! So her body is mine too!' Like that type of ignorance is an adequate defense."

Judge burquette went on, saying, "But I commend you, Mr. Ginn, for being a model citizen, a successful businessman, and a dominant pillar in the community. But it does not justify the action. It does not make it right…" Judge Burquette paused briefly before he continued, "Nor…does the accomplishments make you above the law, sir!"

Judge Burquette was speaking in an overly aggressive tone toward Richard, making sure that Richard understood his point of view. Judge Burquette was talking as if Richard was at his mercy.

Judge Burquette went on, saying, "The horrific crime of sexually violating your wife, that you have been found guilty of sir, is inexcusable…"

Richard was sitting there, fighting the urge to say something to Judge Burquette to defend himself. And words were forming on Richard's tongue, almost spilling out of his mouth, just when Mr. Davis nudged Richard with his elbow every time he thought Richard was foolishly about to blurt out a word to the judge. And it might have been a good thing that Mr. Davis prevented Richard from doing so.

Judge Burquette went on, saying, "Mr. Ginn, you have scarred your wife emotionally for possibly the rest of her life and your daughter for the rest of her life because she witnessed the assault against her mother, sir!"

Richard began to become noticeably angrier and angrier. He was holding his tongue, speechless, hoping that it would pay off in the end when the judge sentenced him to whatever term probation that he would do and put this nightmare behind him and just move on with his life.

Judge Burquette was talking to Richard as if he was some sick, twisted, and scary weirdo. But Richard tried his best not to make the situation worse. So he just allowed the judge to speak uninterrupted. And Mr. Davis kept nudging Richard, as if to say, *Remain silent and get out of here. Don't say anything. Let the judge vent, right or wrong.*

Judge Burquette continued, "Now what if your daughter thinks that she shouldn't tell men no because the men may sexually assault her also? And that's why, for the crime that you have been found guilty of—sexual assault and false imprisonment—I sentence you to..."

Richard's heart rate sped up extremely fast. Richard was hyperventilating and panicking in overdrive. Richard was bracing himself for what Judge Burquette was about to sentence him to, especially after that tongue-lashing. And the word *sentence* was a terrifying word that Richard was not accustomed to hearing nor ready to hear.

Judge Burquette's voice, to Richard, was sounding as if he was in a disoriented drunkenness. Like a record slowed down and dragging in a deep tone, almost like an satanic evil sound.

Judge Burquette's closing statements of sentencing Richard continued, "Mr. Ginn...I sentence you to a minimum term of five years, but no more than ten years. To be served in the Minnesota Department of Corrections. And I really do hope that you can change your way of thinking and live a healthy lifestyle upon your return back into society." Judge Burquette paused briefly to thumb through some papers.

Judge Burquette looked back up at Richard without batting an eye, saying, "I am recommending...mental health treatment as well to help you...hopefully. Good luck to you, sir. Court is now adjourned."

Chapter 15

Richard remained standing at the podium. He was emotionlessly stunned, still not believing what he had just heard. Richard had thought to himself, *How did a ten-year plea deal, then so-called phantom probation sentence, turn into a five-year prison sentence!* Richard was baffled.

Richard began to ask himself as he thought about Mr. Davis constantly telling him, the echo that was still ringing in Richard's ears, *I'm the lawyer...I'm the lawyer...I'm the lawyer...*clouding Richard's mind. Also the other words that still echoed of Mr. Davis, *This is my job! This is what I get paid to do! So just relax!*

All Richard kept hearing play over and over in his head were Mr. Davis's words of, *This is what I get paid to do...This is what I get paid to do...*A ringing echo in Richard's mind.

Richard stood up at the podium next to Mr. Davis, furiously steaming. And it probably was a good thing that the bailiff walked over and handcuffed Richard when he did. Because Richard was very seriously thinking about beating Mr. Davis unconsciously. Richard could picture himself choking Mr. Davis until he literally died from not being able to breathe.

It didn't make the situation any better when Mr. Davis, unaware, made the same exact comment that he made when Richard got found guilty. The comment which all lawyers say, but they don't even believe themselves, "Don't worry, you will get back on appeal." Richard just stood there, numb, while he kept hearing those words echo in his mind as well.

But as soon as Richard heard those same words for the second time throughout his trial, he lost it and snapped! Right then and there, in an instant, in the courtroom. It took six police officers to restrain Richard and carry him out in handcuffs.

Richard continued screaming while being carried out of the courtroom. "I'm innocent!! I didn't rape my wife! I'm innocent! I'm trying to tell you! You have to believe me! Please! Please! Don't do this to me! Nooooooo! This is bullshit!"

Richard was still tussling with the police officers. And the police officers were restraining Richard and trying to carry him out of the courtroom while Judge Burquette calmly looked on, emotionless.

*****

Richard was locked up in prison and now serving his five-year prison sentence. Richard was sitting and thinking, *I can't believe that I got sent to prison for raping my wife! I can't believe that Kim lied on me like that! I would have never believed that in a million years! That's a crime that I didn't do and would never do! I love Kim too much to ever think about doing something like that to her. Me? In prison?*

But to Kim, Richard sitting in prison for something that he didn't do was the furthest thing from her mind. Kim started court procedures to finalize taking complete control over any and all assets that Richard owned.

Kim wanted to take everything from Richard, and the sooner the better. She wanted everything that she and Richard had built together to be all hers and only hers. And she stood a good chance to own it all because her husband, Richard, was gone—gone—sitting in prison for rape.

Richard rarely came out of his prison cell. He had seen prison shows on television that painted the gruesome and violent life of behind prison walls. The prison shows that Richard had seen had depicted men wearing makeup and dressed up like women, engaging in homosexual activity. The show had prisoners on there that were victim of rapes and gang rapes. Stories of extortion, fights, stabbings, and even murders.

Prison was just a world of hopeless and violent convicts hunting for easy prey. And Richard was completely terrified every time he had to leave his cell, even to go eat chow, which he skipped occasional breakfast, lunch, and dinner meals. Stressing and looking thinner, Richard was terrified if another prisoner walked by his cell and looked at him.

Richard knew that prison life wasn't the life for him. And nothing in the world could have ever prepared him for it either. Richard thought to himself as he looked around at all the other prisoners feeling right at home, working out, lifting weights on the yard, playing poker, gambling, smoking marijuana, and drinking homemade alcohol with corrections officers. Richard saw some prisoners finally going home after twenty, thirty years. And Richard saw some prisoners come in just sentenced to twenty, thirty years.

Richard saw prisoners congregating with their chosen and racially divided group. After observing all of this chaotic activity, Richard thought, *I don't fit in here. And I know that I stand out from all the rest of the other prisoners,* because he didn't look like and he didn't talk street slang like almost all the other prisoners.

Richard felt as if he would be easy prey and targeted by the most hardened convicts with everything to gain and nothing to lose. Richard was surrounded by convicted felons that were sentenced to never going home again. This was their home. At least until they died.

Richard was sitting on his prison bunk, thinking, *If someone asked me what I am in for, I can't tell them that I'm in for rape. I know that for a fact from watching those prison shows. A guy with a rape case will get ate alive! Extorted and raped themselves! That's their way of letting a guy see what it feels like to be raped.*

Richard continued brainstorming for different lies to tell someone if they asked him what he was in for. He thought of a couple more lies.

But Richard thought that those lies weren't good enough or even believable. Richard excitedly thought, *That's it! I could tell them that I'm in for murder! I bet they won't attempt to test me then!*

Richard looked into his prison cell mirror, practicing different faces. Faces that prisoners will look at him and automatically assume that he was a cold-blooded killer. Then Richard thought, *Nah, that wouldn't work because I don't look like a killer.* Richard was still staring into the mirror on his cell wall above his toilet. He was intensely focused practicing eight different killer faces. But Richard could only muster up about two good seconds of angry killer-face energy before his face slowly returned to normal.

Then Richard thought, *Nah, I'll just say that I'm a rob-ber!* with anxious excitement. *I'm in for robbing a bank!* But then Richard thought, *Nah, that's not believable either*, sounding mentally exhausted and as if he had given up. Then Richard began practicing in his barely visible scratched and worn jail cell mirror, pretending as if he was telling someone his make-believe lie of his crime. But he couldn't complete the sentence without nervously stuttering. He couldn't even get it out to sound believable.

So Richard went with his gut feeling. And he finally came up with an idea. Richard thought, *I'll just say that I have a drug case. And that I got set up in a big drug sting. And I had ten thousand in drugs!* Richard was excited that he had finally discovered the lie that he was going with.

One day Richard was sitting at his desk in his prison cell, drawing cards for his daughter, as he had always done. And an inmate walked up to Richard's cell bars as he was pushing a dust mop through the catwalks. He asked Richard, "Hey, man, you new?"

Inside Richard was intimidated but quickly had thought that he needed to play the role and get into his prison character. Richard put on his tough prison demeanor so that the prisoner wouldn't think that Richard was soft or easy prey.

Richard made a serious angry face as if he hated the world! Then he slowly and dramatically looked up from the card that he was working on for his daughter. Richard asked, "Why! Who wants to know? You know me or something?"

Richard was feeling confident about how good he was playing this role that wasn't really him at all. But behind the angry face that Richard was making, he was terrified, hoping and praying that it was working because he really didn't want any confrontation at all.

The prisoner pushing the dust mop had an ear-to-ear smile on his face, as if he saw straight through Richard's phony act. The inmate chuckled delightfully and said to Richard, "It's all right. Just don't kill me, man…"

Richard replied, "My bad. I apologize, man. I'm just the new face on the block. And I don't know who to trust."

The prisoner replied, "Aww, man, you don't have to apologize. You're right to be cautious in a place like this here. We're surrounded by killers and weirdos 24-7, 365. But trust me, you don't have to worry about me…I'm just trying to get back home to my daughter. I know she misses her daddy!"

Richard was listening to the prisoner and casually agreeing with him as the prisoner went on, "I only got six months left, and I'm outta this hellhole. Thank God!" The prisoner made a peace sign with his fingers, then kissed them.

Richard slowly began to ease his guard down and opened up to the prisoner with the dust mop. Richard felt like he and his new friend had something in common—they both have daughters.

Richard, finally feeling comfortable with the prisoner just on the other side of his jail bars, finally answered the question that the prisoner had asked earlier in their introduction. Richard replied, "Yes, I'm new here. I just got here a couple of days ago."

But the prisoner with the dust mop already knew that Richard was the new face on the rock because that particular prisoner's institutional job is he helps with the intake of all new ride-in prisoners.

He gives them their blankets, sheets, clothes, kites, and their bedrolls. And the prisoner had been watching Richard from the very first time he had stepped off of the county jail bus. Richard didn't know it, but the prisoner thought that Richard was cute the first second he laid eyes on him getting off the bus.

Chapter 16

The prisoner paid extra special attention to Richard much more than all the other inmates that came in with Richard. Richard didn't remember him because it was so much commotion and chaos going on at that particular time. And he was still in a dazed shock of being sent to prison by his wife and for a crime that he didn't commit. But the prisoner remembered Richard. And quite well at that.

Richard's new friend, standing at his jail bars, was the same man that handed all of the men in intake towels to dry off with as he watched them go through the shower completely naked, back-to-back, sizing them up.

The prisoner, still standing at Richard's jail bars, said, "My name's Dan. But everybody around here calls me Baby Food. My mother gave me that name when I was just a li'l thing. Because I loved to eat that baby food that came in those li'l Gerber jars. I know you remember those! I even ate them as a teenager!" the man joked as he told Richard, and they both laughed about the memory of baby food together.

The prisoner still continued to gain Richard's trust as Richard lets his guard down more and more. The man asked Richard, "So whatcha in for, dude? When you getting outta here?"

Dan had a hidden motive. He wanted to befriend Richard and gain Richard's trust so that Richard could and would confide in him. Dan was hoping to turn Richard against all the other prisoners. And Dan was smiling and salivating inside because he could tell that his strategy of deception was effectively working. Dan could tell because Richard was more relaxed and wasn't as uptight as he was when Dan first walked up to his jail bars. Richard was opening up.

Richard answered Dan, saying, "Yeah, I got popped with some drugs. Knocked with some caine. I got five years. But my lawyer put an appeal in. I'm in the courts. So I should be getting out soon."

That's the same sad song that all the prisoners told each other on the yard all the time because they all actually thought and believed that they would get out on appeal. But rarely, if ever, after conviction does a prisoner get out of prison before his sentence is up. But it's very common that a prisoner stays much longer than his minimum sentence.

Some of the same prisoners spent ten years or better on the same yard repeating that same story—"I'm in the courts. I should be getting out on appeal soon"—with ten years in. But half of the prisoners aren't in the courts. And the other half don't have the kind of money that it requires to "get out soon."

Dan listened to Richard's story of a drug conviction. But he already knew the real truth about why Richard was serving time in prison. Rape! Because Dan had read Richard's prison file while Richard was coming through intake.

Dan wanted to get to know Richard and fast too because Richard was cute to him. Dan read Richard's file, and it read that Richard was in for the rape of his wife. And that instantly turned Dan on! That's just what Dan wanted to hear—that Richard was aggressively freaky! Dan was really loving his chances of being with Richard sexually.

Dan knew that Richard was lying about what he was in for. But Dan didn't mind one single bit. It turned Dan on and gave him chills, just thinking about Richard. So Dan just let Richard tell his lie as he pretended to be shocked by Richard's drug conviction story.

Dan replied, "Oh yeah? Drugs? Daaaaamn. What? You were like Noreaga? Gotti! On some big-time kingpin shit!" Richard and Dan chuckled together while Dan made fun of Richard while still trying to sound serious. The more Dan pretended to be impressed, the more animated Richard became.

Dan said, "Yeah, I'm on my way out off of an armed robbery. I robbed a McDonald's. And since the cashier only had fifty bucks, I robbed them at gunpoint for a cheeseburger and large fries." Richard was seriously listening to Dan's story until he said cheeseburger and large fries. Then they both laughed again.

But Dan was lying to Richard about what he was in for also and how much time he really was doing as well. Dan wasn't actually serving prison time for armed robbery. And he definitely wasn't on his way home anytime soon. Dan's crime had made every national news across the country, including *CNN*.

Dan, a.k.a Baby Food, was notoriously known around the country as the school ground serial rapist who abducted, raped, tortured, murdered, and cannibalized high school girls walking home from school. Or in the early wee hours of the morning while the girls stood at their bus stop, waiting on their school bus. That's really how Dan got his name—Baby Food—known throughout the entire prison system. Even the officers that work at the facility called Dan by his nickname, Baby Food.

Dan was sentenced to five consecutive life sentences in prison. But with Dan's smile and friendly approach, Richard never suspected or had a clue about Baby Food's crime. And Richard actually saw Dan's case on the news when it first broke. But Richard just couldn't place Dan's face to that crime.

In the back of Dan's mind, while he and Richard were conversing, he was smiling and thinking, *I'm getting him right where I want him.* Dan told Richard, "Yeah, man, you really have to be careful around here. Because these guys are thieves and homosexual predators. And I see it all the time. They will try to be your friend just to get you. But…that's what they do."

Really, Dan was describing himself to Richard—a thief and a homosexual predator, preying on the new inmates. The ones that look vulnerable and don't know anything about prison life or its traps. Dan knew what to look for in a new prisoner. And he could really spot those kind from far away.

Dan's plan was working; he was baiting Richard in, slowly but surely. Dan told Richard, "I gotta go right now before these flashlight pigs getta talkin' shit. But I'll swing back by and check on you a li'l later."

Richard was feeling like he had made a real genuine friend, was appreciative, telling Dan, "Okay, man, thanks for the advice. And nice to meet you again."

Dan smiled and said, "Ahh, man, no problem at all. That's what we do in here, look out for each other. Ya know?"

Helping Richard really wasn't a problem in Dan's eyes because Dan was putting in the work to hopefully be rewarded in the end. And getting Richard would be his reward.

As Dan walked away, Richard thought to himself, *Damn... it's actually some good genuine guys in here. Everyone in here isn't bad.* Richard sat back down at his desk and continued drawing the I-love-you-Jessie cards for his daughter.

But in the meantime, over the next six months, Richard and Baby Food had become extremely close and real good friends. Richard even saw his friend Baby Food get into a few altercations on the yard during recreation. But Richard pretended that he didn't see anything and hurriedly walked the other direction.

Richard was scared and didn't want any trouble from the big muscular dudes that worked out, lifting weights all day on the yard. The guys that Richard saw in the altercations with his friend Baby Food looked like some big muscle jerks out of those weight lifting magazines on steroids. Richard thought, *Those guys would rip my body in half with just their bare hands!* So Richard went the other way.

But every time Richard saw Baby Food later on that same day of every scuffle, Richard would ask, "What was all that about on the yard, Food?"

Baby Food would lie and fuel his deception of Richard. "Those clowns were talking about how they wanted you!"

Richard had a look of confusion all on his face. Richard asked, "Wanted me? Wanted me how?"

Baby Food replied, "You know how they want you. I mean what other way would another man want you? A man that's been locked up in prison for years without having sex with a woman!"

But really that was a premeditated act that Baby Food had constructed with those big muscle-bound workout jerks. Those were all

Baby Food's friends. And they all liked the same thing—men! Their crew took turns running schemes on new fresh meat.

Baby Food was really just testing Richard to see how he would respond to the idea of being with another man. So then he would at least know if he had a straight up chance with having sex with Richard.

But Richard adamantly replied to Baby Food, "Man, hell no! I don't have anything against people that do that, if that's their thing! But me, I don't get down like that! I'm married with a wife!"

Baby Food told Richard, "All right, Rich, damn, man, I get the point already. You act like I said that to you or something. I was just keeping them motherfuckers off your ass! You're my buddy, man."

Richard was listening to his friend Baby Food, the only real true friend that Richard felt he had. And he was beginning to feel bad for going off on Baby Food like that.

After feeling bad for snapping on his friend Baby Food, Richard said, "Nah, I know you don't roll like that either, Food. So I wasn't directing that toward you in any way. And thanks for keeping those perverts off my ass!" Richard shook Baby Food's hand and told him, "Thanks again, Food, for being a friend. You're right, I can't trust nobody! The only person I'm trusting is you."

Baby Food was nodding his head to Richard's every word, as if he was agreeing with him. And then they both went their separate ways.

Chapter 17

Days had passed, and Richard was doing what he had always done—worked on his I-love-you-Jessie cards. Richard sat the card on his desk and began preparing to take a shower and call it a night.

Baby Food walked past and saw Richard looking like he was preparing to take a shower. Baby Food was becoming stimulated, he had an instant erection. Baby Food couldn't control or restrain himself any longer. Baby Food quickly ran to his own cell.

Baby Food quickly grabbed his bath towel, soap dish, and his underwear so he could "coincidentally" bump into Richard in the shower. *At least that's what Richard was going to think*, thought Baby Food.

Baby Food watched Richard's every move, letting Richard go into the shower first. Baby Food was hoping to catch Richard just as he was getting undressed to see him naked. Then Baby Food followed, seconds behind Richard.

Baby Food stepped into the shower, and just as Richard was getting undressed, he looked up and saw his buddy Baby Food. It wasn't uncommon in prison to show up at the shower at the same exact time as other prisoners. Richard said, "Hey, what's up, Food? I'm surprised to see you this late."

Baby Food replied, "Yeah, normally I would be dead sleep by now. But they had me doing some extra cleaning tonight. But it's cool, I got paid a few extra dollars' overtime for it."

Baby Food and Richard stood up under two separate showerheads as they showered and conversed. Every time that Richard had closed his eyes so that the shampoo wouldn't go into them, Baby Food would stare at Richard naked and fantasized about him.

Until finally Baby Food couldn't take just staring at Richard's naked body and fantasizing any longer. Richard had closed his eyes one more time, rinsing the shampoo out of his hair, and Baby Food quickly rushed over toward Richard's direction. And before Richard's eyes could open, Baby Food was trying to grab Richard from behind. He was forcing his arm around Richard's neck into a headlock position. Baby Food had Richard into a submissive choke hold.

Baby was desperately trying to force Richard to submit. But Richard relentlessly struggled and fought his way out of Baby Food's choke hold. Richard was fighting back like his life depended on it. They were both covered in soap, slippery, wet, and scuffling.

Baby Food had finally gained an advantage as they both took a hard fall to the shower floor. Baby Food had ended up on the top of Richard's backside. He was straddling Richard's back. Baby Food used his body weight to pin Richard down. He had one hand to cover Richard's mouth from screams for help. And the other hand to forcefully hold Richard still as he forced his erected penis inside of Richard's buttocks.

Baby Food was raping Richard as Richard tried to scream from the excruciating pain of being torn.

Richard's screams for help went unheard as the screams were muffled out by Baby Food's tight grip over Richard's mouth. The whole time that Baby Food raped Richard, he was telling Richard, "Shut up…you know you like it. You know you like this. You led me on, Richy. So moan, scream louder."

Richard kept trying to fight back and struggle with Baby Food. But Richard's strength was no match for Baby Food who strong-armed men in prison for years.

Baby Food continued whispering in Richard's ear while he raped him, "You know this is what all rapists get in here, Richy…so don't feel bad, it happened to me too. You'll thank me later and say I was the best you ever had, Richy. Tell me harder, you freaky li'l rapist."

Finally Richard was so tired and exhausted that he gave up and just lay there, half-covered with soap bubbles until Baby Food finished, and it was over.

Baby Food got off the top of Richard and began drying off as Richard remained lying there on the shower floor. Then Baby Food said to Richard, "Really, it's nothing personal, Richy. It happened to me too. It happens to all of us with sex crimes and rapes here." Baby Food put his clothes on and then left the shower.

Chapter 18

Richard went back to his cell and angrily cried all night. All he could hear in his head was the voice that kept repeating itself. The voice that wouldn't stop that Richard heard was Baby Food's voice, saying, *This is what all rapists get here…This is what all rapists get…*Richard was beyond furious! And those very words had sparked something deep, dark, and severely eerily evil deep down inside of Richard.

This empty soul of cold bitterness feeling that Richard was now feeling, he didn't ever believe was possible to exist inside of him. Richard was furious because he wasn't a rapist and was in prison, being tortured for something that he didn't do.

All Richard could think about was his lawyer, Mr. Davis, and how many other lawyers out there that are just like him. If you don't have any money to pay them, they don't give a damn about you or your freedom!

Richard had now grown an uncontrollable bitter-fueled hatred to despise all lawyers. Richard was feeling as if Mr. Davis didn't fight to prove his innocence and how many other innocent men were sitting in prison with their lives, freedom, family snatched away for a crime that they didn't do, or may have done, but their attorney still didn't put forth the effort to have their client's best interest at hand, which was painfully obvious that Richard's lawyer, Mr. Davis didn't do his best at all to defend Richard.

Richard thought, *It's bigger than Baby Food. If I would have never got sent to prison, that shit that Baby Food done to me would have never happened. Because I would still be out there, free! I blame my dumbass attorney!*

Richard stayed up all night, tossing and turning, not being able to sleep, thinking of a way to get even with all lawyers that are like Mr. Davis.

Richard wanted to do something big, real big, that could and would catch each and every lawyer's attention. Richard wanted to shock the world and set the tone straight in his home state. The same state that robbed him of his freedom, future, and, last but not least, his manhood.

Richard wanted to make all lawyers across the country totally aware of the lives that lawyers have and still are throwing away—and throwing away without a conscience or a second thought about it. Richard was coming up with thought after thought to shake up and put fear in every lawyer across the world just to let the lawyers know that contrary to what they may believe, their jobs just aren't another day at the office. And that their jobs of being a lawyer has much more at stake than what they may think their jobs do.

Richard came up with a few ideas to get even with lawyers. But he thought, *Nah, not good enough to catch the whole country's attention.* Then Richard thought, *It is some good lawyers out there too that actually fight to defend their clients. Not all lawyers are pieces of shit.*

Richard didn't want the lawyers that didn't compromise their integrity for any amount of dollar to suffer for the selfishness of their colleagues.

Richard wanted all of the selfish, money-hungry, and greed-driven lawyers that threw away lives to pay the ultimately price directly. So they would see how it feels to be separated and ripped apart from their families.

Richard brainstormed on a few more ideas deep into the wee hours of the night. But all of the ideas that he kept coming up with, Richard thought, *Nah, still not good enough to wake up and shake up the judicial system of lawyers.* Richard thought to himself, *Nah, I have to get every lawyers attention so that they know and fully understand… this shit is for real life and death!*

Because of this one lawyer, Mr. Davis, making Richard's life a living hell for neglecting to defend him to the best of his ability, Richard finally came up with an idea! A fool-proof idea that would put every lawyer, judge, and police officer in the judicial system on severe pins and needles and on high alert all across the country. Richard thought, *There it is! I got it! I'll go on a killing spree! Yep! That's it!*

Richard made a fist pump animated move as if he punched the air. He continued saying it, as he envisioned it all playing out, "A killing spree…Killing crooked-ass lawyers! Yeah! A killing rampage at the courthouse. Just killing random lawyers as they crowded courtrooms and exited the court buildings."

Then Richard thought, No! *nope! I can't kill all lawyers…Some lawyers give their all to prove their client's innocence. Not all lawyers are selfish, greedy, or corrupt. But then again…I should shoot and kill them all. Just to make sure that my message is clear. And just to make sure I shoot and kill the right ones.*

But Richard wanted his shooting and killing spree on lawyers to be more personal. More of a justified vendetta against all of the guilty lawyers. Richard thought, *I want just the lawyers that are guilty of* not defending *their clients, I want them to pay! And to be made examples out of! So all of their families, friends, and new lawyers coming behind them can be a witness of what can easily happen to them as well.*

Richard quickly sat up in his bunk. He was looking as if a little light had just popped on inside of his head. Richard had a bright look on his face that said he was onto something. Something special. Richard had a sinister look of a new discovery. A justified revenge killing spree. A personal vendetta against the guilty lawyers directly and indirectly involved.

It was easy to see, the instant look of gratification as excitement set in all over Richard's face. Richard couldn't stop smiling. He was possessed with death-gripping revenge as he sat on his bunk in the wee hours of the morning, picturing himself on his shooting and killing rampage, terrorizing lawyers in Minnesota and throughout the rest of the country.

Richard was overly excited about his new plan. And he thought, *It's very possible to carry out and get even with those bastards before they even realize who, what, or why the judicial system was brought to its knees.*

But Richard was thinking hard, trying to answer the one question that he had. Richard asked himself, *How can I separate the guilty lawyers from the innocent lawyers? How?* Richard was stumped as he sat on his bunk, one leg anxiously bouncing rapidly up and down as he rubbed his chin in deep thought.

Richard kept looking around his cell from wall to wall, from the ceiling to the floor, and then back around again. He was pausing for a second at each stop and thinking, thinking, thinking.

Richard was becoming frustrated, asking himself that same question that he struggled to find an answer for. He thought, *How can I separate the two?* Richard fell asleep asking himself that question that he just couldn't answer.

Morning had arrived by now as Richard opened his eyes, stretched, and slowly sat up in his bunk. His buttocks was still sore from Baby Food raping him in the shower. Richard finally sat up, and that's when he said, "I got it! I got it! Yeah, now I can get even and have every lawyer across the country at my mercy. And force them to pay attention!"

Richard was smiling to himself as he thought about his fool-proof plan that he was beyond anxious to put into action. Richard thought, *I'll go on a killing spree of lawyers. And how I'll know the guilty of not doing their jobs, from the innocent? The innocent that work hard for their clients' defense, day in and day out? The perfect idea—I'll separate the lawyers by their wins versus their losses! Yep… Wins vs. losses!*

Richard continued thinking to himself, *Yeah, by their cases won and their cases lost. If the lawyers have more losses than wins, then that means that they don't give a damn about their clients. And they don't take being a lawyer as seriously as they should. They don't give a shit if their client is sent to prison or not. And it's obvious by their losses.*

Richard went on, saying, "Their wins versus their losses will determine if that lawyer lives or if that lawyer dies! I'll separate them from their families the same way that I and like so many other people were separated from our families."

Richard was now on his journey to go do the research to find all of the lawyers in the Minnesota area that had more courtroom losses than wins. They would be the first to make Richard's list of the lawyers killings spree that he planned to carry out.

Richard went to the prison law library and asked the librarian for the lawyers' bar journal and all of the other necessary information that he needed to carry out his task. Richard wanted a list of all the lawyers' names to take a good look at their performance inside of the courtroom.

*****

Richard continued to dig a little deeper and dig a little further. He was digging for more intense research. He was totally preoccupied over the next two to three years. He was trying to get all of the lawyers' records of wins and losses and the lawyers addresses from off of different Internet sites with assistance from his buddy John.

Richard called his best friend, John. He told John that he needed a list of lawyers and their wins *vs.* losses. Richard's reason to John was so that he could get a good attorney for his appeal. Richard's buddy John was sending Richard a new list of lawyers and their wins *vs.* losses every week consistently.

The corrections officers would pass Richard's cell daily at the same time every week as Richard laid back on his bunk, reading and waiting for the mail to hit the floor in front of his prison bars.

John was trying to help his buddy Richard get out of prison. He told Richard when he bonded him out of jail that if he ever needed anything, to not hesitate to call him. So Richard was taking his buddy John up on his offer. But Richard wanted to keep his request simple because he didn't want to be a hindrance either.

Richard told John that was his reason for needing the lawyers' names and their wins *vs.* losses. But Richard had something totally different planned for the list of lawyers that his buddy John had sent him.

Richard sat at his prison cell desk many nights, using the perimeter lights atop of the prison gates, shining through the bars on his outside window from the yard. He was doing his research, going through a large stack of papers. Going through lawyers' names, weeding out, and writing down the lawyers that stood out to him the most.

The list of lawyers' names consisted of male lawyers and female lawyers. Richard didn't discriminate. Any and everybody had to get it! Richard thought, *Shit, they didn't waste their time discriminating me and sent me to this piece of shit dump...So why should I?*

Richard had the long list of lawyers' names that he was narrowing down. He had the list spread out and lain all over his prison desk. The papers were lying all over and covering up the cards that he continued to draw during the day for his daughter, Jessie. Two to three years later, still no answer back from his daughter.

Richard had only one year left before he was scheduled to see the parole board and possibly be back out, free again.

Richard was getting asked what he was in for and how much time he was doing by prisoners for most of his four years so far. But in prison, that's just basic conversation when a prisoner introduces himself. And Richard always told everyone the same lie.

Richard had told the same lie so often that even he was beginning to believe his own lie—that he was a big-time drug dealer that got caught with $10,000 worth of drugs. But the last time that Richard was asked what he was in for, he told the same lie again to the man sitting at the table with him during dinner in the mess hall.

Richard told the man what he was in for. But the man looked confused and replied, "See, I knew these dumbass idiots be lying! They don't have shit else better to do but gossip and twist shit up!" The man seemed frustrated and upset about the prison politics.

The man went on, "That's the very reason why these dudes be getting the business! Stabbed up, stomped, and killed. Sent home to their mama in a pine box! You know?"

Richard was in total and complete shock, still holding his spoon in front of his mouth, frozen. Richard was stunned and didn't know what to think as he stared at the angry man, trying to figure out what exactly the man was talking about and what had the man so pissed off.

The angry man was so pissed that he couldn't even finish the rest of his food. The angry man just furiously stared down at his tray of hamburger with one bite mark in it that he didn't even get a chance to completely bite after hearing Richard tell him what he was in for.

Richard asked, "Why? What they say?" Richard was looking confused himself.

The man answered, "It was a rumor going around here that you raped your wife!"

Richard replied, "Raped my wife? How does a man rape his wife! Nah...not me. They got me confused with someone else. It's drugs, baby. I push heavy drugs. I get money. Real money."

The man's eyes lit up wide open as Richard told him how he was locked up for getting heavy money. The man was actually thinking that he was eating at the table with a heavyweight drug dealer. Richard really sounded believable to the man. The man was all in. The man was happy and relieved that Richard wasn't in for rape.

The man was smiling while Richard was telling him his drug story. But when Richard finished, the man's face instantly returned back to a look of fury and anger that people would go around spreading lies and rumors on a good man. The man just got up from the table, dumped the rest of his uneaten food into the trash can, and walked away without saying a word.

Richard shrugged his shoulders, looking confused as he watched the man walk away, and thought, *Wowwwww, okay, that was weird.*

Richard was beginning to grow leery if rumors of his real crime was beginning to go around the compound. Richard had gotten a little worried because he knew prison wasn't too kind or easy on prisoners with rape cases.

If it was true that rumors of his case was going around, Richard knew that he would be a target until the day that he would leave prison. If anybody were to find out that he wasn't in for drugs but locked up for raping his wife, even though he was innocent. But who would believe that? In prison, everybody with a rape case is innocent and didn't do it if you ask them.

Richard thought, *My crime has to be going around. It has to! And that would explain why somebody keeps breaking into my cell when I'm gone for the day. And that's probably why my TV, music player, shoes, and all of my other shit kept getting stolen. And I know them punk ass police officers let them into my cell because that was the only way to gain entrance. The police had to let them in.*

Richard put two and two together and realized that the police had to know about his crime too because the police were even against him and harassing him now. It made Richard mad because he was going through all of that torture as an innocent man.

Richard thought, *I'm sitting in prison being raped and harassed for a crime that I didn't do. But I bet you, I would not even be in prison, and never would have seen prison, if my lawyer had fought to prove my innocence!*

The police were looking for any reason to take Richard to solitary confinement just to punish him for his crime of being a sick rapist.

The police officers went out of their way from the time they punched the clock to harass Richard. And they told their coworkers so they too would harass Richard. All of the officers hated child molesters and rapists because most of the officers had daughters or nieces themselves.

From the very moment that Richard had opened his eyes until he fell asleep, even during his sleep, until he woke up the next morning, for years, the police officers went out of their way to make Richard's time in prison hell inside of hell on earth! One officer even told Richard, "I'm going to retire making your life as shitty as possible. Enjoy your stay. Ha ha ha ha."

And that's exactly what it was for Richard—*hell inside of hell on earth!* Most of Richard's day was saturated with consumption of thoughts of a horrific justified vendetta. Revenge to get even against all of those lawyers that he had been writing down.

Richard stared at the names on his long list of lawyers that was growing more and more as each day came and went. Richard had a system that he did. He would write a lawyer's name down, and then see how it looked fitting in with the rest of the lawyers' names that had more losses than wins.

Richard would stare at the names, smiling and thinking, *Yeah, it's coming, baby…It's coming along perfectly.* Richard was becoming more and more satisfied the bigger the list grew.

Richard could barely sleep at night, thinking about finally having a chance to put the names of lawyers into motion. Richard thought, *I can just see it now, the whole United States shitting in their pants. And the president putting the entire country on high alert. Yeah…*

He has to do it. Or I'll just keep killing lawyers and more lawyers until he does. That's just more lawyers with bullet holes in their heads.

Richard was smiling from ear to ear with an evil sinister smirk, picturing himself on his mission of appointed vengeance. As corrections officers continued to harass Richard, he did his best to bite his tongue, restrain himself, and not say anything back. Richard was patiently waiting on his turn to get even. He endured it all just to get back out and fufill his mission.

Richard thought, *And the sooner the better.* As an officer hollered from the officer's podium on the lower gallery, "Lights out, ladies!" Richard, with a look of exhaustion and anger written all over his face, reached up, turned his prison cell light out, lay down on his prison bunk, and threw his blanket over his head.

Chapter 19

Richard was closing out his last and final year of his five-year prison sentence. Judge Burquette recommended mental health rehabilitation classes to help Richard try to understand why he felt the need to rape his wife and to further help contain those sexual urges instead of acting on them.

Richard's name had just made it to the top of the mental health waiting list. And he had just recently begun those classes. Richard was attending three-hour sessions, three times per week, in a twelve-month program.

Richard was very upset and frustrated that he had to attend those classes and also upset that he was surrounded by, as he called them, sick and perverted freaks! Richard thought, *I'm nothing like those sickos! I don't think nothing like the rest of that class thinks!*

Richard was an innocent man attending sexual assault prevention classes. And because he was an innocent man, he felt no need to participate in the mandatory mental health sessions. Richard was uncomfortable being in the presence of those types of individuals. But Richard knew that he had to participate in group activities in order to get his parole and to get out of prison. Time was quickly approaching for Richard to go up for parole review in front of a three-member board.

Richard successfully completed the sexual offender program. Although he hated every second of the day of the class with a passion. Richard had approximately six months left before he was scheduled to see the parole board.

And now most of Richard's days consisted of completing his kill list of lawyers. Lawyers that had more losses than wins rounded out Richard's murder list. Richard worked on his list most of the night into the early morning. And he was still using the light from the prison yard, shining through the bars over his window.

Richard was trying his best to narrow his lawyer kill list down to ten names. But it was a challenge as Richard thought, *It's hard picking him over her. Or him over him. Or her over him. Really...All of them need a bullet right between their eyes.* Richard had a hard time choosing the names that stood out the most to him.

Richard had a lot of crumpled and balled up papers with law-yers' names scattered all around his prison cell. The papers were on Richard's bunk, desk, and floor and next to his waste basket. Some lawyers' names were shuffled around, and some were scratched out. And some were even replaced with better names that Richard thought were much more deserving of being killed. Richard replaced those lawyers' names at the last second.

Richard was smiling as he sat there and stared at his perfectly pieced together masterpiece. Richard was very satisfied with the shape that his list was taking, especially the more he refined and cri-tiqued it.

Richard's last six months continued to quickly fly by. Each day was moving rapidly. Richard didn't know why. And he didn't care why either. He just hoped his days kept flying past on his way out the door to go home.

The day that he had been anticipating had finally arrived. Richard, full of anxiety, saw the parole board. And he liked his chances because he had completed his five-year-minimum sentence, and he stayed out of trouble, which could have prevented him from going home at his earliest time possible.

Richard went in front of the parole board, but he refused to admit guilt for the crime, and he had also stood adamantly firm on not accepting responsibility for his actions of the crime.

The parole board sent their decision through the mail to Richard. The officer stopped by Richard's cell, as he did every day with mail. Richard had been on pins and needles, waiting to hear back from the parole board.

The officer dropped Richard's mail onto the floor and kicked it under Richard's cell bars. The officer didn't want to touch Richard's hand because he didn't want his hand anywhere near a rapist's hand.

Richard opened up the parole board letter, and it was a unanimous decision to give Richard a twelve-month continuance. Richard was extremely disappointed, frustrated, and visibly angry. Richard thought, *A twelve-month continuance! What? I didn't do that bullshit to my wife! And these bastards want to keep me in here in prison longer! I don't get it! What more could they possibly want from me!*

Richard continued reading the letter from the parole board, trying to figure out why they had given him a twelve-month continuance. Richard read a little more until he came across their reasoning of why they done what they did to him.

The reason read, typed at the bottom of the decision said:

> Prisoner Ginn 249793 does not seem to be remorseful, doesn't accept responsibility for his actions. And it is of our opinion that he still has a very high probability to repeat offense. It is also of our opinion that Mr. Ginn is not rehabilitated at this time. Mr. Ginn is an immediate threat to society.

Richard stood at his bars, reading the white sheet of paper that had big bold print at the top of the page that read *Parole Board Disposition.*

Richard was steaming furious! He just stood there at his bars, thinking, *Hell no! I'm not admitting to that! No way! It's not going to happen! We can do this for the next fifty years. I don't give a shit! I didn't do it! Those assholes want me to admit to some shit that I didn't do! I'm innocent, and that's not an option!*

Richard went on to read the last paragraph at the bottom of the page. It read, "The parole board recommends continuing of sexual assault mental health treatment. Twelve months' treatment."

Richard angrily crumpled the paper up and said, "I recommend you stupid motherfuckers to a lifetime of kissing my ass! Now get some mental health treatment for that!" And he flushed the letter down the prison cell toilet. *Whoosh!*

Richard stood over his sink looking into the mirror. He was hearing that voice again, saying, *This is what happens to all rapists*, echoing in his brain.

Instantly Richard was furious all over again, thinking about his old lawyer, Mr. Davis. Richard reached over and picked up his long kill list of lawyers that he had beautifully written out and strategically critiqued and swore to separate the lawyers from their families, the same exact way that they separated him from his.

*****

Richard painfully completed another year of sexual classes. Three hours per day, three sessions per week, for another twelve months. An extra year that he was held up past his first out date to go home.

Richard thought, *Now I gave them an extra year. I should have been out a long time ago. Now they can't deny me!* But the psychiatrist told Richard, "The board sent me a notice stating that they refuse to see you this time. And they unanimously recommend a twelve-month continuance to ensure that the public is safe with you out in society."

Richard was now into his second twelve-month continuance, which had him now two years past the time that he should have been out free in society. Richard was now doing seven years on a five-year sentence which should have originally been probation if his lawyer would not have dropped the ball. And all for a crime that he didn't commit.

Richard couldn't control himself anymore after falsely being accused of a crime that he didn't do, could have gotten probation, but instead sent to prison, raped, stolen from, ridiculed, and insulted. And on top of that, being two years past his earliest release date. Richard now had a total of seven years in prison.

Richard thought about everything that he had been through over the last seven years. And he just exploded! He just lost it in an instant! He snapped! The officers ran into Richard's cell, fifteen-man army with shields and protective helmets on. They were trying to restrain Richard while roughing him up in the process as he fought back the best that he could.

Richard had just completed his sexual assault mental health sessions for the second time, and that's when the psychiatrist told Richard the parole board's latest decision.

Richard tried to withhold his emotions while the psych was talking as long as he could. But Richard couldn't take it any longer. His mind was already fragile and his spirit broken beyond repair. He was a lifeless shell of himself. Psychosis and hallucination were beginning to invade his mental space.

Richard lost it! He spent thirty days in segregation for threatening behavior of a prison psychiatrist.

While Richard was in segregation, during his thirty-day stay, this time the psychiatrist recommended another twelve months of mental health classes. But only this time, the recommendation was for anger management, conflict resolution, and impulse control.

Mental health programming stemming from the way Richard lashed out in a violent, aggressive, and intimidating manner. The psychiatrist's evaluation stated, "Prisoner Ginn 249793 is still in denial about his crime."

Richard had to do an additional year, for a total of three extra years past the five years that the judge had sentenced him to.

Richard was on his seventh year for a crime that he didn't commit on top of the five years that the judge originally sentenced him to. And now another extra year recommended by the psychiatrist. For his diagnosed anger, impulse control, and conflict resolution problem, Richard was now eight years in on his five-year sentence.

But to Richard, it all was just more fuel added to his fire. His fire of revenge against his lawyer, Mr. Davis, and all other lawyers like Mr. Davis. Richard was thinking, *That's all right. Those extra years just gave me more time to make sure my killing spree on them motherfuckers is fool-proof. Air tight.*

Richard continued, *Just more time for me to critique my action plan of murder. Appointed vengeance.* Richard was smiling and nodding his head in certainty. He was picturing himself shooting lawyers and taking them out. One by one.

Chapter 20

After being sent to three different mental health classes, with a total of three extra years past his five-year-minimum outdate, Richard knew exactly what it took to achieve his goal. First freedom, and then his mission of appointed vengeance against all the lawyers topped out his kill list.

Richard thought, *I know what it takes now. I'm just as smart as you guys. Yeah. I'm going to beat you at your own game and tell you what you want to hear. Oh... You want me to say I raped my wife? Okay, sure why not? Of course I raped my wife. And I am sorry, so sorry. Please accept my apology, sir, ma'am. I promise I won't do it again. Those sexual assault classes really turned my life around. And I strongly recommend that people take them.*

Richard was acting out everything that the parole board wanted to hear him say. Richard was talking to himself, as if he were talking to them.

Richard told himself that he would agree with everything that the parole board and the psychiatrist was saying. Even though they were painting him as some sick rapist. And this time, Richard played that remorseful role to win an Oscar nomination. He was tremendously remorseful of the rape of his wife that he didn't commit.

And Richard wasn't surprised in the least way that this time it worked. But an extra three years later on top of the five that Judge Burquette had sentenced him to. Richard was now a free man after serving a total of eight years for a heinous crime that he didn't even commit. But he had to bite the bullet and save face just to be a free man once again.

Richard missed eight long years of his daughter, Jessie's, birthday. Jessie was now eighteen years old, now a young lady. Richard was still extremely bitter about being accused of rape. Still just as angry today as he was then when his lawyer, Mr. Davis, didn't put forth any effort to prove Richard's innocence.

Richard was furious that he was sentenced to five years in prison after his lawyer, Mr. Davis, told him that he would get probation. Richard had a laundry list of reasons why he was furiously pissed. And that was just the tip of the iceberg.

Richard was angry and bitter about being raped in prison and having his manhood violated by the only man that he trusted to be his friend. Richard was furious that he not only had to take sexual assault classes for a rape that he didn't do but take the sexual assault classes twice because the parole board said, "Prisoner Ginn is not remorseful and does not accept responsibility for his actions."

Richard grew angrier and angrier the more he thought about all that he had endured. And he didn't know how in the hell he made it through it all. But then again, Richard knew how and why he made it through. Just to make it out of prison and fulfill his mission of a vengeance lawyer-killing spree. And that's the only reason he remained strong enough to make it through.

But going through all of what Richard just went through had only made Richard into something evil and cold that he thought he could never become. He was desensitized, detached, now a cold and distant man of no compassion, sympathy, remorse, or heart. He was now an empty shell of a man with total disregard for human life.

Spending his last eight years, twenty-four hours a day among some of the state of Minnesota's most cold-blooded, hardcore, convicted felons that had nothing to lose because they all had absolutely nothing to live for. And that environment shaped Richard's mind.

His years were spent with serial rapists, murderers, thieves, robbers. You name it. They're all at one place, at one time, planning, plotting, and scheming every second of the day. It all had shaped Richard's way of thinking. Richard didn't leave prison as the same man that went in.

The prison environment and experience had taken its toll and turned Richard into a hardened hardcore prisoner himself. Richard was a completely different person from the Richard before prison life.

All that pain and betrayal had turned Richard into—into a monster with murderous intentions of revenge saturating every inch of fabric in his mind. Richard was now out of prison as a free man. And all he had to his name was his car, his 2005 black Impala SS.

Richard thought, *Good thing I paid that car off in my name. Or Kim would have tried to take that from me too. I mean…She took everything else from me.*

Because now eight years later, Kim owned everything. She took everything that Richard had worked hard for. It was now hers.

Richard's buddy John picked Richard up from the bus station where the prison transportation had dropped Richard off at. It had been eight long years since John had last seen his buddy Richard. John was happy to see Richard and happy to see Richard was okay. Richard and John took a second to hug each other. Richard was excited to see his friend John as well. The last time that Richard had heard from John, he was sending Richard another list of lawyers to help with Richard's appeal. That was just a few months ago.

As John hugged Richard, he instantly noticed that his best friend, Richard, didn't look the same. It was a dramatic change. Richard tried his best to hide it. But by John being Richard's close friend, he knew just from Richard's body language.

Richard tried his best to hide his bitterness. But prison life for the last eight years had gotten the best of him. But John didn't say anything or mention it to Richard.

John just asked what he had always asked Richard, "How are you doing? Richy, are you okay? Do you need anything?" John was staring at Richard after he backed up from hugging him.

Richard answered, "No, no, no. I'm fine, John, really. I just need to get to my car." All Richard had on him was what he left prison with, that piece of paper with the ten lawyers' names on it that he planned a murderous revenge against to shake up the country and get the full attention of each and every lawyer out there.

John told Richard, "Just be careful. That's all I care about." John pulled up to Richard's car. Richard's car was kept in John's garage with a tarp covering it while Richard was away in prison. And Richard's car was still looking brand-new when Richard removed the tarp.

Richard was smiling while thinking about all of the old memories of his car and his family before he was sent to prison. It was painful for Richard, but he was proud of how far he had come today—finally out of prison.

John was tightly holding out a fifty-dollar bill for Richard while Richard held onto the other end of it. John looked Richard into his eyes without blinking and repeated himself once more, "Just be safe! You hear me, Richy?"

Richard was tightly grasping onto the other end of the fifty-dollar bill. Richard was looking his buddy John directly back into his eyes, answering, "I will, John. Don't worry. I will."

Richard got into his Impala SS, backed out of his buddy John's garage, and drove off down the street as fast as he could. John could tell that Richard was in a hurry to make it somewhere.

Richard was in search of a place to sleep and also to get something to eat for the night, with plans of reporting to his parole officer and finding a job first thing in the morning.

Before Richard was released from prison, he was told that he had twenty-four hours to report to his parole officer, or a warrant will be issued for absconding. And he would immediately be sent back to prison for parole violation. And Richard had no plans of going back to that life of hell ever again.

Richard drove off down the street, thinking, *Before I go back to that shit, they're gonna have to kill me! That's the only way I'm going back!* Richard promised himself that he would never go back to prison. And he meant that.

Richard was headed to the homeless shelter, hoping that they had some available room before it got too late, and they turned him away. Richard was going to hopefully get himself a good night of rest after being in prison for all of those years. He was mentally and physically exhausted.

Richard was headed to the homeless shelter in downtown Minneapolis. Richard knew that he would have to park his car a couple of blocks down the street because he figured the chances of them letting him stay there were slim to none if they saw him getting out of a newer Impala SS but was claiming to be homeless.

Richard parked his car a few blocks down and around the corner from the homeless shelter where he had intended on sleeping for the night.

That particular homeless shelter was the skid row community of Minneapolis, where all of the outcast from society lived among each other in this part of town. This well-known crime infested area of the city was full of homeless people that had just recently lost their good jobs due to the pandemic and was now homeless.

Richard was going back to a place where it was all heroin and crack addicts, robberies, assaults, and occasional murders. Low level street corner drug dealers peddled their drugs out of their closed fists and handed out their cell phone numbers to potential drug addict clientele. And pimps and prostitutes swarmed the streets twenty-four hours out of the day while the Minneapolis police patrolled the streets.

Richard saw a prostitute out on the stroll, walking the street as if she were looking for a client. She had on a form-fitting waist-high very provocative fishnet red miniskirt and some matching red scuffed-up six-inch pump heels.

Richard had to take a second look at the prostitute walking up and down on the strip because Richard thought that the stripper was his wife, Kim, for a second. Richard couldn't believe his eyes! Richard asked himself, "Wait a minute, is that—no. It can't be…" Richard pulled his car up alongside the woman to get a closer look.

Richard pushed his passenger seat button, and the window slowly lowered. Richard asked the woman that resembled his wife, Kim, "Excuse me, missus…"

The prostitute immediately stopped in her tracks, thinking she had a bite. The prostitute turned around and walked up to Richard's passenger-side window and asked, "What's happening? Fifty for sex, twenty for some of this A-one head. You looking for some of this action, sexy?"

Richard was tightly grasping that fifty-dollar bill that his buddy John had given him. He was relieved to see the woman's face and that she wasn't his wife, Kim. Richard thought, *Whew! That was too close.*

About forty-five minutes later, the prostitute said, "Thanks, baby. I'm right here anytime you need me. Just look for this skirt, hun."

The prostitute walked away, hollering—"What's up, baby?"—to another car passing by, which looked like another client looking for some fun. And the car's break light lit up, slowing the car down to talk to the prostitute.

Richard took off driving around a few more blocks, then parked his car in an alleyway. He walked a couple of blocks back toward the homeless shelter. Richard was thinking, *Damn...I need some money.*

But he walked inside and checked in at the front desk of the homeless shelter and was approved to stay the night there. Richard fell asleep thinking of a way to get some quick money. He needed food, gas, and a place to stay before the weekend came because that's how long the homeless shelter approved him to stay for, until the weekend which gave Richard one week. And then he would have to give his bed up.

Richard woke up the next morning with plans of looking for a job to get some extra money and plans to report to his parole officer. Richard thought, *I'll go see my PO first. Everything else can wait! I ain't going back to prison*

After reporting to his PO, Richard was on the hunt for a job doing anything. It didn't matter. He just needed a job. And a job quick so he could eat and pay for a place to stay. And Richard thought, *To keep my parole officer off my case so I can breathe a little bit.* But revenge on those lawyers wasn't too far from the thoughts of Richard's mind.

Richard was recalling all of the times that he sat on the prison yard, went to the law library, walked early morning laps to stay fit and in shape, and the many different conversations that he had with other prisoners in the barbershop with every inmate that was in prison because of their lawyers' inability to defend them for whatever reason.

Richard heard seven to eight different stories from prisoners for years on an everyday-all-day basis. They all were wronged by their lawyers' ineffective assistance of counsel. Richard listened to as many of the prisoners' stories that he could. And he wrote each and every lawyer's name down, acting like he wanted to hire them so that he wouldn't send off any red flags.

But every lawyer's name that Richard had written down on that list was ultimately his lawyer revenge kill list. Richard related to every story that he had heard for years while in prison. The inmates told stories of how they were stripped away from their families and sent to prison.

Some of the prisoners received life sentences—guilty or not! Richard spent many nights sitting on his bunk and thinking, *Those bastards didn't do what they swore under oath to do which was fight effectively to the best of their ability to defend their clients. I can't stress that enough.*

That was the only point that Richard wanted to drive home to every lawyer across America—all of them—that lawyers just can't take people lives, family, and freedom as light as they did. In Richard's eyes, this was a very serious matter that shouldn't and wouldn't be overlooked.

Richard was determined to change the way that lawyers thought about their clients, guilty or not, and make sure that lawyers fought for their clients' lives, family, and freedom till the bitter end.

Richard drove around for hours, still looking for work. He drove to grocery stores, liquor stores, mechanic shops, fast-food restaurants, but no one was hiring. But as Richard was looking for work, he passed a couple of gun shops. And all he could think about was getting a good-quality high-powered gun from out of there to carry out his premeditated murder spree against any and all lawyers on his vengeance kill list.

Each time that Richard had passed a gun store, he asked himself, "How can I get a gun out of there?"

Richard really wanted a high-powered sniper rifle. Richard passed a few gun stores while riding and looking for a job. And his mission quickly went from looking for a job to looking for the perfect murder weapon.

Richard thought to himself, *I want the biggest gun that I can find to blow theses lawyers shit for brains out from at least over one hundred yards.*

Richard drove around and made another circle back to all of the gun stores that he had passed. His plan was to get a closer look at the guns. So Richard was going to act like he was a hunter looking for a high-powered rifle to hunt big game with.

Richard entered the store and told the gun store owner, "I'm hunting for black bears. I need a rifle that can lay a grizzly down with ease."

The gun store owner replied, "Well…this is what you want right here."

The gun store owner pulled out, from a huge polished silver gun case, a huge revolver. The revolver was almost the entire length of Richard's forearm. It was by far the heaviest handgun that Richard has ever held! Richard picked the revolver handgun up, awestruck and speechless. He was mesmerized by the handgun's size and beauty.

Richard was flipping and turning the revolver from one side to the other as he looked at both sides of the gun and smiled on the inside. Richard was picturing a lawyer dropping like a sack of potatoes from one headshot. Richard smiled, nodded his head, and said, "Yeah, yeah, I like this…What kind of gun is it?" he asked with a puzzled face.

The gun store owner answered, "That there…is the grizzly bear gun that you had asked for… .50 cal right there. Yes, sir." The gun store owner was smiling with his seal of approval about the type of damage that .50 caliber would do to a five-hundred-plus pound grizzly as the gun store owner began describing the gun to Richard.

Richard smiled, still picturing a lawyer's skull from one shot. Richard then said, "Yeah…I really like this. I'm going to go home and see what my wife thinks. And I will check back later."

Richard was lying. He was strategically casing the gun store. Looking for alarms, security system cameras, motion detectors, etc., so he could come back later on, as he had promised. But not to purchase the gun but to break in and steal the gun and other guns. This was the last store that Richard had made his stop at. And ironically, it was the easiest store with the least amount of cameras and security systems.

Richard looked around and thought, *It only had one camera. And that one camera didn't work because I could see that the monitor wasn't on in a small room in the back of the gun shop.*

Richard also noticed while he was holding that .50 caliber that every time that a customer purchased a gun, knife, or some hunting gear, the owner always took the money back to the same back room with the broken monitors in it. And the owner put the money in a little metal box.

The box had more cash stuffed inside of it, pulled out from a double-door wooden cabinet. Richard thought, *Yeah, this burglary's a piece of cake! Especially after everything that I learned while in prison.*

Prison had quickly taught Richard how to be a top-five criminal expert throughout the entire prison compound. A compound that housed over 1,200 other well-seasoned criminal experts that honed their skills after several years of being behind prison bars.

Richard left the gun store with plans to come back later on that night and break inside. Richard thought, *I really need that cash! I need that hunting rifle that I saw! And I need that .50 caliber that shoots rocket missiles!* Richard was anxious to see what that .50 caliber slug could do to the front of a lawyer's skull, male or female.

It was time, time for Richard to put his plan into motion—a killing spree of lawyers. Richard drove away from the gun shop, smiling with revenge on his mind.

Richard was driving down the street while looking back into his rearview mirror, seeing the gun store's closing time sign on the entrance door. Then Richard checked the time on his dashboard.

Chapter 21

On Richard's ride back to the homeless shelter, until it was time to put his plan into motion, when the gun store closed, he was thinking of all the things to look for and be mindful of in the gun store so that he wouldn't get caught up because he did something silly in the process of the robbery.

The first thing that came to Richard's mind was all of the snow that was covering the sidewalks and the streets. It was the middle of March, and snow was still falling. Richard thought, *I have to remember about my shoes leaving tracks in the snow just in case the police show up at the scene. They won't be able to follow my tracks and locate me by the direction that my tracks are going in and where they stop at.*

Richard was proud of the fact that he knew about the follow-the-tracks-in-the-snow trick. Richard had seen a burglar get caught that same exact way on a show called *The World's Dumbest Criminals Get Caught.* Richard said to himself, "I definitely can't and won't get caught like that!"

Then the next thing that Richard was saying to himself was, "I have to make sure that those surveillance cameras don't work either! Or if they do work, I'll just cover my face up anyway so the owner and nobody else can identify me.

It looked like Richard's blueprint for the burglary was, for sure, locked to be a fool-proof plan as he drove his car and parked it in the back alley a few blocks away from the homeless shelter, where Richard had always parked his car so that he wouldn't be seen or caught by the homeless shelter employees.

Richard looked down at his gas tank light before he turned off the ignition switch and pulled the key out. Richard's gas tank gauge light was lit up with a bright-red warning light, indicating to the car driver that the vehicle's gas tank was very dangerously close to empty.

Richard pulled the key out of the car's ignition switch and thought, *I need that money from the gun store. And the sooner the better.*

Richard exited his car, closed the driver-side door, and hoped that would be enough gas to at least get him to the gun store to get the money, the guns, and immediately to the nearest gas station for gas. Richard asked himself, "I mean...I really don't have a choice, do I? I'll just try my luck."

It was now dinnertime at the homeless shelter. Richard thought, *I'm just in time. I'm really starving,* as Richard walked through the door and saw men, women, and children, from infants to the elderly, waiting in line, waiting to be served their ration.

Richard was beyond humbled as he patiently stood at the back of the long line, speechless and sad as he watched all of the poor and the homeless people who all seem to be happy, talkative, and appreciative just to have a warm place to sleep from out of the fierce and brutal winter wind and snow, with some food to eat as well. No one inside of the homeless shelter complained.

Richard carefully observed all of the homeless people talking and the little kids smiling as they playfully walked away with their plate of food. Richard was daydreaming and thinking back to all of those times when he rode past this very same homeless shelter and didn't think twice about all of the people out there starving and homeless.

The homeless and starving people would be standing on the corners and asking every car that rode past or stopped at the red light out front, "Do you have any spare change, sir, ma'am? So I can get something to eat for me and my son?"

Then another homeless woman standing on the corner, asking every car that passed or stopped at the red light, "I'll work for food, sir. I haven't ate in two days." The woman's hair was dirty, matted down, and tangled up into knots. Her clothes were filthy, her toes hung out and over the front of her busted-out dirty tennis shoes. And she had also worn a brown scarf wrapped around her neck in eighty-plus-degree weather.

Richard was still reflecting on how he would just continue to sit there at the light, with his windows rolled up, ignoring the man with the child and the dirty woman, as if he didn't see them. Richard was in the cool comfort of his air-conditioning in his car until the traffic light turned green. Then Richard would drive off on the family. And now Richard was one of the very same people that, at one time, he didn't think twice about when his life was as good as he had once remembered it.

Having all that, Richard had worked hard for his entire life and was very successful. Richard had it all, the definition of the American dream—big beautiful home, lucrative-paying job, his own mechanic shop, a beautiful wife that was his high school sweetheart, and a beautiful daughter. All that a man could dream of and want, Richard had it, then lost it all in an instant blink of an eye on his road to prison.

The thought of it all and where Richard was at in his life right now, on parole, standing in line at the homeless shelter and waiting to be fed, it really humbled Richard and gave him a whole new respect and perspective on life. But most of all, Richard thought, *This had given me a whole new appreciation of life.*

The whole time that Richard was thinking about his life, the line for dinner was constantly moving. Richard was the last one to grab his hot Styrofoam plate of sliced turkey, mashed potatoes, broccoli, two slices of whole wheat bread, and a Styrofoam cup of milk.

Richard politely told the woman serving the dinner plates at the window, "Thank you, ma'am."

The lady in her late fifties or early sixties replied, "Oh...You're welcome, hun." Then the lady asked Richard, "What's a young handsome man such as yourself doing in here at a homeless shelter?" The lady continued, "You don't look like a face that I've seen before... Drug addiction?"

Richard quickly answered the woman, "No, no, no, no, no, no drugs, ma'am. I've never ever tried any type of drug my entire life! I lost my job and then my family." Richard was painfully smiling, as if everything was going to be okay and as if he was strong enough to weather the storm.

The elderly lady replied, "Awwww, I'm really sorry to hear that. That's sooooo sad. But God is going to make a way for you. He always does. God does everything for a reason. And he never places anything on your plate that you can't handle." Richard politely smiled, appreciating the woman's encouragement.

Richard was blocking the woman out, pretending to be listening to the woman. But the entire time that she was talking to Richard, the only thing dead front and center on his mind was revenge on every lawyer that he thought wasn't playing fair.

To Richard, not playing fair was having more courtroom losses than wins. And that revenge was what Richard had put his faith in and how he planned to make it through—killing lawyers!

Richard told the woman thank you as he walked off and found a place to be seated to eat. The woman smiled, winked, and said, "I'm going to pray for you." Richard nodded his head up and down back at her in approval.

He then found a table where a mother was sitting and eating with her son. The woman's son had a white sheet of paper sitting on the table in front of him. To Richard, it looked as if the boy was doing homework in between taking bites out of his hot turkey sandwich.

It was painful to see a child in a homeless shelter, eating and doing his homework; it saddened Richard.

Richard sat down at their table and then introduced himself. Richard held his hand out and said to the mother and the young boy, "Hi, my name is Richard. Nice to meet you. And your name is?"

The lady answered with an African accent, "Hi, I'm Yutundae. And this is my son, Omeka."

The woman was shaking Richard's hand with a friendly, warm, and welcoming smile on her face. Richard, caught off guard by the woman's accent, asked, "If you don't mind me asking, I noticed you have an accent. Are you from the islands?"

The lady, still smiling and delighted by Richard's inquisitiveness, answered, "Noooo, I don't mind you asking at all." The lady chuckled and said, "I get asked that…quite often as a matter of fact. But to answer your question, I'm from Africa. South Africa."

Richard was very intrigued and admired the woman's accent. Richard looked down at the little boy still doing his homework. Richard asked the little boy, "And how old are you, Omeka?" The little boy was still chewing the bite of the warm turkey sandwich that he had just bitten.

The little boy finished chewing respectfully, then swallowed before answering. "I'm ten and a half years old!" He was proudly smiling and excited to tell someone his age.

Richard smiled when Omeka added the half onto his age. Richard asked Omeka, "So what are you writing right there?"

Little Omeka answered, "This is how I practice my languages…" He was still writing as Richard talked with him.

Richard, seemingly puzzled by little Omeka's nonchalant answer, asked, "Languages? You know more than one language?" Omeka quickly frowned his face up at Richard's dumb question, thinking everyone knew several different languages as easy as he did.

Omeka answered, "Yes! I know four different languages." Omeka named the languages off one by one as he counted them with each finger. He said, "I know Swahili, Spanish, Italian, aaaaaand Japanese!" Little Omeka counted them all off as if it wasn't any big deal for a ten-and-a-half-year-old kid.

Richard, smiling, looked at Omeka and said, "Yeah, aaand English!" while rubbing the top of Omeka's head, as if he was proud and impressed with Omeka's gift. Richard and Omeka both smiled.

Omeka's mother, Yutundae, watched and listened to Richard and her son interacting with each other. Before she said, "He's very, very smart. Very intelligent. He's only ten years old and on course to graduate high school and attend college by the time he is fifteen years old. He has already picked his college."

Richard, with a puzzled expression on his face, looked at Omeka and asked, "So…What college do you like, Omeka?"

And with a huge and proud smile from ear to ear on his little face, and with a milk mustache from downing his last swallow of milk, Omeka answered, "I'm going to the University of Minnesota! So I can play football for them! And then I'm going to the NFL! And make millions and millions and millions of dollars! To buy my mom the biggest house in the world!"

Omeka went on, saying, "So we won't ever, ever have to live like this…homeless on the streets again! I'm going to be the number

1 draft pick! Watch, you'll see! But if the Lions pick me, maaaan, I might not play for them! Or maybe I will! Because I'll get them their first ring!"

Richard and Omeka's mother were both laughing and enjoying little Omeka's vision, passion, and determination to make his dreams a reality. Omeka got excited when he spoke about never having to live in the homeless shelter again.

Like him and his mother, never living like that again was his whole and only motivation. Omeka was talking fast! And he never once stopped for air as all of his words spilled out.

Richard smiled at Omeka, then said, "And you can do it too! But you have to believe in yourself! That no matter what people say, doubt you, or tell you that you can't do something or be somebody, just work hard and believe in yourself. But most of all, prove them wrong."

The little boy confidently replied with certainty, "I'm going to make it! Just watch! Watch me!" Then little Omeka continued working on his language lessons.

Richard had made his first real friend since being home from prison, little ten-and-a-half-year-old Omeka, future self-projected NFL superstar.

Before Richard had noticed, a couple of hours had quickly passed by. The clock on the wall was now reading 8:05 p.m. And the gun store had just closed at 8:00 p.m., and the shelter's curfew for their tenants was 9:00 p.m. All of the doors at the shelter locked and closed at 9:00 p.m., no coming or going was allowed due to any circumstances. "No exception!"

That is what the huge sign on the front door of the shelter had read. And all of the employees were very strict of that particular rule.

The shelter's number 1 rule was, "If you are not here by the time the lights go out, you are terminated from being a resident here and would have to reapply."

Richard looked at the clock and thought, *I can't take that chance of being out on the streets, but I have almost one hour to get there, get the money and the guns. Get some gas and be back inside of the shelter before curfew time, 9:00 p.m.*

After a few hours in the homeless shelter, spending time with his new friend, Omeka, Richard excused himself. Then he quickly headed to this car. Richard thought, *I don't have a second to waste going to go get those guns and money!* as he drove through the thick slippery winter snow that continued to fall and cover the entire streets of Minneapolis, Minnesota.

As Richard drove to rob the gun store of guns and money, he kept glancing across to the digital clock on his dashboard. He was trying to judge the time and the distance. He was asking himself, "Do I have enough time to get it done? Do I have enough time to get there and back? It's going to be close! But I think I can."

Not only did Richard have that worry about having enough time, but he also worried about if he had enough gas in the tank to even make it to the gun store. And he thought, *I still don't even know if I'm out of harm's way if I do successfully make it to the gun store. Because then I have to make it on that same empty tank of gas to the nearest gas station!*

All kinds of crazy thoughts and doubts began to swirl around, clouding Richard's mind. He asked himself, "Damn, what if I can't get to the money? What if the owner took all of the money home? And there isn't any money? What if my car runs out of gas right now while I'm driving? Or runs out of gas on my way to the nearest gas station?"

Richard was driving, and doubts were beginning to creep into his mind. This was, for sure, a risky dice roll. Richard thought, *That's at least one and a half hours walk back to the shelter. But an even better question is, what if I get caught by the cops? I'm going straight back to prison!*

Richard was still driving while glancing down at the gas tank. He was almost doubting if he could get to the gun store while hoping and praying that he could get there. He really began weighing his options.

Richard was weighing out the reward versus the risk factor. But to Richard, it was well worth the risk because he didn't have any money. And he desperately needed those guns! All Richard's appetite consisted of was causing pain, torment, and terror to each and every lawyer across the country, directly or indirectly. Richard could just taste it.

Richard thought, *Yeah, the same pain, terror, and torment that one of their colleagues caused in my life!* Even the lawyers, way across on the other side of the country, in total different states, Richard wanted them to be terrorized and wonder if the same terror of a lawyer killing spree would strike them and rip through their community, with a domino effect.

It was a twenty-minute drive through slow-moving traffic to the gun store due to the slippery snow and ice that covered the streets before Richard made it to the gun store.

Richard pulled up slowly riding past the front of the gun store. He was looking to see if they were officially closed or if any of the lights were still on. It was all clear. All of the store's main lights were off. Richard pulled around to the side of the building on a residential and small side street. Richard was trying not to look suspicious.

Richard looked down at the digital clock on his dashboard. He was estimating exactly how much time he had to make his move, which was get inside of the gun shop, get the guns, get the cash, and successfully make it back out to his car.

The clock on the dashboard read 8:28 p.m. Richard thought, *I have at least fifteen minutes to get in and then to get out! That gives me fifteen minutes to get gas—that's if I get the money—and then make it back to the shelter before curfew. I'm cutting it close…I don't know? But I'm wasting time just sitting here. It's like they say, no guts no glory!*

Richard was giving himself a last-minute confidence boost and pep talk, trying to build up the courage to do it and get it done. Richard turned the key in the ignition switch off. He paused for a brief moment. He was making one last view of his surroundings, making sure that there wasn't anybody around watching what he was about to do.

Richard suddenly and quickly exited his car. But he didn't close the driver door completely shut. Richard left the driver door ajar so that it would be quicker for him to get back into the car after stealing the guns from the gun shop.

Richard quickly and sneakily made his way to the side of the gun shop where it was a glass door. But Richard was so caught up in the moment, with his adrenaline pumping at such a fast rate, that he didn't even hear his car's automatic alarm set itself as he walked away. *Chirp, chirp.* His car alarm was set without Richard being aware of it.

Richard was looking at the glass door of the gun shop. He was looking at the glass door up and down and from side to side. Richard was looking for the smallest weakness in the door to gain entrance to the inside of the gun shop.

Richard grabbed the security bars on the outside of the glass door, and he shook them. He knew then trying to gain entrance that way was, for sure, a dead end.

Richard walked back to the back of the gun shop. He looked at that door and thought, *Nope! Damn! Dammit! That's all solid steel! Shit!*

Richard took a step back and scanned the gun shop's brick wall. But the closest windows were at least the roof's height. And there wasn't anything around that he saw tall enough to stand on as he quickly looked.

The clock was ticking, and Richard hadn't gained entrance inside of the gun shop yet. Richard was thinking to himself, *I'm running out of time...but I refuse this to be a dry run for nothing! If this is a dry run, I'm out on the streets for sure! Because my tank is on E, and I don't have a way to get back to the shelter.*

Richard began to pick up the pace a little bit in an almost panic. He was scrambling, looking around, kicking through the snow on the ground for a brick, or just anything to help him get in. Richard noticed a trash dumpster and thought to himself, *Oooh, a dumpster! It's always bricks by a trash dumpster!*

Richard ran to the trash dumpster and began feverishly kicking through the snow all around the dumpster.

Richard was in luck! His quick thinking had paid off! Richard's boot had kicked a brick that was frozen completely solid in the ground. Richard hurt his big toe when he kicked the brick. It hurt and sent a sharp pain of shock through every bone in Richard's body.

Richard said to himself, "Take the pain, Richard. Take the pain, Richard. Shake it off. Complete the mission. We're on the clock, baby…we're on the clock…"

After the self-pep-talk, Richard turned around and used the heel of his boot to kick the brick loose from the frozen dirt and ice in the ground. And after a few good kicks, the brick was loose from the ice in the ground.

Richard hurriedly picked the brick up, shook the lingering pain still in his big toe off one last time. He then made his way back to the front door of the gun shop again. The gun shop's front entrance door was facing a busy street. But Richard didn't have an option by now. Richard said to himself, "It's the front door or nothing!"

Richard tiptoed and slid alongside the gun shop's brick wall. He was still cradling the medium-to-large-size brick in both hands like a newborn baby. Richard peeked his head out from around the corner of the building, making sure that there wasn't any traffic coming or going.

But if there was traffic, Richard was going to patiently wait for the perfect opportunity for the cars to either slow down or stop at the traffic light. Richard thought, *That should give me enough time to jump out and break the glass door with the brick.*

The first peek that Richard took at the traffic was too busy to risk it. And the cars slowed down tremendously, not allowing for an opportunity to make a move. So Richard let the last of the few cars that tagged along behind, he allowed them to pass by. And then Richard quickly darted out from around the side of the gun shop's wall and took his chance.

Richard was moving so swiftly that when he turned the sharp corner, he almost slipped and fell, but he regained his balance while his adrenaline was racing. And without thinking twice, Richard mustered up as much energy and strength that he didn't even know his body had, and threw the brick straight through the gun shop's glass entrance door. *Crash!*

But the only problem with that was, Richard had forgotten all about the security bars bolted behind the glass on the inside of the gun shop. So when Richard finally had realized what he had done, he saw the brick that he had just thrown stuck in between the steel bars on the inside of the gun shop and the steel entrance door on the outside.

Richard thought, *It's over now, I'm back on the streets!* But if Richard would have been just a little more patient, he would have seen the big glass picture window that had no bars on it. That window was right beside the door that he had just thrown the only brick that he had through.

Feeling like it was over, Richard turned around to walk back toward his car. He was praying that he had enough gas to make it back to the shelter. But as Richard turned to go back to his car, he noticed several medium-size bricks forming a landscaping circular-shape for a flowerpot in front of the store.

Then Richard instantly thought, *Oh, it's not over for me yet! One of these, and I'm in there!* Richard used the heel of his boot again to kick the brick loose—kick, kick, kick—and by Richard's third kick, the brick was free from all of the ice surrounding it.

Richard picked the brick up, then he looked to see where the next group of cars in traffic were. Richard saw that there weren't any cars close. But he could see dim headlights from a far distance. Those were cars headed toward his direction.

Richard picked the brick up and held it up with one hand next to his ear. Richard held the brick up in a throwing motion and tossed it through the big plate glass window that read "Dean's Pawn and Gun Shop." the brick hit the glass and made a loud crashing noise from the window breaking and falling to the ground. *Tssshhhh!*

Richard didn't have a second to spare. He didn't know how much time he had left. But what he did know was that the time that he thought he had left didn't feel comfortable to him.

Richard knocked the remaining lower half of the glass window out so that he wouldn't cut himself climbing through the glass window. Richard pulled his winter skull cap down that doubled as a ski mask. Then Richard climbed through the broken window.

Richard thought, *Whew! Finally in!* Richard didn't know how much time he had left, but he thought, *As soon as it feels like I have been in for five minutes, tops…I'm getting out of there!*

Richard was inside of the gun store. He ran straight over to the glass case where he had stood holding that .50 caliber handgun earlier in the day. Richard looked into the case, and the .50 caliber handgun was still there. And it was still looking heavy, fat, and pretty as ever.

Richard feverishly searched and looked around for something to break the top of the glass case with. Richard spotted a brass table ornament. Richard picked the brass ornament up in the air, and it felt like it was heavy enough to do the trick. Richard stood over the glass case, holding the brick up in the air, outstretched arms above his head. Richard was bracing himself.

But just before he was about to let the brass ornament go over the top of the glass case, a big bright light shined into the gun shop. The big bright light was shining from one of the side street windows.

Richard instantly thought, *Shit! That light is bright enough to be one of those spotlights that are mounted on the outside of the police cars! Dammit! That's the cops!* Richard immediately dropped the heavy brass ornament to the floor. And then Richard followed by falling to the floor himself. Richard fell to the floor almost as quick as the heavy brass ornament that he had just dropped.

Richard lay there on the floor, trying to be as still as he possibly could. Even though in the back of his mind, he was thinking, *I have to get out of here! I'm almost out of time! Maybe I should just get up and run for it? And just take my chance on getting back to the shelter while the cops are chasing me...or should I just lay here and wait while precious seconds continue to tick away.*

Richard had a rush of sudden thoughts as he panicked. He continued, *Just continuing to lay here might have me homeless, though. Taking a gamble on the cops doing just a random round on the gun store. And hopefully the cops just keep on going past.*

Richard continued to lie still on the floor. He wasn't moving a muscle and hoping the cops were just passing through. As Richard lay there on the floor, he could see the bright light shining over his head, shining through both side windows of the gun store from one window to the next. The bright light was moving up and down and going from side to side all over the walls on the inside of the gun store.

As the bright light was shining through, Richard could see all of the guns inside of the gun store lit up everywhere. The bright light scanned over the many rifle gun racks attached to the wall. And that's when Richard noticed that the gun store owner had a special type of gun rack. A gun rack that locked and secured a long quarter inch thick steel rod. The steel rod went through each of the rifle's trigger guard holes.

Richard knew then that it would be impossible to get those rifles off of that gun rack. And even if he could get past the steel rod securing the guns, he didn't have enough time to even try. So the rifle plan was abandoned for the sake of time.

The bright light shined back through the window but, this time, on the opposite side of the gun shop. The bright light was illuminating the glass case that held all of the handguns. Richard could see all of the handguns lying on their sides with all of the orange oversized price tags tied onto the trigger guards.

Richard saw the one that he had his hands on earlier in the day. The only reason Richard noticed that handgun first was because that handgun was the biggest and the fattest pistol out of all the other handguns in the glass case.

The high-polished stainless steel .50 caliber handgun with the big rubber handgrip. The .50 caliber was very distinctive and stood out from all the rest of the 9 millimeters, 10 millimeters, Glock 40s, the .45 automatics, and the .44 revolvers that were lying on their sides in the glass case as well.

Finally all of a sudden, the bright lights stopped flashing into the inside of the gun store. And all Richard could hear was an engine revved up, foot on the gas pedal speeding off down the street. Richard thought, *Whoever they were, they're gone now*. Richard quickly hopped up to his feet and peeked out of the store's side window just to make sure.

Richard looked to the left, down to one end of the street. Then Richard looked to the right, down to the other end of the street. The entire side street was clear of traffic.

Richard thought, *Good thing I didn't try to break in through the side of the gun shop because I would probably be in jail right now. I'm just glad the cops got another call because if they would have made their way to the front of the gun shop and saw that big plate glass window broken out, or that brick stuck in the entrance door, I would be on my way back to prison.*

Richard quickly and nervously made his way back to the handgun glass case in a panicked hurry. He thought, *Damn...I am definitely out of time now! Just get what I can grab and go!*

Richard picked the heavy brass elephant ornament up and made sure that he was standing in front of the right glass gun case. Richard spotted the big .50 caliber inside.

Richard lifted the heavy brass elephant ornament up and above his head and dropped it directly into the center of the glass gun case—*tisssshhhh!*—quickly turning his face away all in the same motion, trying not to get any glass into his eyes.

Richard lifted the big .50 caliber up, and he blew the little glass that had shattered all over the handgun off. Then Richard stuck the big gun into the front pocket of his winter coat.

Richard saw the boxes of .50 caliber shells on the countertop just behind the glass gun case. He quickly grabbed four boxes of .50 caliber bullets. Then Richard stuck those into the other front pocket of his winter coat. Richard looked right past the rifles with the steel rod laced straight through every trigger guard on the rifles.

Richard headed toward the back of the gun store where he had previously seen the owner taking all of the cash into a room when he was there earlier in the day. Richard turned the doorknob, but the door was locked. And that's when Richard's prison survival instincts took over instantly. Prison had made Richard into something completely and totally opposite of what he was before he went in.

Richard kicked the door in that had all of the cash on the other side of the lock. Or at least, he hoped it did. *Boom!* Then Richard walked straight over to the cabinet, pulled the cabinet doors open. And there it was—all cash, neatly folded in half with a rubber band tightly wrapped around the money!

Richard asked himself, "What? The owner thought locking the door would keep his money safe?" Richard smirked and said to himself, "Huh...silly man. Better luck next time." Shaking his head in disbelief, Richard then stuck the folded-up cash with the rubber band around it into his pants pocket.

Richard thought, It's time to go! It feels like I'm out of time! It has to be nine o'clock!" Richard quickly began walking back toward the front of the gun store. He was going to climb back through the window but only this time, to leave. But that's when Richard noticed the AK assault rifle.

The assault rifle was hanging from the ceiling by two straps over his head. Richard snatched the rifle down from the ceiling. Then he ripped the hanging big orange price tag from off of it and threw the price tag to the floor.

That's when Richard remembered seeing boxes of AK shells on the countertop right next to the boxes of .50 caliber shells. Richard quickly made his way back behind the glass case and grabbed two boxes of AK shells from off of the countertop, along with a couple of boxes of infrared laser sights that he didn't notice were there the first trip when he reached on the countertop to grab the .50 caliber shells.

Richard stuck the AK ammunition into his coat pocket, climbed through the window with his AK-47 in his hands. When Richard made it to the other side of the glass, he adjusted the big .50 caliber that was hanging halfway out of his pocket. It had almost fallen out.

Richard pushed it down with half of the handle visibly showing. Richard quickly made his way back to his car. He was moving swiftly while trying not to look suspicious.

Richard grabbed his driver-side door handle, forgetting that he had already left the door ajar. And that's when the car's alarm went off. Richard's car horn began blowing loudly while his head lights were flashing. *Honk! Honk! Honk!*

Richard panicked as he quickly tossed the AK assault rifle into the passenger seat. Then he quickly began digging into both of his coat pockets. Richard was looking for his car keys to turn the car alarm off. Richard dug around the huge .50 caliber handgun and then the ammunition. And that's when he found his keys—*urt! Urt!*—disarming the alarm.

Richard put the key into the ignition and then turned the key forward to start the car up. But nothing happened. His car was completely and totally silent. Not a sound. Richard, leaving his car door ajar, had drained his car's battery. Richard's car was completely dead! Richard instantly thought, *My car is dead! And so am I because I know I'm for sure out of time now!*

But getting to the shelter was the least of Richard's worries. He was worried about how he would get out of jail because the police were probably within seconds of getting there and catching Richard with the assault rifle, the .50 caliber handgun, the bullets, and the gun shop's stolen money. Not only that, charging him with the gun store's breaking and entering.

Richard sat there in his car, frozen, still in complete shock. He was thinking, *I'm on my way back to prison for sure! It's over for me!* Especially when Richard saw some of the houses in the neighborhood lights turn on, trying to see what all of the commotion was all about.

Chapter 22

Richard nervously sat there in his car, waiting, and hopefully giving his car a few minutes that he didn't have to recharge and hopefully start up when he tried it again.

Richard put his fingers back onto the key to turn the ignition switch and start his car up. But before he gave it another try, he closed his eyes and prayed, "Please, God…please let it start. Please. Come on, car…come on…start, dammit!" Richard still had his eyes closed and his head bowed as he turned the ignition switch over, waiting on the outcome.

Richard thought, *At least the engine made noise this time. It's trying.* The car battery recharged and gained a little more power than it had the first time that he had tried it.

A car pulled up beside Richard from out of nowhere. The man asked, "Hey, guy, need a jump?"

Richard turned his face away from the stranger, toward his passenger window, opposite direction from the man's voice so the man couldn't see his face. Richard answered, "No, no, thank you. It always does this."

Richard was trying to use his body to block the man's view of the big assault lying across his passenger seat. But the man was persistent. He insisted on helping Richard out of the freezing cold of Minneapolis weather. And before Richard knew it, the man was standing in front of Richard's car and yelling, "Pop your hood up! Pop your hood up for me!"

Richard said to himself, "Dammit!"

Richard quickly popped his hood up, trying to get the man to leave as quickly as he could. Then Richard heard the man yell, "Now try it! Try it now!" Richard turned the ignition switch over again. And Richard's car's engine started up. *Vroom! Vroom!*

Richard yelled out of his car window, "Thank you, sir!" And just like that, before the man had barely unclamped the jumper cables from off of Richard's car battery, Richard was gone!

The man just stood there, watching Richard drive away down the street until Richard's car disappeared into the darkness of the night.

Richard looked down at the digital clock on his dashboard. He was absolutely positive, by everything that had just taken place inside of the gun shop, and with his car not wanting to start, that the time was at least nine o'clock. But to Richard's surprise, the time was only eight forty-eight. Richard thought, *Oh! Only twenty minutes passed? Damn, that felt like hours! Long hours at that!*

Only 8:48 p.m., that gave Richard twelve minutes to get gas and cut a twenty-minute drive back to the shelter at least in half to ten minutes. Or hopefully less. Richard thought, *I'm pushing it close! Extremely close! But I think I can pull it off!*

Richard took off speeding toward the direction of the nearest gas station. And the empty gas tank warning light was lit up bright red all the way to the gas station. And Richard was praying all the way there, saying, "Please, God, let me make it…please, God, let me get there…"

Richard didn't know how he made it to the gas station. But he was just relieved that he did make it and riding on gas fumes at that. All Richard could say, as he pulled next to the gas pump, was, "Thank you, God. You answered my prayers tonight. All of them."

Richard filled his gas tank up. Then he peeled a new crispy twenty-dollar bill from the thick rubber band stack of cash and paid the gas station clerk. Then he quickly took off out of the gas station parking lot. He was in a panicked hurry to make it back to the shelter before the curfew there.

Richard was driving as fast as he could through the icy and slippery snow-covered streets. Richard glanced down at the dashboard clock again. He was seeing how much time he was working with. The clock on his dashboard was reading 8:52 p.m. Richard thought, *Damn, I got eight minutes to get back to the shelter. Shit, that's nearly impossible. It's almost a twelve-minute ride from here.*

But Richard stomped the gas pedal down to the floor and gave it all that he had on an all-out race against the clock.

Richard sped through every traffic light that wasn't already green by the time he had made it to it, with a bulging pocket full of stolen cash, coat pockets full of gun ammunition, and a car full of stolen guns. That was the only chance that he had, so Richard took it.

Richard was driving erratically and watching his dashboard clock as he was quickly approaching the shelter. The time was now exactly 9:00 p.m., and Richard had just parked his car down the block and around the corner from the shelter.

Before Richard exited his car, he took off his winter coat with the pockets filled with ammunition. Richard threw the winter coat over the .50 caliber handgun and the AK assault rifle that still laid across the passenger seat. Richard wanted to cover the guns up so that they wouldn't be visible if anyone was to look inside of his car.

Richard got out of his car and closed the driver-side door, making sure that it was tightly shut. And then he quickly walked toward the shelter, through the freezing cold with strong winds blowing rapidly and no coat on.

When Richard finally arrived at the shelter's entrance door, one of the employees was just turning the dead bolt from the inside of the shelter, locking and securing the door, prohibiting any traffic from coming or going.

Richard walked up to the door and tried to walk inside of the shelter, but the entrance door was locked. The man looked at Richard and yelled through the glass window of the door, "You're late! It's nine o'clock! Curfew time!" He was pointing to the shelter's clock on the wall that visibly read 9:03 p.m.

Richard looked at the man with a face that pleaded for compassion and sympathy. But the man just repeated what he had just told Richard a couple of seconds ago, "You're late! It's nine o'clock, curfew time!" The man was yelling through the glass door window and still pointing up at the clock. "I'm sorry!" The man was walking away.

Richard begged the man, saying, "Come on, sir? It's freezing out here. And I don't have a coat on." Richard was waiting on the man's response. The man stopped in his tracks, turned around, and began walking back toward the entrance door in Richard's direction.

Richard's heart was beating and racing rapidly, waiting on the man's answer and hoping that the man would have just a little compassion for him and let him inside. The man unlocked the dead bolt, opened the door, and said, "All right, I'll let you in this time...but next time, you won't be so lucky!" His face was straight as an arrow.

Richard walked inside of the shelter and wiped his feet off on the mat. Then Richard said to the man, "Thank you, sir. I really do appreciate this. And I promise it won't happen again." Richard blew heat into both of his hands to warm them up from coming outside from the brutal cold.

Richard walked to his assigned area where his bed was located. He climbed into his bed, and then he pulled his blanket over him. Richard let out a deep exhale of mental exhaustion, reflecting back on everything that he couldn't believe that he had just gone through. Richard said to himself, "Thank you, God. Whew!" Richard lay there in his bed until his eyes closed, and he fell asleep.

It was breakfast call early the next morning at the shelter. Everyone lined up to eat, women and children first. Everyone had their plates and were sitting down, eating, and casually conversing. But Richard, he was eating his breakfast and thinking about all of his details of carrying out his plan of a justified lawyer killing spree. A killing spree of lawyers that the United States has never witnessed or heard of.

The plan made Richard smile on the inside and feel a deep sense of relief and justification, knowing that he was about to terrorize the entire country and catch the attention of every attorney, aspiring attorney, law students, and law professors within the next few weeks.

With each bite that Richard took out of his meal, he looked at his plan as justified revenge. Richard sat his fork down onto his plate and continued chewing as he briefly closed his eyes and used his index finger to motion a make-believe cross over his chest.

Richard thought, *God, I hope you can and will forgive me on my day of judgment because I owe those lawyers at least that much...I owe this revenge killing spree to my lawyer, his colleagues, and all other aspiring attorneys. For what they have done...and for what they might do. God, my mission is warranted. Look at it this way, God, it's deserved justified revenge.*

Richard picked his fork back up and continued eating as he thought about the AK-47 assault rifle that he stole from the gun shop last night.

Richard felt as if the AK-47 wasn't a good enough rifle to accomplish the mission that he had set out before himself. Richard wanted a hunting high-velocity sniper-type of rifle that had a one-hundred-yard-plus scope with pinpoint accuracy. Richard thought, *That AK-47 is more of an assault-type rifle. Up close nasty crime scene. It's not really what I envisioned for my mission.*

Richard continued eating while brainstorming about the perfect rifle. He thought, *Where can I get a rifle from? I'm not going to another gun shop and going through that again. It has to be a better way...*

Richard asked himself over and over again, *Where can I find a rifle at?* And then instantly, he remembered something. "I got an rifle! My hunting rifle! Yeah, I'll use my Remington R-25. It's for big game hunting and long-range targets."

Richard continued on, "And it has a 2.5 10×4,200 scope! Sighted in to hit dead-on at two hundred yards. But I'm willing to bet one hundred dollars to a bucket of shit that it can drop anything in its path at three hundred yards at least!"

Richard thought to himself, *The only problem, it's back at the house. But I still have the key to my house!* Richard had forgotten but then remembered that fast about his hunting rifle. Richard looked up at the clock on the wall. The time was 6:15 a.m. Richard thought, *Kim is usually out and about, running errands at 7:00 a.m., and Jessie is now seventeen years old, and she should be in high school by now. Damn...high school now? Those eight years in prison sure was a long time. And a lot has changed. But Jessie should be in school by seven thirty. Yeah, I think high school is seven thirty. I hope anyway."*

Richard thought, *I'll just go report to my parole officer first, and then swing by my old house to get my rifle. And then go out again looking for work. Any type of employment. Just something to get some food with and something to get some gas with to get around for now. And anything extra is a plus.*

Richard was feeling a strong sense of relief and feeling good about the fact that his murderous plot against all lawyers was finally coming together.

Richard's plan was coming together the exact way that he had envisioned it. And it was beginning to take shape.

Richard looked up at the clock on the shelter's wall one last time. The time was now reading 6:20 a.m. Richard downed what was left of his Styrofoam cup of orange juice. And then he took off in a hurry out of the door. Richard was on his way to report to his parole officer, then his old house, and then finally out looking for a job.

Richard walked to his car and then opened the passenger door. He grabbed his coat from off the top of the AK-47 that was covered with it. Richard hurriedly put on his coat and quickly looked around, making sure nobody could see what he was about to do next. Richard pressed the trunk release button of his car attached to his key ring.

Richard's trunk popped open. Richard grabbed the AK-47 with both hands and then quickly made his way to the trunk of his car. Richard placed the rifle inside of his trunk and laid it down onto its side. Next Richard pulled the .50 caliber out of his coat pocket and laid the handgun next to the AK-47.

Then Richard reached inside both pockets of his coat, pulling all of the boxes of AK-47 and .50 caliber ammunition out. Richard tossed the boxes of ammunition on top of the rifle and the .50 caliber. And then Richard covered the rifle, the .50 caliber, and the boxes of ammunition with an old sheet that was balled up in his trunk. Richard closed the trunk, got into his car, and made his way to downtown Minneapolis to report to his parole officer, Mrs. Pandleton.

This time, Mrs. Pandleton stressed to Richard that he was skating on thin ice by not having a job yet. Mrs. Pandleton's exact words were, "You really need to find a job, Mr. Ginn. And the sooner the better. Because then you could save me from using some ink that I would rather not waste on you! But…I won't hesitate either!"

Richard quickly got Mrs. Pandleton to ease up off of him when he dug deep down into his pocket and peeled a $50 bill from off of the $1,200 in the breaking-and-entering money that he pulled off at the gun shop late last night. And Mrs. Pandleton instantly forgot all about pressuring Richard for a job. She didn't mention another word about it.

Richard thought, *I really do need to find a job. Because I don't know how much longer she's going to keep letting me slide. And there's no telling how long this $1,200 is going to last me. I can't keep going around breaking into stores like that.*

Richard finished up his parole meeting with Mrs. Pandleton. And then he left the parole office on his way to his wife, Kim's, house. His old house. By the time Richard arrived there, the time was 6:45 a.m. As Richard was approaching the house, he saw two cars parked in the driveway.

One of the cars in the driveway, Richard immediately recognized. It was his wife, Kim's, car. But the other car, Richard didn't seem to know whose it was. It was a small newer style lue Ford Focus. Richard thought, The other car must be Kim's new boyfriend's."

Richard was parked down the block and looking at his old house from a distance. Richard hadn't seen his wife or his daughter, Jessie, since he had been home from prison, fresh off of doing an eight-year prison bid.

Richard continued looking at his old house from a distance and thinking, *Damn, Jessie was just a little girl before I was sent to prison. It seems just like yesterday when I was going to her bedroom window and her classroom window during the winter months. And writing I love you, Jessie into the frost of the window.*

Richard knew that he only had minutes before they both woke up to prepare for school and Kim off to run errands. So he had to make his move really fast.

Richard quickly exited his car. Then he briskly began to walk up the street toward his old house. And once he got there, he walked with his back sliding tightly up against the house, as close as possible through the driveway. And as he passed the unfamiliar car that was parked in the driveway, he looked inside and tried to see some type of clue of who the car may belong to.

But all Richard could see in the car was an old local section of the Minneapolis newspaper. And the newspaper was lying on the passenger seat opened up to the sports section.

Richard turned and continued walking toward the house, making his way toward the back side of the house. He heard a noise in the house and was startled. So Richard quickly made his way back down and through the driveway, down the street, and back to where his car was parked so that he wouldn't be seen or get caught.

Richard patiently waited while watching from a distance for Kim, Jessie, and whoever else was driving the Ford Focus to leave the house so he could go inside of the house and get his rifle out of what used to be his bedroom closet.

Approximately twenty minutes later, Richard saw his wife, Kim, and his daughter, Jessie, leaving the house. Richard hardly recognized his own daughter standing next to her mother eight years later. Richard stared at the both of them, sadly thinking about his daughter that he had lost, his wife sending him to prison, and everything that he had gone through over the last eight years.

Richard also thought about his dysfunctional family as a child growing up. Richard swore his family wouldn't be anything like his family when he was growing up.

When Richard was a little boy, he used to sneak and put his ear up to the brick wall in the family kitchen and listen to his mother and father in their bedroom, talking about him as if he wasn't theirs and how they both regretted him being their child.

It really saddened Richard as he watched both Jessie and his wife, Kim, leaving the house and Kim turning around to lock the side door while standing in the driveway. Richard watched Kim hug Jessie and then gave Jessie a kiss on her cheek.

A tear welled in Richard's eye, feeling the excruciating hurt and fury of a lawyer taking his family from him. There's no greater pain or betrayal.

Jessie walked to the Ford Focus parked behind Kim's car in the driveway. Richard was speechless, thinking, *Wow, Jessie's driving now! Before I left, she was barley riding her bicycle!*

Jessie got into her car and drove off on her way to her high school. And Kim was right behind her, leaving out of the driveway. Kim and Jessie both had split up and left in separate directions.

From where Richard was parked at, he thought, *Now's the time for me to go!* Richard exited his car and quickly made his way back up the street toward the house once more. He made it to the driveway and walked up to the side door. He pulled out his door key that was still on his key ring before he went to prison.

Richard put the key into the door's keyhole, and he hoped that the lock hadn't been changed by Kim. Richard crossed his fingers for good luck and then turned the key to unlock the door. He was in luck, saying, "Whew!" with a sigh of relief as he heard the lock make a *click* noise. The door easily unlocked, as if Richard had never gone away.

Richard stepped inside of the house where he could still smell the strong aroma of breakfast. The smell was still lingering through-out the house. As he walked toward the kitchen, Richard thought, *I haven't smelled food like this in a while! Years as a matter of fact! The only breakfast served in prison was watered down and runny oatmeal with two slices of ice-cold frozen-solid stale bread.*

So the aroma of what seemed to be sausage, eggs, and hash browns instantly made Richard hungry as his stomach growled.

Richard walked over to the stove and saw some leftover eggs and sausage covered up in two different cooking pans. Then Richard walked over to the microwave and looked inside. A thick and fluffy stack of blueberry pancakes were in the microwave on a plate. With a spoon of butter still melting on top.

Richard quickly pulled a spoon, fork, and butter knife from out of the silverware drawer. And then he reached up into the cupboard where the plates were and grabbed himself a plate. Richard helped himself to a little portion of everything.

Richard pulled out a container of orange juice. He poured him-self an ice-cold glass of orange juice. He downed it all in one swal-low and said, "Ahhhh! It's been a long time. Prison even makes you appreciate a glass of orange juice! Things that I never thought twice about. It's true what they say, you don't know what you got till it's gone."

Richard was chewing and swallowing extremely fast, so much that he was almost choking with each mouthful. He finished eating, then poured another half-glass of orange juice. He drank that until the glass was turned upside down in the air and till the last drop dripped into his mouth.

Then Richard headed upstairs to his old bedroom closet to grab his hunting rifle and then get out of there before someone came back home.

As Richard walked through the living room to go upstairs, he noticed over the fireplace a portrait, still hanging up, of him, Kim, and Jessie on the wall, when Jessie was just a week-old baby in his arms.

Richard stared at the portrait and thought, *I will never forget how we all went as a family together and took those pictures. That day right there was one of the proudest days of my life.*

Richard smiled and thought, *Wow, Kim still has my picture up after all that we had been through? I really would like to work things out with her just to keep my family together. Just for the sake of Jessie. But I'm scared of rejection. Or better yet, scared of myself that I may snap one day and only God knows what I'll do to Kim.*

Richard continued thinking to himself, *Maybe we're better off leaving things as is...* Richard shook it off. Then he thought, *I have to get out of here!* Richard walked away, stopped, and then took one last look over his shoulder at their family portrait as he kept walking, making his way upstairs to get his rifle.

Richard made it to his old bedroom door. He turned the doorknob and slowly opened the door. Richard had finally pushed the bedroom door all the way open. He didn't step inside. Richard stood in the doorway, first looking around the bedroom for a couple of seconds. No immediate or obvious signs of his wife sleeping with another man or even having another man.

Richard could breathe a little easier now without holding his breath. And that really made Richard feel like Kim still loved him and that they stood a strong chance to work things out. Also Richard didn't see any signs of Kim having another man around his daughter. So Richard still held onto hope. Richard finally took one step inside his old bedroom. Richard was standing just on the other side of the doorway now. Both of his feet inside, *Richard thought, It's been eight long years since I've last stepped inside of my bedroom.* Richard still didn't touch anything.

Richard walked over to Kim's dresser and noticed a *Thinking of You* card. Richard picked it up, opened it up, and then read it. The warm and loving words inside instantly infuriated Richard.

Richard began reading the words inside.

> To my future husband, Dave. I'm really looking forward to spending the rest of my life with you. I love you more than life itself. Jessie talks about you all the time. She even calls you Dad now. My, how time flies! See, I told ya…we're meant to be.

Richard kept reading until he read to the right-hand side of the card. And that read, "PS, I hope you enjoyed what I done for you last night. Because I did…Smile!"

Richard became even angrier. *Now she has my daughter calling some strange guy named Dave, daddy! I sent Jessie I love you cards from prison for eight years! I'm willing to bet Kim didn't give Jessie any of the cards that I sent home!* Richard took the card and violently threw it across the room.

Richard just happened to look inside of the waste basket that was beside the bed. And there they were. Two freshly used condoms in the waste basket. It was totally covered with runny, watery, and drippy semen from the inside to the outside.

Richard was staring at the used condom in disbelief of his wife, Kim. Richard felt betrayed, angry, and hurt all at once as the used condom was dangling on the end of the pen that Richard was holding out in front of him. He was looking at the semen dripping and leaking from it.

Richard threw both the pen and the condom back into the waste basket as semen dripped from out of the condom onto the floor from the force of being thrown.

Richard made his way toward the bedroom's closet. He opened the double doors up, turned the closet light on, then walked inside. Deep inside of the closet, he pulled the clothes hanging up on hangers to the side. And that's when he saw it—his hunting rifle, still standing straight up in its case, exactly where he had left it before he was sent to prison. Nicely tucked away into the corner.

Next to the rifle was a large black trash bag. Richard used his hand to push and feel around the outside of the trash bag, trying to make out what it felt like it could be on the inside. But Richard couldn't figure out what it felt like was on the inside.

Richard thought, *This feels like a trash bag full of paper trash. But why would it be in the closet?* Richard untied the tightly tied double knot on the trash bag. And that's when he saw all of the cards that he had made and all of the letters that he had written to his wife and his daughter while serving his eight-year sentence in prison. The cards and letters were all inside of the trash bag.

Richard thought, *Jessie probably thinks that I left her, forgot all about her, and that I don't love her anymore. Jessie probably hates me now. After all these years have passed, I'd hate me too. I have to try and talk to her and explain.*

Richard took a couple of letters that he had written to Jessie while in prison out of the trash bag and read them. He stared at one card, thinking about how he felt at that particular time. Richard thought, *I'll never forget this card*, as he held it in his hands.

Another card on Jessie's birthday read, "I'm sorry, Jessie, for Daddy leaving you like this. But I promise to make it up to you when I get home. We'll be together again soon! Real soon! PS, hugs and kisses 4ever!"

It was extremely painful for Richard, reading that card that he had made for Jessie, knowing that she had never read or even seen the card. But it angered Richard even more that his wife, Kim, hid all of the letters and cards that he had made for his daughter.

Richard placed the card back into the black trash bag, then grabbed a couple boxes of ammunition from off of the top shelf right above his rifle. Richard angrily said to himself, "This just added more fuel to the fire. As if I really needed more fuel? This motivated my thirst for revenge even more. I'm going to make the whole world feel my pain!"

Richard put the boxes of ammunition inside of the front pocket of his coat. Then he picked his rifle up and threw it over his right shoulder. It was hanging by its strap.

Richard picked the trash bag filled with his cards and letters up, he turned the closet light out, and then closed the closet's double doors. Richard made his way to Jessie's bedroom. Richard dumped the trash bag full of cards and letters all over her bed. He was shaking the trash bag upside down until every piece of paper, letter, envelope, and card shook its way out onto Jessie's bed.

Richard looked up and noticed Jessie's senior high school picture. It was tucked into the corner of the big mirror of her dresser. Richard walked over toward her picture and got a better look up close.

Richard was staring at how much his baby girl had grown into such a beautiful young lady. Richard shook his head in disbelief. It was a lot of years that he missed out of her life that he will never be able to get back or make up for. But the mission that Richard was on would at least help to ease some of his regrets and his hurt.

Richard, with his rifle still hanging by its strap over his shoulder, smiled to himself, proud of his baby girl and admiring how much she had looked like him. Jessie was flawlessly beautiful. Richard kissed Jessie's picture, stepped back, and looked at it one more time. Then he left her bedroom and closed the door behind himself.

Richard, with his rifle over his shoulder, left the house, locking the door behind himself. And just like that, Richard was off making his rounds around the city, looking for work.

Chapter 23

After a few hours of riding around, looking for work, Richard was still unsuccessful. Nobody was hiring due to the state of the economy. Almost every business or major corporation was either at a standstill or bankrupt.

Richard was driving around when he spotted an old bar on the street corner named Lucky's, and a huge brightly lit light out front that read "Dining Room Help Wanted."

Richard thought about his time in prison when he worked in the kitchen busing tables. He wanted to give it a try. Anything would do right now. He was pulling into Lucky's parking lot. Richard was going inside to take his chances.

Richard was a little nervous. He hadn't worked busing tables out in the free world with regular citizens in society. Only in prison with bad attitude, rude, and disrespectful prisoners with nothing to lose. He wondered if these people out here in the free world would be the same as those people in there. But he really needed the money, so this was his only option.

Richard entered inside the bar where he spotted an heavyset and balding older white gentleman. Richard assumed he was the owner since he was the loudest man inside the bar. Also he was standing behind the counter cracking jokes with the customers while serving mugs of beer.

Richard walked up to the man and said, "Excuse me, I can bus tables really well, and I'm a people's person. I'm looking for a job to make a little money to get some gas and food. Do you have room for me?"

The bar owner looked Richard up and down. The bar owner had a lit fat cigar hanging from out of his mouth. The man was silent for a moment, not knowing what to think. The owner didn't say a word as he stared at Richard waiting for an answer.

The bar owner answered in a raspy voice, "Well…let me see what you got! Go handle those customers. You aren't shy, are ya?" The bar owner laughed to himself, turned his back to Richard, and walked off, back toward his buddies who were all laughing as well. They were all seated at the bar, drinking out of tall beer mugs, as one of the men rudely belched, almost in Richard's face, doubting Richard's skills and figured Richard would just freeze up and crumble to the regular, rude, and disrespectful customers.

But little did the men all know, Richard had just left some of the most rude, disrespectful, heartless, bitter, angry, and most violent people on the planet inside of prison. That Richard dealt with from morning to night, 24-7, for eight years. So anything out here was easy! Piece of cake. Richard thrived comfortably in this atmosphere, nowhere near as worse as what he just lived through.

Richard went over to the customers who were rude, disrespectful, and very inconsiderate. He killed it! And the customers liked Richard so much they tipped him, which those specific customers never tipped in their ten years of coming into Lucky's bar. The owner and his buddies watched, speechlessly impressed. They were very familiar with the customers they knew would eat Richard alive. But they tipped Richard instead.

Richard knew that he didn't have any room for error. His first impression had to be all that he had. And it definitely was. And that gave Richard an edge. The owner and his buddies, all of their mouths dropped with whispers among each other.

Richard's confidence took over as he continued going from table to table with the customers. And they all laughed and enjoyed Richard's company and conversation. Then Richard's confidence shot through the roof. The owner was trying his best to pretend as if he wasn't impressed with Richard's performance.

The bar owner said to Richard, "Yeah…I guess you're decent. I've seen better. You're a little rusty but stop back by in a few weeks, and I'll try to let you know something. One way or another."

Richard excitedly replied, "Yes, sir! Yes, sir! Thanks for your time. I really do appreciate it, sir!" Richard tried giving the bar owner the wadded-up cash of tips he quickly earned.

The owner nonchalantly said, "Nah, man, that you."

Richard quickly said thanks and stuffed the wadded-up cash into his pockets.

Richard quickly drove back to the homeless shelter where he had been living since coming home from prison. Over the next few days, Richard anxiously waited and prayed diligently, hoping to get that gig at the bar to pay for his food, gas, and hopefully get up out the shelter. Richard wanted to find a place of his own.

But as of lately at the shelter, Richard and Omeka had grown amazingly closer as friends. They studied all of the different languages together almost every day all day. Omeka slowly went from slowly pronouncing each word to completely saying a word from each language faster and faster.

It was a fun game that he and Richard came up with to make learning interesting. And Richard was now strong enough in his little knowledge pronunciation of different languages that Richard kept up with every word that Omeka threw his way as a curveball. They really laughed and had a great time together.

Richard was constantly thinking about how low his money was becoming, almost one month later from the time when he had broken into the gun store and stolen that $1,200.

Richard tried to wait it out and not seem too desperate while waiting to hear from Lucky's bar. Richard didn't want to show up at Lucky's bar, asking, "So what do you think? Can I work? Is there room for me?"

But Richard couldn't resist the temptation any longer. The shelter had a thirty-day room/board max time with no children included. Then you would have to reapply after thirty days to give someone else an opportunity for room and board.

Richard was in a bind—no money. And he was almost certain that he would be put out into the streets. Three weeks had passed since Richard tried out at Lucky's bar.

Richard got into his car and went up to Lucky's bar, thinking, *He's gonna just have to tell me no! I'm not waiting any longer!* Richard wanted to talk to Lucky and see if he had made a decision yet on hiring him or not. Richard thought, *If he tells me no, I don't know what I'm going to do next. I've damn near ran through all of that gun shop robbery money.*

In between riding around looking for work, he would ride around for hours looking for every place in town where all of the lawyers on his list hung out at—restaurants, country clubs, bars, workout gyms, and where most of them lived with their families until Richard located them all.

Richard would be in front of wherever the lawyers were at, and the lawyers were unsuspecting of Richard in their presence. He was just one of the guys, undetected and unnoticed, sitting in his car, pretending to be reading a newspaper so that his face wouldn't be visible.

Richard had finally arrived at Lucky's bar and grill. Richard walked inside of the bar where an older lady in her fifties, who was probably Lucky's wife, was serving a drink to a customer.

Richard politely said to the woman, "Excuse me, missus, but I'm looking for the owner—"

But before Richard could finish his sentence, he heard a deep raspy voice hollering from the back of the bar where they prepared food at, "Who's looking for Lucky up there!"

The older woman behind the bar answered, "I don't know, Luck! Some young fella! Hurry up because he's kinda cute too!" The older woman looked at Richard and winked her eye.

Richard was smiling and looking down at the floor. Richard was thinking, *I can't make eye contact with the owner's wife. Never mix business with pleasure. She reminds me of my grandma for Chrissakes!*

The owner of the bar came out from the back through some swinging double doors. He was drying his hands on a meat-loaf-stained dishrag. While drying his hands, he asked, "How can I help ya, fella?" The owner didn't recognize Richard from the last time that he was here busing tables.

Richard answered the man, "Remember me, sir? I was here a few weeks ago, looking for a job here busing tables."

Lucky threw the towel that he had been drying his hands off with, carelessly over his shoulder. Then Lucky asked, "You said busing tables?"

Richard replied, "Yes, busing tables, sir. Remember I took the order for those rowdy customers for you also?" Richard couldn't believe that Lucky didn't remember him.

Lucky closed his eyes, thinking in deep thought of that day. He was silent in thought. Then he excitedly replied, "Oh, you! Well, hell yeah! We sure can use a little bit of live entertainment up in here! Spice it up a bit, ya know?"

Richard asked, "How soon can I start, sir?"

Lucky answered sarcastically, "How soon can you start! Ha ha! You don't even know how much you're gonna make! Ha ha! That's funny!" Lucky jokingly said, "Maybe I'll just hire you as my comedian instead!" Lucky fell out laughing. "Ha ha ha, ooooh!"

Richard politely smiled, trying to figure out the humor in the question that he had just asked Lucky.

Richard said to Lucky, "It really doesn't matter how much you pay me, sir. I just need food, gas, and pay for a place to stay...I just need a job." Richard pleaded desperately to Lucky.

Lucky replied, "So tell ya what I'm going to do...I'm gonna pay ya seventy bucks a night, you keep all tips—and you're really gonna love this—I got a little place in the bar here. You can stay there as long as you need to. Just watch the bar for me, ya know? From those li'l assholes that broke in here twice before. How does that sound? Huh? What's your name, fella?"

Richard excitedly answered, not expecting Lucky's gratitude, "My name is Richard, sir. But my friends call me Richy. And yes, yes, sir, that sounds great! Beggars can't be choosy! Thank you! Thank you! So how soon can I start?"

Lucky answered, "Give me and my wife a couple of days to clean her all up. Get her nice and spiffy for ya to move in. So give us a couple days. Matter fact, what's today? Uhhh, Wednesday, right? Be ready to bus some tables Saturday night, Richy. We have a tough crowd, faithfully, every Saturday night. Be ready or they'll eat you alive in 0.2 seconds!" Lucky laughed, doubting if Richard could handle the tough rowdy crowd on his first night performing.

Richard looked Lucky directly in his eyes, confidently smiled, and replied, "I will be ready, sir. I guarantee I won't disappoint you."

Lucky replied, "It's not me you have to worry about disappointing…you're the one that has to live with it. Not me." Lucky gave Richard a key from off of his key chain.

Then Lucky said to Richard, "Saturday…around…1:00 p.m., move your things in." Then lucky jokingly asked Richard, "Hey, Richy, before I let you move into my place, you're not some type of serial killer with a buncha damn guns and on the run from them TV shows, are ya?"

Lucky laughed hysterically as he walked away back toward the bar's kitchen, thinking Richard looked as harmless as a baby fly.

Richard quickly responded back to Lucky before the swinging doors closed, "Nah, man. Not me, I'm harmless. I wouldn't sneeze in a pepper fight!"

Lucky responded back, saying, "I know, you definitely look like you wouldn't!" Lucky continued laughing from the bar's kitchen area.

Richard heard Lucky and thought, *Yeah, little do you know, you about to have the most feared lawyer killer in the country, living directly above your bar.*

Richard smiled to himself, then winked at the old lady serving drinks to the customers as the old lady paused and watched Richard leave all the way out of the bar with a suspicious eye after hearing Richard's and Lucky's conversation.

To the old lady, something didn't seem right about Richard to her. But she really didn't think too much about it. She thought it was just her feeling weird again. So she shook it off.

Richard only had twenty dollars left in his pocket from the money that he had stolen from the gun store. Richard thought, *I can get me a little gas to get around until Saturday when I will get paid for my first night at the bar.*

Richard only had a couple days left to spend with his little friend, Omeka, back at the shelter. Richard wanted to give him a gift, something to inspire and motivate him to believe in his dreams and something to remember him by.

So before heading back to the shelter, Richard stopped for gas and to buy little Omeka an official NFL authentic football. Richard thought, *I'm not going to tell him I'm leaving or give him the football, not until my last day at the shelter, because I don't know if I can handle leaving my new friend.*

Richard continued thinking, *And I know that he's not going to like it either. We have grown real close at the shelter together. And it's going to be a sad moment for the both of us. I'm sure of it.*

Once Richard arrived back at the shelter, he placed Omeka's football in a paper sack and then rolled the bag down until it was tightly shut. Then Richard tucked the paper sack out of eyesight under his bed. Richard said, "I can't let little O find this before I get the chance to give it to him."

Richard made his rounds around the shelter, speaking to everyone as he had always done. Richard made his rounds until he walked over and met Omeka at their study table where Omeka was already sitting and studying.

Omeka looked up with his signature milk mustache, surprised and excited to see Richard at their regular study time. They both did their cool handshake that Richard asked Omeka to create for every time that they saw each other and every time that they left each other.

It took Omeka some time to create their cool signature handshake. Richard smiled as he watched Omeka every day, hours after hours, endlessly, sitting on his bed, frustrated until he fell asleep, trying and trying his hardest to create the perfect handshake for him and his friend, Richard. Until one night he finally came up with a good one.

Omeka excitedly woke Richard up out of his sleep one night. Omeka was shaking Richard nonstop as he was softly whispering, trying not to wake anyone up.

Omeka whispered, "Richy! Richy! I got it! I got it! I think I got one for us! Come on, look! Hold your hand out!" Richard was still half-asleep trying to focus his eyes and see what Omeka was talking about.

Omeka, excited about his and Richard's cool handshake that he had just came up with, had grabbed Richard's hand and said, "No! Do it like this, Richy!" And it was history. Their cool handshake was born, all in the darkness of the night, assisted all by the back bathroom light glowing on the both of them.

Richard and Omeka did their handshake, Richard was standing up by now. Richard and Omeka gave each other two hand slaps, then they went right into putting the backs of their hands against each other, slid their hands backward toward themselves, until the end of their fingertips touched; they snapped their fingers at the same time, pointed at each other with fingertips still touching, then they both held up one finger, symbolizing the number 1.

Richard and Omeka were both smiling at each other as they were doing their handshake. And then Richard nodded his head up and down, as if he was giving Omeka his approval. They both smiled and gave each other a big hug while Omeka's mother, Yutundae, had awakened from out of her sleep. She was watching Omeka and Richard from afar.

Richard lay in his bed, with the lights out, thinking about the next days to come. Richard thought, *Only one day left before I move into the place at Lucky's, which means that I only have one day before I put my plan into motion. Killing lawyers! I'm going to be a hero. A legend. America will never forget my name.*

Richard continued thinking, *I'm about to have every lawyer in the country regret they went to law school. I can't wait!* Richard lay there in the darkness, bathroom light still glowing, and just thinking, thinking, thinking.

Richard lay there in his bed, smiling to himself, seeing vengeance right at his fingertips, literally within days.

Richard calmly slept all night until morning. He woke up and thought, *Let me tie up all my loose ends because after tomorrow, I'm not looking back! I'm not stopping until my mission is complete!*

*****

Jessie came home and saw all of the letters and cards that her father had made for her while he was in prison. Jessie noticed dates on the postage and realized that her mom was keeping her dad from contacting her from prison. Jessie read each one and thought, *My dad was actually writing me from prison? My dad really does love me.*

Jessie asked herself, "Why would my mom keep this from me? Why would she do that?" Jessie was feeling bad for hating Richard for leaving her. Jessie knew that it was her dad that left the letters on her bed for her to read. She was speechless. She was stumped with a look of confusion on her face. Jessie thought, *No…my dad! He's out of prison? No way!*

Then suddenly, Jessie heard a knock at the door. She quickly grabbed her blanket and threw it over the bed full of letters and cards from Richard—*whoosh!*

Jessie calmed down and tried to act as normal as possible before she answered, "Come on in, Mom!" Jessie threw her blanket over the mail first because she didn't know if her mom knew her father was out of prison. And Jessie wasn't about to say anything about it.

Kim entered Jessie's bedroom and asked if she ate some of the food they cooked the other day for breakfast. Jessie answered, "Yes. That was me, Mom. I went back for more. I was kinda starving." Jessie halfheartedly chuckled, still trying to keep her composure. Kim turned around to leave.

As Kim was leaving, she replied, "Oh, okay. Just let me know next time, hun. Because I was really beginning to think that it was some weirdo in here without us knowing. That's all I wanted, sweetheart. Bye."

And as Kim was closing Jessie's bedroom door, Jessie said, "Yeah, sorry. And I will let you know next time, Mom. My bad. See ya," with slight nervous jitters still in her voice and still trying to calm her heart's erratic pace. She exhaled a deep sigh of relief when her mom left her bedroom—"Whew!"—still trying to mentally process what had just happened.

Chapter 24

Richard had left the shelter by now. He was in traffic. As Richard approached an intersection, he could see a police car stopped at the traffic light in front of him in the other lane. Richard thought, *Maaan, if this light doesn't turn green, I'll be sitting next to this clown at the light with my car full of guns.*

Since being falsely accused of rape and lied to by cops just to get him in handcuffs, and then railroaded by his lawyer, then sent to prison for extra years on top of his sentence and then violated by being raped in prison, Richard had grown to have a very, very strong dislike for the police—a bitter furious hate for the police.

Richard had now hated the sight of any cops. Richard tried to hide the bitter fury all in his facial expression. The closer he had approached the traffic light, Richard said to himself with a whisper, "I hate those pigs!" with an snarl on his face.

It was like a bull seeing red every time he thought about a cop. Richard went from watching and loving every cop show that came on television to now hating them all. Even the cop shows!

Richard remembered times when officers stopped by the shelter while he lived there. It took every bone in his body not to kill them right then and there, run out to his car, grab his guns, and go back and shoot the shelter up just to kill them all! But Richard would just leave the room instead. Didn't want anything to do with them.

His bigger thirst called for bigger murders. Lawyers were priority to Richard, then maybe cops.

Somehow Richard kept his cool as he slowly pulled up beside the cop car. They both were waiting at the traffic light for the signal to turn green.

Richard was looking straight ahead. So straight that he didn't want to make any eye contact with the police officer because he or she would unmistakenly see *murder* written all over his face.

But with a trunk full of guns and ammunition, he didn't want to seem suspicious either. Richard slowly looked over toward the passenger side of his car, trying not to obviously move his head, just his eyes, while he saw the cop car sitting still and both waiting on the light to turn green.

But that's when Richard and the male police officer had made eye contact. The officer politely smiled and nodded his head toward Richard, as if to say hello. It took everything inside of Richard to put on a fake smile and nod his head back at the officer in return, saying hello as well.

The traffic light had finally turned green which, to Richard, it felt like it never would, as if time stood still, and they were frozen. Then they both sped off in separate directions. Richard drove straight ahead, the police made a right-hand turn onto a side street.

Richard was driving to the nearest Catholic Church. He wanted to clear his conscience for the heinous sin that he was possessed to commit—the history-changing and horrific killing spree of lawyers that was about to take place. And it was so necessary.

The pain and the terror caused by the hands of one man, inflicted upon family after family across America. And it knows no color. No black or white, just green, green pieces of paper with dead presidents all over them. Richard said to himself as he was driving, "Even the families that wouldn't directly suffer would still ultimately feel it."

Richard felt sorry for the innocent lawyers' families that took pride in their work and placed integrity and people's lives and family and freedom before a dollar, the lawyers that respected their jobs, the lawyers that carried their jobs out with honesty and respectfully with integrity.

But in order to be taken seriously and change lawyers' thinking in the future, the innocent lawyers had to feel it too because they should be policing and holding their colleagues accountable. And it would have never gotten to this place of no return—lawyer killings.

Richard wanted all lawyers and all families of lawyers to fully understand what's at stake every time they step inside of a courtroom to defend the guilty or the innocent.

Because not only is the defendant's life, freedom, future, and family on the line, but the attorney that is sworn to effectively represent him, his life, family, and future is on the line as well, just as much as his or her client, guilty or innocent or maybe even more at jeopardy.

Richard knew that he wasn't the only person that felt this way. Richard heard hundreds and hundreds of stories from prisoners during his eight long years in prison. And the only thing that all of the prisoners ever talked about was killing their lawyers the very first chance that they get whenever or if ever they were ever let back out on the streets.

But it seemed after all the talk of getting revenge on their lawyers, Richard was the only person with the balls and heart, to carry it out and the bitter fury fueling his unwillingness to forgive and forget that easy. He lost everything, now an empty soul of darkness. He experienced flashbacks as he drove on his way to the confession booth.

Richard said, "I'm doing a good deed for you, God, and any and everybody that has ever been wronged by their lawyers. Now I'm their judge, God. It's judgment day for those lawyers. I'm their jury and their executioner. For their corrupt motives, they must answer to me and only me."

Richard parked his car, then steeped into the Catholic Church. Richard was making his way to the confession booth to clear his conscience and wipe his hands clean of the lawyers' blood that had made his kill list.

A mission of vengeance that Richard felt he was obligated— appointed—to carry out for the souls of the people, even some that he knew, that died in prison while doing decades, from teens to elderly hospice old men because of their lawyers. Richard's deed was for the good of the wronged.

Richard felt like he was chosen. That God had appointed him and only him for this mission of vengeance.

Richard stepped inside of the confession booth. He sat there for several minutes, collecting his thoughts before he spoke.

The whole idea of giving a confession was beginning to feel like it wasn't the right thing to do. Sacred and confidential or not, Richard was beginning to have stronger second thoughts the longer he sat there, confused.

In the state of Richard's confusion, he heard a voice on the other side of the wall softly and peacefully ask, "What's your confession today, son?"

Richard felt a sudden calm sweep over his body as he paused for a couple seconds just to build up the courage to answer.

Sweat dripped from Richard's forehead, down the side of his face, and onto his cheek. Richard was sounding ashamed of something as he slowly and softly answered, "I'm sorry, Father...Please forgive me for I have sinned in my mind against you."

The voice on the other side of the confession booth wall replied, "What or who have you sinned against in your mind, son?"

Richard answered, "I'm afraid that you won't understand me, Father. No one understands me. I have lost everything...I'm nothing in God's eyes, Father...I've been made homeless, and my manhood had been viciously robbed from me. And it can never be gained or given back to me, ever again..."

The voice in the booth softly replied to Richard, "Go on, son. God is listening to your heart."

Richard paused for a moment, then went on, "They can never make what they have done to me, or what they have done to many others...right. So I...I have to make it right for the voiceless. I will be the sacrificial lamb, Father."

The voice replied, "God loves you, son, confess to me."

Richard responded, "I am the chosen one, for appointed—" Abruptly before Richard could finish his confession, Richard hollered in an extremely loud outburst, "Noooo! Can't do this!"

Richard struck out of the confession booth as fast as he could while he heard the voice from a distance, screaming at him, "Wait! Wait a minute, son! Confess to Godddddd!"

Richard swiftly ran through the church, down the stairs, and out of the huge wooden double doors. The wooden double doors were almost as tall as the ceiling. Richard got back into his car and drove back to the shelter.

Richard was mentally and physically exhausted after going to the church. He climbed into his bed and took a nap. Before he dozed off, he lay there, thinking about all the chaotic events that took place since early in the morning.

By the time Richard had awoken, it was dinnertime. Richard ate, and as he had always done, he conversed with his little friend, Omeka.

As Richard conversed with Omeka, he thought, *This is my last full day with my friend. My only real true friend that doesn't judge me or look at me any differently. I want to spend as much time as I can with him before I go. And it's killing me inside, just looking at how happy he is whenever we're talking and playing. And he smiles with his milk mustache.*

Richard continued thinking, *I'm going to miss you, little O. But the mission must go as planned. I've waited, meticulously planned, and dreamed of that day. But I promise to never forget you. And I will always love you, little buddy.*

Richard had already packed up all of his belongings over the last few days. He was more than prepared to move into his new place above Lucky's bar. All of Richard's belongings were in his car. All except the football that he bought for Omeka. It was still in its paper sack, tightly rolled down shut and safely tucked up under Richard's bed.

Chapter 25

Richard and Omeka did their little cool handshake and then went off to their individual beds to go to sleep.

Richard woke up bright and early the next morning, prepared. The day was a happy but sad day for Richard. He was ecstatic about finally being able to leave the shelter. It was a long time coming.

But on the flip side of the happiness, Richard was depressed and sad. Sad because he was leaving his little friend, Omeka, behind. Omeka and his mother were still back at the shelter, struggling daily to find a way out, trying to find a decent job, for a place to stay.

Just the thought was almost bringing Richard to tears. Richard said to himself, "They're beautiful people. They deserve better. So much more." Richard didn't want to see Omeka give up on his dream of playing football in the NFL, just to sell drugs in the streets, like so many other young and talented kids that throw their future and talents away for the fast life of drugs, money, and guns. Because so many kids come from a background of poverty and struggle.

Richard knew how much Omeka hated to see his mother struggling to feed him and buy him decent clothes for school. Omeka had always spoken to Richard about it.

Omeka would always look just outside of the shelter's window while he studied and watch the saturated busy traffic of young drug dealers, eleven and twelve-year-old kids his age, on every street corner peddling drugs just on the other side of that door. And most of them were talented and gifted just like him.

Omeka played ball with most of them every day down at the park. But now, most of them were young dropouts, locked up, or dead. Promising futures lost down the drain.

Richard feared that it wouldn't take much for Omeka to be sucked into the temptation of that dead-end lifestyle. Because for most inner-city kids, all it took was a pair of Jordans on their friends feet from selling drugs. And most kids were all in.

Richard was on his way out of the door. But before he left the shelter and set out on his mission—a killing spree of lawyers—he wanted to see Omeka and Yutundae once more. Because depending on how this all ends, there was a very real and strong possibility that this could be Richard's last time seeing the both of them.

Richard left out of the shelter to put the rest of his belongings into his car that was now finally parked right out in front of the shelter.

Omeka and Yutundae were both watching Richard take big black trash bags back and forth to his car. They were trying to figure out what Richard was doing. They were confused and didn't understand.

Richard had made his last trip out to his car while trying his best not to make eye contact with Omeka or Yutundae. Richard was purposely looking in the opposite direction of where they both were standing. But they stared at Richard each time that he passed them.

On his last trip in, Richard walked over to his bed and just stood there. The only thing that he had left on his bed was a tightly rolled-down-shut brown paper bag with an official NFL football inside of it.

Richard had picked the brown paper bag up, then walked over to Omeka and Yutundae. who were standing together. Richard exhaled a deep breath to speak to Omeka first. Omeka was silently anticipating Richard's every word. His little heart was beating faster than normal, fearing the worst.

Richard said to Omeka, "I found a job. A way for me to make a decent living and be able to buy food and gas, to try and survive out there. And the job offered me a place to stay as well." Omeka frowned his face up as he sadly and slowly dropped his head. He was looking down at the floor.

Richard went on, saying, "O! Don't look down! Never look down! You always hold your head up high! And look adversity directly in the eye! And remember, no matter what you may go through in life…you keep your eye locked on the prize! The things we go through in life build resilience and will only make you stronger!"

Richard was still looking Omeka directly in his eyes as he finished by saying, "And the prize is what, O? The prize is your dream! Your dream of playing football in the NFL! And buying your mom the biggest house on the planet! Or did you forget that?"

Omeka, without saying a word, had a half-smile on his face as he sadly shook his head from side to side, saying, "No, I didn't forget. I understand, Richy. I hear you."

Richard handed Omeka the brown paper sack that he was holding behind his back, out of Omeka's view so that he couldn't see it. Richard said, "This right here, it's for you, O. This is your and Mom's ticket out of here."

Richard handed Omeka the tightly rolled-down-shut brown paper sack. Omeka excitedly tore open the paper sack almost to shreds as he screamed, "Aaaaaawwwwwe! Look, Ma! Look, Ma! My own NFL football! Look, Ma! It says *NFL* real big on it! This is the coolest present that I have ever got my whole life! This is sick! Thanks, Richy! Thank you!" Omeka jumped up and hugged Richard as tightly as he could.

Omeka's mother was staring at the both of them and smiling to see her son happy. Yutundae kept smiling as tears welled in her eyes and slowly ran down her cheeks. Yutundae gave Richard a big hug, squeezing him and her son at the same time. All three stood there, holding one another and hugging for a moment.

When they all finally stopped hugging after a few seconds, Richard looked Yutundae in her eyes and said, "Yutundae, you'll make it out too. Just don't give up."

Yutundae replied, "Thank you. Thank you for everything."

Richard looked back at Omeka and said, "Oh yeah, before I go, Omeka, this is what I want you to do every time you score a touchdown in college and in the NFL. That'll let me know that you didn't forget me."

Omeka briefly quit tossing his football up into the air. He was staring at the big *NFL* letters spiraling around. He looked at Richard, waiting to see what Richard wanted him to do.

Richard said, "I want you to do this." Richard grabbed both of Omeka's arms. Richard placed Omeka's left arm directly across his chest in front of himself. Then Richard grabbed Omeka's right arm straight up and down, making a fist in the air. Both of Omeka's arms were connecting, the left arm's fist connecting with the right arm elbow, making an L-shape.

Omeka didn't understand what it was supposed to mean. So Omeka asked Richard, "You want me to hold up the letter *L*?"

Richard assuredly answered, "Yep! Every time you score a touchdown, I want you to hold up the letter *L*."

Omeka replied, "I don't get it, Richy. That's kinda weird. But all right. I'll do it for you. So when you see me on those sports television highlights, in college and in the NFL, holding up an *L* in the end zone after I score a touchdown, you know that's me! Scoring a touchdown for you!"

Richard smiled. Then instinctively, they both did their cool little handshake that Omeka made up for the both of them.

Richard proceeded to make his way out of the shelter's door. Richard looked back at Omeka, who was still staring in awe at the letters *NFL* on his football. Richard asked Omeka in Italian, "Not the Detroit Lions?"

Omeka smiled, then answered back in Italian, "I'll get them a ring."

Richard winked at Omeka; Omeka smiled back. And just like that, Richard was gone. Moving closer and closer toward putting his plan of attorney murders into action.

*****

Richard met up with the bar owner, Lucky, as planned. Lucky gave Richard the key to the place above the bar. Then Richard began moving what little bit of clothes and belongings into the place.

Before Richard had brought his .50 caliber handgun, his AK-47, or his hunting rifle up to his apartment, or anywhere near his new apartment, he didn't want Lucky or anyone else to see the guns or the ammunition because he didn't want to risk being out of a place to stay or potentially end up back in prison.

It turned out to be a good thing that Richard decided to wait to bring the guns and the ammunition into the apartment because Lucky and his wife came up to Richard's apartment, just above their bar, just to help Richard get familiar with the place and how to use the appliances.

Forty-five minutes later, Lucky and his wife were gone for the last and final time. Richard said to himself, "Geez! Thank God already!"

But before Lucky left, he told Richard, "I'm going to give you tonight off. So you can get settled in and relax a bit. But tomorrow… It's showtime! So be ready to rock and roll, babeeee!" Richard cringed at how loud Lucky's raspy voice increased as Lucky rubbed his hands together, really looking forward to and anticipating tomorrow.

Richard took a seat on his couch for a moment, soaking it all up. He finally found a little motivation to get up, take a shower, and then he dozed off until the wee hours of the night.

Richard woke up several hours later. He looked up at the clock, then hurriedly ran down to the parking lot. He took a few trips out to the car. He brought the guns and the ammunition inside of the apartment.

Finally they were all inside. And they were all laid out on his dining room table as Richard sat there at the dining room table, with his lawyer kill list in hand, as he was staring at each gun—both guns from the gun store robbery and his hunting rifle. Richard was trying to match each gun to a lawyer's name.

Richard was trying to pick which gun would be the best one for each murder. Richard was going down his lawyer kill list, trying to match each gun to a name.

Whichever lawyer had more losses than wins, to Richard, that was a more up close and personal murder. He wanted to inflict as much pain as possible on that specific lawyer.

Richard's lawyer kill list had grown to nearly twenty names to be executed. And some lawyer names were much worse than others. Richard thought, *Some of these bastards have way more losses than wins than others on here. But you all have made my lawyer kill list for one very specific reason.*

Richard went on, thinking, *A very valid and justified reason. And my reason is to just kill, kill, kill, and then kill some more. And end the lives of lawyers that have more losses than wins in the courtroom. I'm making a traumatic statement to America, to every lawyer and to every law school with aspiring lawyers in the United States. That their ineffectiveness will no longer be tolerated! At least not by me. The lawyer killer.*

It really excited Richard that the name lawyer killer had a nice ring to it. He kept saying the name back to himself in every different way possible and in different voices that he could think of, pretending to be news anchors, police captains, and international news services.

Richard, in a high-pitched woman's voice, said, "The lawyer killer." Then in a news anchor's delivery, "The lawyer killer has struck again early this morning..." Then as a chief of police department's voice, "The lawyer killer is at large..." Richard had fun pretending to be those personalities.

So this specific list of attorneys' lives had to come to an end, unfortunately. And Richard anxiously but patiently anticipated and strategically waited for the perfect time. And the time was now.

Tomorrow would be his first day of providing services at Lucky's bar—and also Richard's first attorney murder which was also providing live entertainment for himself and everybody else that thought like him but never ever mustered up the guts to carry it out.

Richard thought, *The very first name that I pick to kill has to shake up the city! But it's too early for them to detect a motive. So it won't be that alarming yet. Just an unexplained crime under investigation. But that murder will set the tone of the lawyers' killings so that lawyers all across the world know, without a shadow of doubt, that whoever is out there killing lawyers means serious business!*

Richard didn't want lawyers or aspiring lawyers in school to make any mistake about his intentions or his motive. Richard meant 1,000 percent *business!*

After Richard brought his guns up to his apartment, he sat down on the couch and watched some television until he fell asleep. He wanted his mind and his body to be well rested for his big debut tomorrow—at Lucky's and on the news.

Richard woke up the next morning bright and early. He went and sat at his dining room table. He was staring at his kill list of lawyers that was lying down on the table in front of him.

It was still very early in the morning, around 5:00 a.m., and the sun hadn't yet arisen. Richard was thinking 'bout the situation and his mission at hand.

Richard was a strong and wholehearted believer in the United States justice system. That is, up until the tables turned. And he found himself on the other side of the law. Richard had always thought, like so many others, that the justice system is fair and just. And that anybody convicted of a crime was guilty and got exactly what they deserved.

Richard had hit rock bottom and couldn't pick up the pieces. He had lost everything. And that triggered a murderous killing spree. Richard was angrily staring at the very first name at the top of his kill list.

Richard began thinking about when he was locked in prison and homeless, living at the shelter. All of his too-many-to-count sleepless nights of nightmares, locked up in a prison cell, feeling like the walls were closing in on him while he tossed and turned, waking up in the middle of panic attacks and cold sweats. Just the thought of it all had Richard sweating profusely and hyperventilating again.

All Richard heard in his nightmares were deep, dark, and evil-sounding demonic voices. It was the same voice talking to Richard and repeating itself. All Richard could hear the voice saying was, *Public pretender...Public pretender...* Followed by eerily evil and demonic laughs of court-appointed lawyers.

Lawyers that got another person that couldn't afford adequate and legitimate legal representation sent off to prison.

Richard was still furiously staring at his attorney kill list up and down, from the top to the bottom. back from the bottom up to the top, trying to pick a name that deserved his attention and reprimand next.

Richard was literally living among kids in prison, just thrown away by some lawyer that didn't give a damn if they got sent to prison, or care if he could have helped them get a second chance at their future.

But instead of helping a young kid get a second chance, some lawyers just threw them to the predators that used deceptive intelligence and fear against vulnerable little kids. Richard couldn't bear to watch it.

Lawyers would trick you into pleading guilty or carelessly rush you through trial, if you weren't stupid enough to plead guilty, forfeiting your childhood, freedom, and future.

Richard had finally picked a lawyer's name. The next attorney to be murdered on Richard's kill list was Mr. Howard Loney.

Mr. Howard Loney was a very successful attorney, but only if you paid him. He was a high-priced lawyer that had a flamboyant ego. Mr. Howard Loney has a well-known reputation around the inner city. Street dudes loved him and rolled out the red carpet for Howard. He mingled with killers that worked on hit list payrolls. And he worked for federal-level big-time drug dealers. Howard beat murder and drug indictments for them.

Howard specialized in natural life sentence offenses. He beat over 93 percent of his cases. Howard knew his shit. And Howard knew that he knew his shit.

But on the flipside of Mr. Howard Loney's reputation, every time his name came up for a pro bono obligation for legal representation, he lost a large number of those simple routine cases and, most of the time, purposely.

Howard felt like he paid his dues early on out of law school just to have his name what it was today. Out of Howard's own mouth, as he talked with a client over the telephone, a client that was slow with paying Howard to postpone and prolong his court dates. Howard told the client, "Look, dude, it's like this, pimp, if you can't pay that ticket, then I guess you're just shit out of luck! It's not personal...It's just business, baby. Peace out!"

So arrogant that Howard had hung his telephone up from off of the intercom, and when the client called right back after Howard hung up, he just would let it ring and turn his surround sound music up in his office to drown the telephone out, paying it no attention.

Richard's plan was, "I can kill him coming out of the bar." The bar that Richard was referring to was a bar called The Underworld where a strictly upper-class crowd, mostly of young lawyers or kids in law school, partied at after long hard days of classrooms and court-rooms. They all frequented the bar and hung out regularly.

Richard thought, *I can catch ol' Howie coming out of the bar and put two slugs in the front of his skull. I want to see if this big shot flamboyant lawyer got enough of that same money to buy his life back.*

Richard sat there at his kitchen table, staring at Howard's attorney at law photo in his phone. Richard circled Howard's name on his attorney kill list. Then Richard screenshot Howard's picture in his phone.

Richard had plans to kill Howard in club Underworld's parking lot after his work shift at Lucky's bar tonight. Richard had already envisioned how he would pull it off. The plan was set. Howard Loney was the first attorney to be a murder victim.

After hours had passed, it was time for Richard's first night of work at Lucky's. He headed down to the bar. Richard walked inside the bar, trying to see through the thick cloud of tobacco smoke. The smoke blanketed the entire inside of the bar like thick fog. Richard could barely see one foot in front of the other.

Richard spotted Lucky. Lucky signaled over to Richard, waving his hand. Lucky was hollering over the music, "Richy! Come over here for a second! I got some good ol' country folks I'd like you to meet. Come on over here, partner!"

Richard shined like a star his first night at Lucky's. They loved him.

Chapter 26

The time was now one o'clock in the morning. Richard was smiling after collecting his tips and politely exited the bar. Turning his murder mentality instantly on like a light switch, he went to a zoned-in mode of vengeance and murder in literally seconds.

Richard walked out to his car, sat inside for a second, then he reached under his driver's seat to pull out his .50 caliber handgun. Richard was driving to club Underworld to murder Howard Loney. The lead off name for the lawyers' killings.

Richard pulled into club Underworld's parking lot. He circled around the club once, seeing how the doors and the perimeter was set up. Then Richard parked in a neighborhood behind the club. The neighborhood was on the back side of the club, a little side street.

Richard got out of his car, tightly holding his .50 caliber gun in hand. The gun was so large that it was halfway hanging out of his coat, barely fitting inside his large pocket.

Richard was walking toward the club's side door. After driving around the club's perimeter once, he noticed people enter through the front, but they exited out the side door.

Richard thought, *If all these people are lawyers, I should've brought that AK and ran in there, just spraying motherfuckers, thirty or forty all at one time. I know some of them guilty too. Even if they didn't make my list. Fuck it, then that'll be for what they might do.*

Richard was walking through the club parking lot, almost right at the club. It was close to club Underworld's closing time. It was a lot of traffic coming out and leaving the club as cars hung out, slowly driving around the parking lot with their music systems loudly blasting.

There were crowds on top of crowds of people leaving and running around, scrambling for last-minute sexual encounters. Almost everyone was drunk and over the alcohol legal limit.

Richard was leaning against the club's brick wall next to the side door of the club. He was smoking a cigarette and looking at a picture of Howard in his phone. Richard was comparing every face that exited the club to the picture of Howard in his phone. The weather was cool with a medium drizzle of snowflakes falling to the ground.

Richard could hear the club's DJ announcing over the loudspeakers, "Y'all better make y'all last-minute booty calls! 'Cause you ain't got to go home, but—"

The leftover people still partying inside of the club finished the DJ's sentence. They all hollered at the same time, "You gotta get the hell outta here!"

Richard thought, *Oh, that's why everybody is in such a big rush—last-minute booty calls!* as Richard watched all of the men and women scrambling and running around for their last-minute booty calls like the club was on fire.

Richard was smiling and making small talk with the people that walked past him to their cars. The club's door opened up again. *Thump! Thump! Thump! Thump!* Richard was feeling the vibrations from the music's hard bass and nodding his head to the beat.

Richard had his phone in the palm of his hand, comparing every face that exited the club while taking long drags on his cigarette and blowing large clouds of smoke out. Richard thought, *Damn, what's taking this guy so long to come out?* The door opened again, music still blaring. *Thump! Thump!*

But only this time, Richard ran up to the door and quickly peeked inside. There were still a nice amount of people still at the bar, mingling, dancing on the dance floor, and standing around conversing.

While Richard still had the club door slightly opened, a car pulled up behind him and startled him. The car honked their horn. *Honk! Honk!* Richard swiftly turned to look behind him. It was a very small compact car, full of what seemed to be five or more young college girls. Richard lost count.

The car was so small that all of the girls were sitting on top of one another's lap. The passenger side female had her window down. They were all laughing and giggling uncontrollably, smoking marijuana, visibly sloppy drunk.

The passenger side female couldn't stop laughing as she tried to holler and ask Richard, "Hey! You want a ride? I can sit on your face!" Then she quickly lifted her shirt, flashing Richard and exposing her breast.

The young college girl caught Richard off guard. He wasn't expecting her to flash her breast at him as he quickly turned his head away and closed his eyes. He didn't want to disrespect the young teenager.

Richard answered, "No. No, thank you. I'm just waiting on a friend to come out." Then a female sitting in the back seat of the small car, on her girlfriend's lap, hollered out to Richard, "I hope he's as fine as you are." Then she drunkenly stood up out of the sunroof, laughing and flashing her breast at Richard.

The female driver of the car turned the radio up to the maximum and then sped away as fast as her little weighed-down-in-the-back car would go, disappearing into the light drizzle of white snowflakes.

Richard turned back to the club's door and opened it, still waiting and looking for Howard to exit the club. Richard didn't know that Howard was upstairs in the VIP room, sniffing fat lines of cocaine with complimentary hundred-dollar bills spread out carelessly all over the table.

Howard was with his childhood buddy Keith and surrounded by some beautiful strippers that were stripping, dancing, and drinking.

Howard kept looking down at his custom heavy diamond watch. He knew that he had to be home to his wife shortly. He had a habit of coming home in the wee hours of the morning, even though he had a wife and children at home.

Howard sniffed his last half of a line. He leaned back on the couch for a few minutes, holding his head back. He was trying to control the drain from the uncut cocaine that had his nose running.

Richard was still peeking inside of the club. He saw a man that resembled Howard about to exit the club and thought, *This has to be him! About time! Now I can spill your brains all over your high-priced expensive loafers.*

Richard quickly ducked off, adjusted his skull cap, pulling it snug down to his eyebrows. Then Richard made sure that his collars of his winter coat were up and around his ears, covering his face as much as possible.

Richard looked at the picture of Howard in his phone again, being absolutely certain that the man leaving the club was Howard.

Richard quickly grasped the .50 caliber in his hand, down at his side. Richard heard the beat to the music get louder as the club door opened up again. *Thump! Thump! Thump! Thump!*

The first man stepped out. Richard compared Howard's picture to the face of that man, looking from the man's face to Howard's picture, then from Howard's picture back up to the man's face. And it was confirmed. Richard said to himself, "That's him! Howard, buddy...you can kiss ya ass goodbye, baby!"

Richard took the big .50 caliber off safety, placed his index finger on the trigger. The man that Richard confirmed to be Howard came walking out of the club by himself as the club's door closed behind him. Richard was walking behind the man, getting closer and closer without the man noticing.

Richard started raising his gun up, about to shoot him twice in the back of his skull. Just as Richard was about to apply pressure to the trigger, squarely aimed at the back of the man's skull, instantly the club's door flew open, and a man ran out, hollering, "Hey, Matt! Hey, Matt!"

Richard quickly lowered his gun, then made a detour.

The man that Richard was literally within less than a hair of a second about to put bullets into the back of his head, the man Richard thought was Howard, turned and answered, "What's up, Gabe?"

Gabe replied, "Hey, man, if it's not a problem, do you think you can give me a lift to my pad?"

Matt turned around and answered, "Sure, come on, dude. I'm going that way anyway."

Gabe answered, "Thanks, dude. I'll give you five bucks for gas." Matt and Gabe got into Matt's car and drove away.

Richard walked back to the wall of the club's door. He continued to stand and wait on Howard while thinking, "Damn, Matt, you were in the wrong place at the right time. You almost got your brains scrambled for another man's sin. So sad…but oh well."

Then suddenly the club's door opened again. Richard ducked his head back down into the collars of his winter coat. Two men exited the club. They both saw Richard standing there with his head buried deep inside the collars of his winter coat. But it was lightly snowing. So the two men didn't think twice about Richard being covered up.

The two men both said what's up. Richard politely spoke back as the two men stood there for a second and continued to converse with each other for a brief moment. Richard was waiting on just the right time to make his move. And the club's parking lot was almost cleared by now. It was confirmed by Richard, one of the two men talking was Howard.

Richard thought to shoot Howard as he stood there, talking with his friend. But he second-guessed it and thought better. Richard thought he'd shoot Howard in the back of his head as he walked away toward his car.

The two men turned their backs to Richard and began walking toward their cars. Richard eased his .50 caliber gun out of his coat pocket, then quickly held it to his side. Again, finger on the trigger and ready to shoot. Just as Richard was about to take a step toward the two men, Howard stopped in his tracks, turned around, and asked Richard, "Hey, man, need a lift? I'll take you."

Richard was stunned that Howard was that drunk that he still cared enough about a perfect stranger's well-being. Richard thought, *He probably thinks that I'm one of his brotherhood attorneys or in law school. And that's the only reason he asked me.*

Richard answered, "Yeah, sure. Thanks for asking, man. I didn't know how I was going to get home." Richard quickly put his gun back into his pocket so that Howard or Howard's friend that was riding with him wouldn't see it.

Howard said to Richard, "Come on, follow us, man. I'm parked right over here. I got that spankin' new Benz straight off the floor. Oh, I forgot…The only one in the city like it." Howard was bragging as usual and walking toward his Benz.

Richard followed the both of them to a triple-black Benz with blacked-out twenty-inch rims and offset chrome lips. Richard just stood there in awe, staring at the beautiful wheels that Howard had sitting in the parking lot, parked sideways in an angle taking up two parking spaces, as if Howard was too above anyone else to park their car by his.

Richard's assumption was right because that's when Howard said, "Yeah, I park my shit sideways to keep these hating clowns from ACCIDENTALLY scratching it. You know how that is. And then IIII'm going to have to need a lawyer after I kill their dumb ass!"

Richard chuckled as he agreed, saying, "Yeah, man, I don't blame you. This is nice!"

As Richard climbed into the back seat, Richard thought, *This shit is a waste of money. Especially since you won't be able to drive it dead.*

Howard push started the engine while he sat there going through songs on his sound system through his phone. Howard was still pushing buttons on his phone, trying to find a song. That's when he asked Richard, "So what law school are you in, dude? Or are you done?"

Richard replied, "I forgot the name of the school. I just recently began classes. I'm from out of state. But I got it here in my pocket."

Richard began digging into the front pocket of his winter coat. Then Richard said, "Oh, here it is right here. I got to—" Richard slowly pulled out his .50 caliber and shot Howard and Howard's friend once in the back of both of their heads. *Bang! Bang!*

Richard quickly grabbed the back seat door handle. He got out of Howard's car and closed the door with Howard's engine still running. Then Richard ran off into the darkness of the night, running toward his car.

Calmly driving, Richard made his way back to his apartment. Richard hurried to his television set. Richard wanted to see the lawyers that he killed on the news for himself. Watching news reporters report on the murders made Richard feel like some type of celebrity or something, knowing that he was the cause of lawyers being killed, exactly how he planned it. And then following the news to see if the lawyers actually died and didn't survive.

Richard couldn't wait to see the news to see exactly what type of terror, if any, that he was putting his city through. This was the best that Richard had felt in years. Richard had a look on his face that said, *Yeah, people say life is good. But I say revenge is even sweeter.*

Chapter 27

Richard didn't see anything on the news yet. He waited and waited—nothing. So Richard fell asleep. He woke up the next morning and went to report. It was report day. He saw his parole officer, Mrs. Pandleton. And as he finished up, before Richard left, he asked Mrs. Pandleton, "So how have you been doing, Mrs. Pandleton?"

Mrs. Pandleton answered, "Not too good. My morning didn't begin quite the way I anticipated."

Richard asked Mrs. Pandleton, "Why do you say that?"

Mrs. Pandleton answered, "You didn't see the news this morning? Where have you been?"

Richard's heart began to beat erratically as anxiety and optimism set in of the unknown. Mrs. Pandleton showed Richard her phone that she had pulled the news up on. It read, "Two lawyers killed in an attempted carjacking," and a photo of the crime scene at club Underworld.

The same Mercedes Benz that he was sitting in late last night/ early this morning, just a few hours ago. The black Mercedes Benz had yellow crime scene tape all around it. Richard's whole body was tingling with euphoria as he read and stared at the photo of the crime scene.

Richard handed Mrs. Pandleton her phone back and said, "Wow! Yeah…It's really crazy out there. I'm scared to leave my own house."

Mrs. Pandleton said, "I don't know…It's a lot of sick people out there with nothing to do." Mrs. Pandleton said, "Yeah, the police say it's too early to make assumptions or jump to conclusions. But it's mysterious that it just happens to be lawyers."

Richard was looking baffled when he asked, "Lawyers! Somebody's out there killing lawyers? That sounds like another jealous coworker to me. You know those lawyers can turn greedy real quick. It's always over jealousy or money."

Mrs. Pandleton looked at Richard, thinking for a moment. She had a look that said Richard sounded like he was onto something. Richard's logic was making sense to Mrs. Pandleton. Richard went on to say, "Yeah, you never know...it could be a fellow lawyer gone bad."

Mrs. Pandleton was still looking at Richard and thinking. Richard was making sense. Mrs. pandleton said, "Yeah...That's very possible. That's the first thing I thought too." Mrs. Pandleton was lying because she didn't want to make it seem like a convict was smarter than her. She felt embarrassed that she didn't think of that before some prisoner that was beneath her.

Mrs. Pandleton said, "It's difficult to think straight while some crazy psycho is out there killing lawyers. I really hope that he doesn't confuse me for a lawyer!"

Richard left his parole report with Mrs. Pandleton and headed to the gas station. He bought some gas, and before he left, he pulled up the news article on his phone just to see it for himself uninterrupted, a little longer. Then he was headed back to his apartment.

Richard returned back to his apartment. He sat at the dining room table, staring at his phone, looking at the crime scene and reading the article again but aloud. "Two lawyers killed in an attempted carjacking."

Richard kept reading the article. He was mesmerized and feeling like an anonymous celebrity. He spent a few seconds staring at the Benz roped off in yellow tape. He was thinking, *Daaaamn, I did that? I was actually sitting in the back seat of that car! I was actually talking to them before they were killed.*

Richard read the bottom of the article, "Just a random coincidence? Highly unlikely. We're following up on leads of suspended attorneys and attorneys that have had their licenses revoked. That could possibly be motives. Any tips, call Sgt. Beckford at 819-794-4310."

Richard thought, *Damn, it's getting serious. That's how you set the tone! And get these coward ass dirty lawyers and everybody's attention.*

They don't know who done it or why. So smart but so stupid. So the next piece of shit lawyer I slaughter should really open their eyes.

Richard picked up his kill list of lawyers. The list had one lawyer's name that he had killed, circled. Howard Loney had a line drawn through his name. His friend was just a throw-in bonus named Keith Pike.

Keith Pike was attending law school to be an attorney to partner up with his childhood friend and start a law firm together. Richard was marking lawyers off as he killed them, keeping tally of who he murdered thus far.

Richard picked up his writing pen and added Keith Pike to his attorney kill list. Richard was smiling as he circled Keith's name and drew a line through it.

Keith was a good message to send to the friends of lawyers and to the family members of lawyers. That now really isn't a good time to be seen or be around a lawyer—friend, family, or not—because it could cost you your life too! Guilty by association.

Richard was 100 percent correct because that was exactly how the friends and family of lawyers felt. They weren't taking any chances. They kept their distance from family and friends that were lawyers or going to school to be lawyers.

If you were in law school or were already an attorney, family and friends barred you from going anywhere near them! Family and friends demanded that you stayed away, at least until you either quit your job or quit going to law school or at least until the killer was caught.

Richard's plan was working; he didn't know it yet for himself, but it was questions and concerns and suspicions swirling about the lawyers' murders. And that ignited fear. It was separating family and friends. Richard was making a dramatic statement. And word was quickly spreading throughout the entire city, throughout the entire state, and quickly making its way across the entire country.

Lawyers and law students studying to be lawyers, all across the country, were helplessly waiting to see if there really was a lawyer killer on the loose. And they were praying the two murders were just a freak coincidence.

But it wasn't. Richard had his next attorney murder locked on his list. Daniel. Daniel Maynor. Richard circled Daniel's name, and with a sinister smile, he said out loud, "Daniel...you're up, baby. So enjoy the next few days of your life. Live every day like it's your last... literally."

Richard heard his television in the background, "Minnesota gunman targeting lawyers? Anticipating and fearing another lawyer killing."

Chapter 28

Media coverage and fear throughout the United States continued to circulate, and some customers at the bar were angry, saying, "It can be anybody on that lawyer killing spree! I heard of some of those damn lawyers railroading people, especially if you couldn't pay them."

At Lucky's bar, another customer said, while drinking a big glass mug of beer and visibly drunk, "If that's true, then that's what their dirty money-hungry asses deserve!"

Some customers stared at the man, not knowing what to think about his harsh opinion, until he finished his statement, trying to clear it up by saying, "I'm not justifying anybody being killed. I'm just saying maybe now lawyers will learn from those lawyers of how not to handle business."

Richard heard customers at grocery stores. "Those lawyers need to start caring a little more! And put a little more effort into their damn jobs! Money or not! Or fucking quit! Everyone isn't going to keep accepting being shit on!"

People waiting in line at the movies were saying, "See, this is exactly what you get, exactly what we have now. Some sick mother-fucker out there running around the city, blowing attorney's heads off! Feeling wronged! Vindicated and justified by revenge. Call me crazy, Steff, but I see exactly where this shit is going."

At the gas station yesterday, Richard overheard some police officers eating doughnuts and talking. One of the police officers said to the other, "Yeah, this crazy lawyer killing shit might end up turning into the newest and the latest thrill-killing epidemic, like Columbine. You see how popular it got to shoot up schools and class-rooms? Schools were getting shot up every year, it seemed. But this time, instead of students being shot up—"

Richard loved and enjoyed the topic of discussion. Debate and fear everywhere that he was the mastermind behind.

Richard was beyond anxious to draw a line through his next murder victim that he had already drawn a circle around.

Big-time lawyers were having constant meetings to determine if courtrooms in Minnesota should be shut down for the safety of lawyers. At least until further notice.

Richard looked through his phone until he found Daniel Maynor Law Offices. Richard looked at Daniel Maynor's business hours. His business hours were from 8:00 a.m. to 4:00 p.m. Richard dialed Daniel Maynor's Law Offices' telephone number.

Daniel Maynor's secretary answered, "Daniel Maynor's Law Offices, good afternoon."

Richard replied, "Good afternoon. I would like to set up an appointment with Mr. Maynor today. But I have a few meetings that I need to attend today. So…what's a good time?"

Daniel Maynor's secretary answered, "I'm sorry, sir. But Mr. Maynor's schedule is completely full until two o'clock."

Richard asked the secretary, "Well, can I make an appointment with Mr. Maynor for two o'clock?"

The secretary answered, "Mr. Maynor has a very important meeting to attend at two o'clock elsewhere. He'll only be here up until then. But can I reschedule, sir?"

Richard answered, "No, that's okay. I'll just call back some other time. You have a blessed day."

Mr. Maynor's secretary replied, "Thank you, same to you, sir." They both hung up.

Richard was calling Mr. Maynor's office to try and get a feel for when and if he could find out if Mr. Maynor was leaving his office.

Richard was in luck his gamble paid off. Mr. Maynor's secretary told Richard everything about Mr. Maynor that he needed to know, except for what he was eating today. Richard now knows how long Mr. Maynor will be at his office today.

Richard walked back to his bedroom. He stopped at his doorway and just stood there. He was staring at his bed where he had all three of his guns laid out. Richard was trying to decide which gun would be the best weapon of choice to murder Daniel with.

Richard walked over to his bed and picked up his AK assault rifle. He grabbed it and held it up. He looked at it, then began nodding his head, saying, "Yep...Yep...I like this, I love this one."

Richard took the long banana-shaped clip from out of the bottom of the rifle, looked at the long pointed bullets, and said, "Shit! That's a lot of bullets! What, at least thirty or forty?"

Richard pulled Daniel Maynor's name back up in his phone. He got everything prepared to go. He killed a little time, then left his apartment at roughly 1:14 p.m. Richard thought that would give him enough time to drive to Daniel Maynor's office building and wait on him to come out.

Richard's plan was to shoot Daniel Maynor multiple times with the assault rifle as Daniel sat in his car. It was time for Richard to put his plan into motion.

Richard grabbed a blanket from off of his couch and wrapped the AK assault rifle up to carry it to his car unnoticed.

Richard put the AK into his car while still leaving it wrapped up in the blanket. Richard arrived at Daniel Maynor's law office roughly at 1:30 p.m. Richard watched and waited for a car to leave the law office for almost thirty minutes, but still no car movement.

Richard was parked across the street from Daniel's law office. Richard pulled out his hunting binoculars from the car floor of the back seat. He was constantly looking over at Daniel's parking lot. Still no Daniel, and it was after two o'clock.

Richard suddenly observed a man come out of Daniel's building. The man stepped out, exited the door, threw his scarf over his shoulder, and patiently waited on the front steps. Richard held his phone up with Daniel's picture and looked through his binoculars, trying to confirm the man was Daniel Maynor.

Richard thought, *Yep! That's Danny boy!* But Richard couldn't figure out who or what Danny was waiting for. Richard started his car up, waiting a few seconds for Daniel to make his move to his car. And that's when Richard observed an eggshell-white-colored BMW pull into Daniel Maynor's parking lot.

The eggshell-white BMW was the same exact match to the BMW that had already been sitting there in Daniel's law office parking lot. The BMW pulled up and parked in front. A woman exited the vehicle as Daniel began walking down the steps toward her.

Daniel and the woman embraced and then pecked lips for a kiss. After they kissed, the woman walked to the passenger side of the car she exited, opened the door, and got inside. Then Daniel opened the driver side door of the same vehicle and got inside.

Richard thought, *Oh, great! Your pretty little wife gets to be killed with you? Aaaaaaawe, I think that'll be so cute! Bleeding in each other's arms! I'm tearing up. Why didn't I think of that?* Richard was having fun, humorously being sarcastic but just as serious, though.

The white BMW that Daniel was now driving had pulled out of the parking lot and was waiting for an opening to get into the flow of traffic. Richard meticulously watched Daniel's every move without blinking, not once.

First the BMW that Daniel was driving darted out into traffic—*vroom!*—then Richard allowed three cars to pass him so he wouldn't be noticed before darting out into traffic tightly behind Daniel. *Vroom!*

As Richard was driving, he was reaching over to the passenger seat, unwrapping the AK-47 assault rifle from out of the blanket. After a few traffic lights, Daniel turned left onto a side street. Then another left onto another street. Now Richard was the only car driving behind Daniel.

Richard was observing Daniel and his wife laughing and conversing as Richard continued to follow undetected. They were now riding down a street that had a yellow flashing caution light and a yield sign that they were quickly approaching up ahead.

Richard thought, *Now is the perfect time to gun their asses down. No witnesses.* Richard reached over and grabbed his AK-47 that he was unwrapping out of the blanket while driving. It was resting on the floor, leaning against the passenger seat.

Richard laid the AK-47 across his lap. He was anticipating Daniel slowing down at the yellow flashing caution light at the intersection ahead.

Richard's plan was to pull up beside Daniel's car and shower AK-47 bullet holes through the passenger-side door, where Daniel's innocent wife would get the bulk of the thirty-something hot bullets spraying.

Richard calmly pulled his car around from the back side of Daniel's BMW. He was almost right beside the passenger-side door where Daniel's wife was still facing toward him, laughing and talking. She was oblivious to what was about to take place just on the other side of her car door. Daniel and his wife were too caught up in the topic of their conversation to even notice Richard's car pulling up on the side of them.

Daniel and Richard both stopped side by side at the stop sign. They were both waiting on the vehicle across from them that had the right away.

Daniel's wife was completely oblivious to the AK-47 that Richard was holding in his hands. It was resting on Richard's driver-side door window that was down. Richard had one hand off of the steering wheel, tightly grasping the AK with his foot on the brake pedal.

Richard put his finger on the trigger of the rifle. Then Richard said to himself, "Goodbye, Danny and wifey." And just as Richard's finger was applying pressure to the trigger, a little girl popped her head up in the back seat of Daniel's car. Richard said, "Dammit!" As the little girl was behind the passenger seat, smiling and waving at Richard.

The little girl had a heart-shape balloon in her hands. She was playing a game of peekaboo with Richard, covering her eyes with her hands, then quickly snatching them away to look at Richard, hoping that he would play back with her.

Richard fought with himself; he still had finger pressure on the trigger. Kid or not, it had to be done before the little girl wanted to grow up and be a lawyer like her dad. Richard reluctantly thought against it. And it took everything inside of Richard to do so. His mind wasn't made up yet to call it off.

The little girl had a huge innocent smile on her face as she was tapping on her mother's shoulder, trying to get her mother's attention to look at the stranger that she was just playing peekaboo with in the car next to theirs.

But before Daniel or his wife could look over at Richard, he eased the AK-47 back down from out of the window and onto his lap. When they finally looked over, Richard was smiling and waving at their daughter.

Richard took one hand off the AK and the other hand off the steering wheel just to play peekaboo back with the little girl. Daniel and his wife politely smiled and waved back at Richard.

Daniel drove straight through the intersection. And Richard made a right turn onto a side street. Richard said to himself, "Fuck! Fuck! Fuck!" He pounded his steering wheel, driving away furious.

As bad as Richard wanted to kill another lawyer and his wife, and add another dead-lawyer news article to his collection that he was saving and stacking up in his phone, Richard couldn't bring himself to kill Daniel or his wife in front of their daughter.

He had a daughter himself and didn't want to risk killing a child. That would have been on what little of a so-called conscience that he had left—which wasn't much, if any at all.

Richard didn't hesitate to kill a lawyer or anybody with a lawyer because they've been warned by the first lawyers' murders. Richard was driving home back to his apartment. The AK-47 was still lying across his lap.

Richard arrived back at his apartment, wrapped the AK-47 back into its blanket, then took it upstairs. Richard walked inside of his apartment and sat the AK-47 next to him on the couch. Then he looked at Daniel's picture in his phone and deleted it, thinking, *Lucky day today.*

Richard sat down at his dining room table, back to the drawing board. He was looking over his attorney kill list. He drew a question mark next to Daniel Maynor's and made a little sidenote that said "come back to."

Then Richard continued looking over his kill list to see who was in immediate need of his reprimand. Richard thought, *This time I'll use the scope and rifle. Yeah, that DC sniper shit,* as his eyes intensely scanned up and down the attorney kill list, looking for the next perfect victim.

Richard finally spotted his definition of the next perfect victim. The next lawyer Richard planned to kill was a big-time Minnesota superstar clients' sports agent. And her name is Christina Brookerfield.

Richard wanted to protect his friend Omeka from being exploited by some sports agent, crooked sports agents taking his friend's money while making a name for themselves. Richard felt he had to kill Christina before she got to his friend Omeka.

The few times Richard worked out and trained with Omeka, before he bought him his own football, Richard saw Omeka really had some serious catching and elusiveness skills.

All Omeka watched were receivers' footwork and catching skills. He mimicked his favorite NFL players perfectly. The hardest catch, the over-the-shoulder catch, was hands down the most difficult catch for all receivers. But Omeka flawlessly made those high-stake catches consistently. Richard saw Omeka's immense talent and potential that he possessed at an extremely young age. Omeka was focused.

Richard heard a lot over the years about Christina Brookerfield's sports agency shady dealings in the dog-eat-dog world of sports entertainment.

When Richard worked at the plant as an automotive engineer and at his hot rod automechanic shop, Christina and her dealings were almost always the top conversation piece or debate throughout the mornings.

Christina was constantly in the local newspaper for allegations of illegal contact with junior high, high school, and college athletes. And they all were big-time young superstars, destined to generate millions and millions of professional dollars. She was a vulture. No age was off limits as she frequented grade schools scouting talent.

Christina signed several young athletes in the state of Minnesota and all regional surrounding states.

Allegations of tricking young superstar athletes into signing her deceptive contracts, and with their parents' approval, Christina would mostly target and pursue poor inner-city families that didn't really have a choice in the matter.

Once Christina teased families by purchasing expensive gifts, jewelry, luxury vehicles, expensive homes out of the ghetto, lavish vacation trips on yachts to reserved islands, the families couldn't resist her smooth snakelike moves.

Whatever it cost, whatever it took to get their child to sign the contract, she went the distance. The families couldn't and wouldn't refuse. How, when the family didn't even know how they would even eat most of the time and were one government assistance check missed away from being homeless, living on the street.

All she cared and loved was the child's potential to make her richer than what she already was.

The entire sports world of Minnesota knew that Christina's sports agency was guilty! Even public opinion, but they just couldn't prove it. She had top superstar athletes that played professionally for the state of Minnesota and also tennis and golf professionally. Christina had her hands into everything worth putting hands into, first.

Christina had brokered athletes' and musicians' commercials, shoes, and endorsements. This year Forbes' list even named Christina one of the country's most influential sports agencies. She was also named the fastest sports/entertainment lawyers to reach a quarter-billion dollars. One of the magazine CEO's quote read, "Christina accomplished the unthinkable in a matter of just under twenty months. Keep up the excellent work!"

Richard thought about everything that he had read and heard about Christina over the last almost-two years, about how the sports committees could never prove any wrong dealings against Christina. Although they were certain that she was guilty. And Richard was convinced that she was guilty as well.

Richard said to himself, "Another snake lawyer that misuses her clients and slithers her way up out of situations that would destroy her and her agency." Richard continued saying to himself, "Christina, this time, me and you are in a contract agreement you just don't know about yet. I guess it's kinda like an unwritten contract. The only bad thing…it's just not any money coming to you. Just a gruesome murder." Richard sarcastically finished by saying, "Good for me, though…Bad for you," with an evil smirk.

Richard fully understood that if he didn't kill Christina now, that one day—and one day real soon—Christina and his little friend, Omeka, would eventually cross paths on his way to the NFL or NBA.

Richard refused to let some lawyer kill his little friend's dream of making millions and millions of dollars and buying his mother "the biggest house in the world!"

Richard remembered a story of a student that sprung off to the NFL. Christina had given him advice to come out of school after two years. The student was a number 1 receiver drafted that year. But that student constantly stayed injured, never really playing a full season. And then in his final year of his rookie contract, he suffered a career-ending injury.

The draft pick was dead broke with no education to fall back on. He was back in his hood, slinging crack on the corner, and back living in his mother's basement after she lost her house as well, with his fiancée and two children. Christina didn't think twice about him.

Christina used to tell the kids, "Once you have millions, who needs an education? You can just pay people to think for you," she jokingly but seriously told the parents while they all laughed it up.

Richard circled Christina's name on his attorney kill list. His mind was made up. "Yep. You gotta go."

Several hours had passed. It was now time to go to work at Lucky's. Richard worked his shift, finished, and was back at his apartment. He was preparing for bed. But before going to sleep, he looked at his lawyer kill list again. He was looking at how many more lawyers were left that he had planned to kill. And last but not least, who was next.

Richard looked at the lawyer kill list until he came across Christina Brookerfield's name again. Richard thought, *I'll call her first thing in the morning*. Richard turned his living room light out and fell asleep.

The next morning had arrived. Richard made himself a cup of coffee and turned on his television to watch the news as he tried to collect his thoughts, still half-asleep. Richard watched and listened to the news reporter reporting the latest update on the lawyer killings, almost one week of Minneapolis terror and two bodies later.

A Minneapolis man was being held in custody for questioning in the connection to the attorney slayings. It was reported that he had given a confession to a jailhouse snitch and that he himself had confessed to the homicide detectives."

Richard watched and listened in total disbelief as he chuckled and said, "Law enforcement up to their bullshit again. Guess they gotta put it on somebody." He shook his head in amusement.

Richard turned the television channel to another news station that was reporting, "Breaking news on attorney serial killer." They didn't release the suspect's name. but they did show a mug shot of "the lawyer killer" suspect arrest last night.

The suspect's eyes were blackened, his lip was cut, his head was bandaged, and his face was swollen and bruised. "The suspect tried to resist arrest late last night. And the officers used justifiable force to subdue the suspect. And the person of interest that we currently have in custody clearly matches the witnesses' description of the suspect for these lawyer serial homicides."

Richard thought, *Suspect? In custody? He's responsible for the lawyer killings? They have to know that man is not responsible for some shit that I did! They just don't care about who goes down for it. Just as long as somebody goes.*

Chapter 29

Richard called Christina Brookerfield's agency. Her secretary answered the telephone, "Brookerfield and Associates Sports Agency. This is Melissa speaking."

Richard replied to the woman on the other end of the telephone, "Yes. I was referred to Christina Brookerfield by a very close friend of mine that plays professional basketball. My friend told me that Mrs. Brookerfield could possibly help me out."

Melissa responded, "Oh, I'm sorry, sir. But Mrs. Brookerfield isn't available to accept personal calls. But if you could leave me your name and your telephone number, I will definitely give her the message."

Richard knew that he had to take the stakes up higher just to get Christina to bite. Richard answered, "No. I would rather not leave a message. Maybe you can help me. I heard that Christina pays people for scouting talent for her. And I really think that she is going to love what I got for her."

Melissa replied, "Oh, really? Well…what do you have for her?"

Richard answered, "I found the next superstar fourteen-year-old two-sport athlete." Richard had Melissa's complete attention because she thought maybe she could get a little something off that finder's fee as well.

Melissa replied, "Two-sport athlete?"

Richard answered confidently, "Yes, basketball and football. But…I guess that's her loss. I'll take my business elsewhere. Thanks anyway."

But before Richard could hang his telephone up, Melissa nervously tried to stop Richard, saying, "No, no, no, no! Please wait a minute, sir! I apologize for the entire misunderstanding." Melissa was sounding as if she could lose her job if she let this one get away.

Melissa quickly forgot all about the finder's fee. She was now trying to save her job.

Melissa said to Richard, "I didn't know that you wanted to introduce Mrs. Brookerfield to new talent, sir. Goofy me. Please hold on, and I'll put you through straight to Mrs. Brookerfield."

Melissa pushed a button on her telephone, and the background fell completely silent on Richard's end for a few seconds. Then a woman answered, "Hi, this is Christina Brookerfield. How can I help you?"

Richard replied, "Hey, Christina. How you doing? A friend told me you love sports talent?"

Christina cheerfully answered, "I'm doing good now that you called!" Richard and Christina cheerfully chuckled. Then Christina asked, "I hear you have a gift for me?"

Richard replied, "As a matter of fact, yes, I do. A couple hundred million, or maybe even more of them!"

Christina was listening with all ears as she lit up and answered, "Say no more! I got the picture! You know they probably have every phone in place tapped. They've been trying their best to take me out of the game for a minute now. I know you've probably heard. Just a bunch of lies, though. No worries." They both shared a laugh again.

Christina went on talking. But she switched it up, talking in code now. She asked, "So I hear it's a double, huh?"

Richard answered as if he had the only hidden treasure in the world, "Yes, it's a double. Are you familiar with the name Omeka?"

Christina replied with excitement, "Yes! Hell yes! Sure I am. Who isn't! The kid's from…I think…Africa, right? Yes, I think that's him! He's next on my—oops. There I go again, flapping off my big mouth. I'll tell you what, mister…"

Richard, excited that he got Christina to easily bite, was caught up in the moment when he mistakenly answered, "Ginn. Richard Ginn." Forgetting all about his sole purpose, intent, and motivation for calling Christina—which was to kill her. *Murder!*

After Richard had mistakenly given Christina his name, he instantly thought about what he had done. Richard got quiet while she was still talking. Richard said to himself, "Shit! Fuck! Damn! Why didn't my dumb ass give her a fake name!"

Christina finished her sentence, saying, "If you're not too busy, Mr. Ginn, maybe we could get together this evening and discuss further details over some lattes or something?"

Richard replied, "No, never too busy when it comes to moola, baby!" Richard went on, "Sounds good. Almost as good as that cup of latte. You like lattes, huh? Well, I'm buying then."

Christina answered, "Hells yeah! I love lattes! Especially free ones. They taste so much better when someone else pays for them!" They jokingly laughed together.

Christina went on, saying, "Seven o'clock, sharp? Bigbees downtown? Look for the blond-haired lady, wearing some knee-high Uggs with the cute little fur around the top of the boots. I'll be standing in front, waiting on you, Richard."

Richard replied, "I'll see you then." They both hung their telephones up.

While talking on her telephone, Christina was writing a note to herself on her yellow sticky paper. The note read, "Richard Ginn, 7:00 p.m. Bigbees."

Richard hung the telephone up, angry at himself for slipping up and telling Christina his name. he cringed every time he heard Christina say his name after he told it to her. But then he thought, *Oh well, she'll never get a chance to tell. Dead people can't talk.*

Richard hung around his apartment until roughly 6:30 p.m. He looked at his clock, picked up his high-powered rifle with the scope. He was practicing shooting Christina, looking through the scope and saying, "Pow!" with rifle recoil.

Richard turned around, looking out of his apartment window at people walking. He was looking through the scope, aiming his rifle, and softly whispering, "Pow! Pow!" pretending to see Christina fall from the gunshot, as if he was actually picking people off with his rifle.

Richard put on his winter coat, winter hat, and gloves. He racked one live round into the rifle, then put the rifle on safety, and headed out the door.

Richard didn't want to be rude, showing up late to his appointment of lawyer murder with Christina Brookerfield.

Richard drove to the Bigbees coffee shop. He parked a couple of streets down, in front of a park, across from the public library that was closed for the day.

Richard exited his car and put one dollar's worth of change into the parking meter next to his car. He was thinking, *Hopefully one dollar should buy me enough time, sitting and waiting without the meter maid coming around, giving me a ticket for expired time.*

Richard got back into his car. But only this time, he was sitting in the back seat where his rifle was laid. Richard picked up his binoculars and looked over toward the coffee shop's direction. He wanted to be absolutely positive that the angle his car was positioned gave him an unobstructed view and a clear dead-on shot to the coffee shop.

Richard put down his binoculars and said with certainty, "Perfect! Don't get no better than that."

Richard had already rolled the back seat passenger-side window down, just enough so that he could barely stick the muzzle of the rifle outside of the car without being noticed. Richard pulled his leather gloves up tightly on his hands, making sure that he had enough grip on the rifle from the recoil when he shot.

He only had one chance to get his shot perfect on Christina. But that was all Richard needed, one shot. He was confident in his hunting skills and knew he was a certified marksman.

Now all Richard was waiting on was his target. He had his eye focused into the scope, safety off, and his finger on the trigger. Richard said, "Come on, Chrissy, show your face, girl. Front of the coffee shop. Come on."

Richard kept glancing down at his watch. The time was now 6:57 p.m. Richard was counting, "Three more minutes…Threeee more minutes…" Then Richard suddenly heard—"Breaking news! Breaking news! Lawyer killer update"—come through his radio station.

Richard quickly pulled his rifle out the back window. Then he pulled his skull cap up from covering his ears, making sure that he heard his radio loud and clear. Richard tuned in, listening to every word.

"The sergeant of the Minneapolis Police Department released a statement earlier this morning saying, 'The state of Minnesota and its citizens can finally breathe a sigh of relief today after the person of interest for the double attorney homicide is scheduled to be formally be arraigned today in federal court under terrorist acts.'

"The statement went on, saying, 'This is a result of a great collective effort from all of the Minnesota police agencies. Congrats on the outstanding work and making our community and citizens safe again. Justice will be served to the highest degree. Thank you.'"

Richard thought, *The suspect is in custody?* Richard pulled his skull cap back down over his ears and looked at his watch. Richard said, "Oh shit! Damn! It's 7:04 p.m.!

Richard hurriedly picked his rifle back up and stuck the tip of the muzzle back out of the back window. Richard was looking through the rifle's scope toward the direction of the coffee shop's entrance door.

That's when Richard noticed a blond-haired woman standing and waiting on someone in front of the coffee shop. She was holding a white plastic bag with two cups of coffee inside of it. The bag was hanging from her right wrist.

Richard thought, *There she is, holding our cups of coffee. That was nice of her.* Richard slowly and methodically placed his finger back onto the trigger of the rifle. He was looking through the rifle's scope, aimed directly at the center of the blond-haired woman's forehead.

Richard calmly took a deep breath, inhaling and exhaling, trying to regain his composure. Once Richard gathered himself, he relaxed, then tensed his body up tight, bracing for the rifle's recoil after he pulls the trigger, and the bullet fires.

Richard looked down at the woman's shoes. "Yep, knee-high Uggs with fur on upper boots. That's what she described." It was Christina, staring to the left, then staring to the right, as if she was looking or waiting on someone.

Richard focused his rifle directly in the center of the blond woman's forehead. Richard was talking to law enforcement in his head, *While y'all patting yourselves on the back for catching the lawyer killer suspect, don't forget to put this body on him too.* Richard chuckled and said, "Fuckin' geniuses."

Richard braced himself, then pulled the rifle's trigger. The gunshot sounded like a loud firecracker. *Clow!*

The gunshot was unbearably loud and almost deafening to Richard's ears as it echoed throughout the inside of his car, barely escaping through the tiny crack in his back seat window.

Richard paused for a brief second after he pulled the trigger. He still was looking through the scope, seeing what damage, if any, that he did by shooting Christina directly in the center of her forehead.

The impact from the fired bullet's force and power made Christina stumble when she was struck by the bullet. Then all in one motion, she dropped her and Richard's bag of lattes as she was still falling in slow motion. She fell to the ground instantly.

Christina lay there in the cold snow on the sidewalk, lifeless, in a big puddle of red and brown lattes. Red and brown lattes because it was mixed with her blood on the sidewalk.

The bullet went through her skull and out the back, then traveled through the coffee shop's huge plate glass window, shattering it instantly. *Tissshh!* The bullet finally came to a stop when it lodged into the coffee shop's cash register, almost taking out the cashier.

Richard was still looking through his scope of all of the chaos, panic, and fear on the inside of the coffee shop. The bullet forced the cash register drawer open.

Richard climbed in the front of his car, and just as he was driving off, when he turned the corner, he looked through his rearview mirror and saw the meter maid making rounds, checking meters exactly where Richard had just pulled his car from.

Richard arrived back at his apartment, laid his rifle down on the kitchen table. He checked the news to see if the news was reporting the shooting at the coffee shop yet. Richard kept the news on the channel and just waited.

*****

But days later, it was back to the normal routine: work at Lucky's and checking off attorney's names on his lawyer kill list as he strategically picked them and murdered them. The news was a firestorm.

*****

Four months had passed and twelve lawyer killings later, the news named the serial lawyer kill list. The news article read, "The lawyer killer list keeps growing, twelve attorneys and still no answers."

The news named the lawyer killings' victims and place of homicide: Patricia Gallium, grocery store; Mathew Tramque, shopping mall; Trey Burnway, fishing; Monica Troop, jogging; Frank Sumny, visiting gravesite; Ashley Tenderson, exit ramp; Kaytie Parker, at the zoo; Jackson Hemmingway, music concert; Mark Mapleton, golfing; Sara Solemon, book club; Sal Manson, theater; Garrett Larson, football game; Annie Dillson, local bar.

Richard proudly kept in tune with the lawyer killer news updates. He was hell-bent on his lawyer killings mission of vengeance.

This was the latest news updates after the well-known celebrity sports lawyer Christina Brookerfield was shot and killed at a downtown coffee shop.

Richard walked into his bedroom and picked up his lawyer kill list. Richard looked at the attorneys' names that he had killed so far with lines drawn through their names. Richard stopped twirling his pen while biting on it in his mouth and drew a line through Annie Dillson.

Richard looked at the rest of the attorneys' names left on his list to be killed. Richard looked the kill list up and down, carefully picking his next best victim to be killed.

Chapter 30

Richard woke up the next morning with his next lawyer-killing mission in motion. The name that was next on his layer kill list was a fresh-out-of-law-school rookie named Mrs. Janice Stevenson.

Richard left out of his apartment door to carry out his next murder. He didn't know what number it would be. By now it was too many lawyers to count.

Jannice worked out of her home office. Her hand was visibly shaking while pouring her and her husband's fresh cup of coffee. It was during breakfast at the kitchen table, Jannice was telling her husband how upset she was about losing her first trial case.

Jannice's husband put down the newspaper that he was reading, then said to Jannice, as he was trying to comfort her, "Baby, don't get so down on yourself." Jannice's husband got up from the dining table and walked up behind Jannice, who was still seated at the dining room table.

Jannice's husband massaged her shoulders, comforting her, applying a little pressure with his thumbs, getting deep into the muscle to relax her as he kissed her on her cheek.

Jannice's husband went on to say, "They're not really real cases to worry about anyway, babe. They didn't have any money to pay you to beat the case. Did they? So they don't matter. The people with no money is just practice. They are how you're going to get better. That's all they're for."

Jannice angrily and quickly cut her husband's comforting opinion off. She snapped, replying, "No! See, you don't understand! It's not about the money to me. I fight my butt off for each case and for each of my clients! Guilty or not! My job is to prove my client's innocence! That's it! The same way that I would want my attorney to fight his butt off for me! Even if I couldn't afford it!"

Jannice's husband was listening to Jannice with shock. He knew that she loved her job. He just didn't know that his wife was this passionate about her job. He remained speechless and in complete shock as Jannice continued.

Jannice went on, saying, "I fight for the people with no money that much harder just because they don't have the money to hire top lawyers to defend them! I fight each case whether it's trial or trying to get my client the best plea deal possible just before trial!"

Jannice's husband replied, "I didn't mean it like that, Jannice. I just didn't want you to be so down on losing your first trial case, honey."

Jannice adamantly replied, "I swear, babe, if it takes every breath in my body, I'm going to change the way those lawyers think. It's not always about the money! It's about keeping families together. That's my fight!" Jannice barked, still visibly upset about losing her first trial case.

Jannice forcefully dropped her fork and excused herself from the table. She was getting ready for her second trial at the court building scheduled for 7:30 a.m.

Jannice's husband replied from the kitchen, while Jannice was no longer visible, "Yeah, honey, I guess you're right. That was kinda selfish of me thinking like that."

Jannice answered from the back office, "Well…I have to go to work, babe. I'm finishing up my second trial this morning. And I'm going to win this one! Or I'll be on trial next for murder, and I'll be looking for a good lawyer!"

Jannice and her husband both chuckled. Trying to ease the tension, Jannice went on, saying, "Then after I win, we're going to celebrate tonight, honey. I'm going to put on something real nice for you too."

Jannice was walking back towards her husband's direction, smiling and purring like a kitty cat as she winked at her husband. Jannice and her husband both hugged each other, then kissed on the lips. Then Jannice kissed her daughter before her husband was to take her off to school.

Jannice kneeled down, scratching their house dog playfully under his neck and chest area, as she was baby talking to him, "Yeah, yeah, I know, baby. Mommy has to go to work. But Mommy will be back soon. I promise. Okay, baby? Yeah, that's a good boy." The dog's tail was wagging, and he was barking and jumping in excitement onto her legs.

Jannice picked up her briefcase in one hand and put her purse over her opposite shoulder. Then she headed out to her car parked in the driveway as her husband stood in the house doorway, making sure Jannice made it out to her car safely.

Jannice didn't know that she wasn't alone in the early wee hours of the morning. Richard was squatting down, completely hidden in the pitch-dark next to a bush that separating their driveway from the neighbor's driveway.

Richard was watching Jannice dig into her coat pocket, trying to get her car keys out. Jannice's husband asked her, "You need some help, honey?"

Jannice answered, "No, no, no. No, thanks. I got it, babe." Jannice took her briefcase from off of her shoulder, then sat it on the ground for a moment. Jannice finally found her car keys. She pushed the keyless entry button to unlock her car door.

Richard was carefully watching Jannice's every move. He was timing when to perfectly make his move. Richard had his .50 caliber in hand, at his side, and ready to shoot. Jannice's keyless entry had unlocked her car door. Jannice kneeled down to pick her briefcase back up with her husband still watching her. But as soon as she grabbed her briefcase and looked up, Richard had the .50 caliber in hand, finger on the trigger, aiming directly at her face. And the next thing heard was—

To Be Continued

Book 2 Coming Out
The Epidemic

About the Author

Willie Peters Jr., born and raised in Lansing, Michigan, was an award-winning author in school. A talented songwriter, musician, and music producer, with musical projects in production. He possesses a natural gift, talent, and keen sense of translating illustrated vision, utilizing gripping descriptive words that paints the picture and breathe life into the reader's imagination, as if they are watching a movie and becoming the actual characters themselves.

I created this larger-than-life character, Richard Ginn, the hero/villan to be the only person to have the courageous conviction of being the self-appointed merciless lawyer killer of vengeance to carry out what countless others left as vulnerable prey abandoned by their legal counsel had always had empty threats about doing but never pursued until the idea took root into the wrong individual's mind. And the idea hangs by a frayed thread of being snapped and creating the "lawyer killer" a catastrophic American nightmare.

CPSIA information can be obtained
at www.ICGtesting.com
Printed in the USA
LVHW022019151121
703363LV00001B/73

9 781636 929644